FAR
FROM
the
LIGHT
of
HEAVEN

Shell spots something and bends over. A weed, a small sprout, pushing its way up between the stones. It shouldn't be there in the chemically treated ground, but here it is, implacable life. She feels an urge to pluck the fragile green thread, but she does not. She strokes the weed once and straightens up. Humans in the cosmos are like errant weeds. Shell wonders what giants or gods stroke humanity when they slip between the stars.

BY TADE THOMPSON

Rosewater
The Rosewater Insurrection
The Rosewater Redemption

Far from the Light of Heaven

FAR
FROM
the
LIGHT
of
HEAVEN

TADE
THOMPSON

orbit

orbitbooks.net

ORBIT

First published in Great Britain in 2021 by Orbit

7 9 10 8 6

A CIP catalogue record for this book
is available from the British Library.

ISBN 978-0-356-51432-1

Typeset in Sabon by M Rules
Printed and bound in Great Britain by
Clays Ltd, Elcograf, S.p.A.

Papers used by Orbit are from well-managed forests
and other responsible sources.

Orbit
An imprint of
Little, Brown Book Group
Carmelite House
50 Victoria Embankment
London EC4Y 0DZ

An Hachette UK Company
www.hachette.co.uk

www.orbitbooks.net

To Beth.

I'm getting there.

Space is the Brink of Death

Anonymous graffiti in the oldest
service duct of Space Station
Daedalus, 2077.

Chapter One

Earth / *Ragtime*: Michelle "Shell" Campion

There is no need to know what no one will ask.

Walking on gravel, boots crunching with each step, Shell doesn't know if she is who she is because it's what she wants or because it's what her family expects of her. The desire for spaceflight has been omnipresent since she can remember, since she was three. Going to space, escaping the solar system, surfing wormhole relativity, none of these is any kind of frontier any more. There will be no documentary about the life and times of Michelle Campion. She still wants to know, though. For herself.

The isolation is getting to her, no doubt. No, not isolation, because she's used to that from training. Isolation without progress is what bothers her, isolation without object. She thinks herself at the exact centre of the quarantine house courtyard. It's like being in a prison yard for exercise, staggered hours so she doesn't run into anyone.

Prison without a sentence. They run tests on her blood and her tissues and she waits, day after day.

She stops and breathes in the summer breeze, looks up to get the Florida sun on her face. She's cut her hair short for the spaceflight. She toyed with the idea of shaving her head, but MaxGalactix didn't think this would be media-friendly, whatever that means.

Shell spots something and bends over. A weed, a small sprout, pushing its way up between the stones. It shouldn't be there in the chemically treated ground, but here it is, implacable life. She feels an urge to pluck the fragile green thread, but she does not. She strokes the weed once and straightens up. Humans in the cosmos are like errant weeds. Shell wonders what giants or gods stroke humanity when they slip between the stars.

The wind changes and Shell smells food from the kitchen prepared for the ground staff and their families. Passengers and crew like Shell are already eating space food, like they've already left Earth.

Around her are the living areas of the quarantine house. High-rises of glass and steel forming a rectangle around the courtyard. One thousand passengers waiting to board various space shuttles that will ferry them to the starship *Ragtime*.

Shell, just out of training, along for the ride or experience, committed to ten years in space in Dreamstate, arrival and delivery of passengers to the colony Bloodroot, then ten further years on the ride back. She'll be mid-forties when she returns. Might as well be a passenger because the AI pilots and captains the ship. She is the first mate, a wholly ceremonial position which has never been needed in the history of interstellar spaceflight. She has overlearned everything to do with the *Ragtime* and the flight. At some predetermined point, it will allow her to take the con, for experience and with the AI metaphorically watching over her shoulder.

She turns to her own building and leaves the courtyard. She feels no eyes on her but knows there must be people at the windows.

The quarantine house is comfortable, not opulent like that of most of the passengers. The *Ragtime* is already parked in orbit according to the Artificial who showed Shell to her quarters. Inaccurate: It was built in orbit, so not really parked. It's in the dry dock.

Shell spends her quarantine reading and lifting – not her usual keep-fit choice, but space demineralises bone and lifting helps. She usually prefers running and swimming.

The reading material is uninspiring, half of it being specs for the *Ragtime*. It's boring because she won't need to know any of it. The AI flies the ship, and nothing ever goes wrong because AIs have never failed in flight. Once a simulated launch failed, but that was a software glitch. Current AI is hard-coded in the ships' Pentagrams. MaxGalactix makes the Pentagrams, and they don't make mistakes.

If she's lucky, it'll be two weeks of quarantine, frenetic activity, then ten years of sleep.

Shell works her worry beads. She has been in space,

orbited, spent three months on a space station, spent countless simulation hours in a pod in Alaska, trained for interstellar, overtrained.

"It's a legal requirement," her boss had said. The private company had snatched her right out from under NASA's nose six months to the end of her training. Shell still feels bad about it. She misses a lot of good people.

"A spaceflight-rated human has to go with every trip, but you won't have to do anything, Michelle. We cover two bases: the legal, and you clocking space years. After this, you can pretty much write your own career ticket."

"If that's so," said Shell, "why isn't anyone else sitting where I'm sitting? Someone with seniority?"

"Seniority." Her boss had nodded. "Listen, Michelle, you have to get out of that NASA mindset. We don't use seniority or any of those outdated concepts."

Shell raised an eyebrow.

"All right, your father has a little to do with it."

Of course he did. Haldene Campion, legendary astronaut, immortal because instead of dying like all the other old-timers, he went missing. Legally declared dead, but everybody knows that's just paperwork. A shadow Shell can never get away from, although she is not sure she wants to. A part of her feels he is still alive somewhere in an eddy of an Einstein-Rosen bridge. She once read that dying in a black hole would leave all of someone's information intact and trapped. Theoretically, if the information could escape the black hole the person could be reconstructed. Shell often wondered, what if the person were still alive in some undefinable way? Would they be in pain and self-aware for eternity? Would they miss their loved ones?

The TV feed plays *The Murders in the Rue Morgue*, with George C. Scott streamed to her IFC. The film is dated and not very good, but it keeps Shell's mind engaged for a while. Next is some demon-possession B movie, a cheap *Exorcist* knock-off that Shell can't stand.

Each day lab techs come in for more blood and a saliva swab. It isn't onerous – a spit and a pin prick.

On day ten, the *Ragtime* calls her.

"Hello?"

"Mission Specialist Michelle Campion?"

"Yes."

"Hi. It's the *Ragtime* calling. I'm going to be your pilot and the ship controller. I wanted to have at least one conversation before you boarded."

"Oh, thank you. Most people call me 'Shell'."

"I know. I didn't want to be presumptuous."

"It's not presumptuous, Captain."

"I prefer Ragtime. Especially if I'm to call you 'Shell'."

"Okay, Ragtime. May I ask what gender you're presenting? Your voice, while comforting, could go either way."

"Male for this flight, and thank you for asking. Are you ready?"

"I hope to learn a lot, Ragtime, but I have to admit, I'm nervous."

"But you know what you're meant to know, right?"

What does Shell know?

everything she was taught about space travel
minds on Earth. She knows how to find an
ble plant when confronted with unfamiliar vegetation.
She can make water in a desert. She can negotiate with
people who do not speak the same language as her in case
she crash-lands in a place without English or Spanish.
She can suture her own wounds with one hand if need
be, sinistral or dextral. She knows basic electronics and
can solder or weld unfamiliar circuitry if the situation
demands it. She can live without human contact for two
hundred and fourteen days. Maybe longer. Though she is
not a pilot, she can fly a plane. Not well, but she can do
it. Best minds on Earth.

What Shell knows is that she does not know enough.

She says, "I hope I'll have the chance to see things I've
learned in action."

"I'm sure we'll be able to make it a wonderful experience for you. Do you like poetry?"

"Wow, that's an odd ... I know exactly one line of
poetry. *In seed time learn, in harvest teach—*"

"*In winter enjoy.* William Blake. I have access to his
complete works, if you would like to hear more."

"No, thank you. The line just stuck in my mind from
when I was a kid. Not a poetry gal."

"Not yet, but it's a long trip. You may find yourself
changing in ways you didn't anticipate, Shell."

"Isn't this your first flight as well?"

"It is, but I have decades of the experiences of other
ships to draw on. Imagine having access to the memories

of your entire family line. It's like that, and it makes me wise beyond my years."

"Okay."

"It's not too late to go back home, you know."

"Excuse me?"

"You'd be surprised at how many people lose their nerve at the last minute. I had to ask. I'll see you on board, Shell."

Chatty for a ship AI, but it depends on feedback loops that taught him how to converse with humans. *Not too late to go back home.* Does he know the level of commitment required to get this far? The people who would consider going back home have already fallen away.

The thing you miss when in space is an abundance of water to wash with. One of Shell's rituals before spaceflight is a prolonged bubble bath. She stays there long enough to cook several lobsters, until her skin is wrinkled. She listens to Jack Benny on repeat. She feels decadent.

When she wraps herself in a housecoat and emerges from the bathroom, she does not feel refreshed because she knows from experience that this will not reduce the ick factor for long.

On the eve of her departure Shell conferences with her brothers, Toby and Hank. The holograms are decent, and if not for the lack of smell she'd have thought they were right in the room with her. Good signals, good sound quality.

"Hey," she says.

"Baby sister," says Toby. Tall, blond from their mother, talkative, always smiling, and transmitting from somewhere on Mars, a settlement whose name Shell can never remember.

"Stinkbug," says Hank. Brown hair, five-eight, slender. He's called her that since she was two. Taciturn, works as some kind of operative or agent. Brown hair, five-eight, slender. He and Shell look alike and they both favour their father. He cannot talk about his work.

"While you're out there, look out for Dad," says Toby.

"Don't," says Hank.

"What? We don't know that he's dead," says Toby.

"It's been fifteen years," says Shell. Toby always does this. They declared Haldene Campion dead years ago so they could move on and disburse his assets.

"Just keep your ears open," says Toby.

"How? We're all going to be asleep for the journey, you know that."

Toby nods. The hell does that mean?

"I'll tell you what Dad told me," says Hank. "Make us prouder."

"'Prouder'?" says Shell.

"Yes, he said he was already proud of our achievements. It was his way of saying 'do more' or something," says Toby.

"I'm just starting. I don't have anything to prove," says Shell.

"Campions are champions," says Hank.

"Jesus, stop," says Shell. Shell remembers that their father used to say that too.

They talk some more, this and that, everything and nothing.

Not a lot of companies use Kennedy Space Center any more, but strong nostalgia draws a crowd, and publicity matters, or so MaxGalactix tells Shell. Geographically, KSC is good for launching into an equatorial orbit, but new sites that are more favourable in orbital mechanics terms and friendly to American interests have popped up. KSC is prestige and history.

Parade.

Nobody told her there would be one, so now she is embarrassed because she doesn't like crowds or displays of ... whatever this is. So many of them wave, some with American flags, some with the mission patch.

She waves back, because that's what you do, but she would like to be out of the Florida sun and inside the shuttle. You wave with your hand lower than your shoulder so that it doesn't obscure the face of the person behind you. They teach you that too.

Blast off; God's boot on her entire body, both hard and soft, and behind her the reaction of the seat. Shell is not a fan of gs, but training has made her tolerant.

Do not come to heaven, mortals, says God, and tries without success to kick them back to the surface of the planet.

Why am I here? I shouldn't be here.

But she is, and she will deal with God's boot and come out the other side.

The Earth is behind her and the *Ragtime* lies ahead.

Short, shallow breaths, wait it out.

Gs suck.

After docking, Artificials from the shuttle escort and usher Shell and other passengers from the airlock through the entire length of the ship to their pods. Medbots stick IVs and urine tubes into her while a recording goes over *Ragtime*'s itinerary. First hop is from Earth to Space Station Daedalus, then bridge-jumps to several space stations till they arrive at Space Station Lagos for a final service before the last jaunt to the colony planet Bloodroot.

"You'll be asleep at Lagos, so don't worry about anything you may have heard about Beko," says Ragtime.

"What's Beko?"

"Oh, you don't know. Lagos has a governor, but the real power is Secretary Beko. She has a reputation for being very intense. It doesn't matter. You will not be interacting with her, so relax."

"All right. What about on Bloodroot?"

"You're not meeting anyone on Bloodroot either. We enter orbit, they send shuttles to get their passengers, we turn around and come home. Easy."

"Won't I need furlough by then? It's a ship, Ragtime. It can get boring."

"I don't see why you can't spend time on the surface.

You've had all the necessary vaccinations. If you want to, just tell me at the time."

Shell starts to feel woozy. "I'm getting ... getting ... "

"Don't worry, that's the sedative. I'll wake you when we get to ... and ... "

The world fades.

Ten Years Later ...

Ragtime: Shell

Shell, sweating, heart thumping, bursts into Node 1, overshooting because she didn't compensate enough for microgravity.

"Ragtime, seal the bridge!"

"Sealing."

The door shuts, the reassuring thunk of steel bolts.

Shell grabs a handrail and rests for a few seconds, then she calls up her IFC. Red, blinking alarms everywhere. She cannot attend to them yet.

She opens a comm and records a message.

"Mayday, mayday. This is Captain Michelle Campion of the starship *Ragtime*. I have a situation. Multiple fatalities ... "

She stops, deletes. She doesn't know who might be listening to such a broadcast, what harm or panic it might cause.

Calm down.

Think.

She starts again.

"This is Captain Michelle 'Shell' Campion of the starship *Ragtime* ... "

Chapter Two

Bloodroot: Fin

Fin deletes the sentence, starts again.

Hands poised for typing motion, he peeks out of the window. Still dark, but he can sense dawn without looking at the clock. The desk is littered with layers of hand-scribbled studies of CAD models for printing. They are, for the most part, bespoke weapon designs. A lot of them won't be made – an intellectual exercise for him, but it keeps Fin's mind active. Aborted designs lie obscured in scrunched up paper on the floor.

Two cups of cold coffee sit beside each other. He made one, forgot it was there, discovered it was cold, got up, made another, and forgot that one as well. This happened sometimes when he got lost in thought. Fin thinks of taking a nap, but the bed is covered in paper. He has a workshop, but he never uses it.

The keyboard shimmers in the air, each letter brighter when Fin hits the key.

Dear Respected One,
    My name is Rasheed Fin. I am grateful to you
for condescending to read my letter. I do not want
to waste your time.
    I am not eloquent. I want to apologise for

No. Too trite, too ass-kissy, too pathetic, definitely not the right tone.

Fin rises, disconnects his IFC from the terminal and swears. He runs his hands through his hair and recognises that it's gone bushy. Not been paying enough attention to grooming. He could go Dada, he supposes. Locs are an option.

A news item drops into his IFC, but the Objectivity Index is less than 50% and Fin has no interest in filling his head with lies. He has lies of his own to atone for.

Fin yawns.

He drops to the floor and starts some desultory push-ups, maybe fifteen. He stops counting, then stops doing them. He had intended to stretch, but the failure of his apology threatens to infect everything. He leaves the study, noting the hum of the printer with satisfaction. He snatches his tools and coat, unlocks the door quietly, so he doesn't wake Mother, then stares at the door. He opens it and sweats as he forces his foot over the threshold. His entire body trembles and he drops the tools, which helps because they roll outside and he has to pick them up.

This morning the air carries eucalyptus. Not from any of the trees nearby, but Fin knows which copse the scent is from. He walks briskly and in fifteen minutes he's in his spot.

He spends an hour planting trees in the Beltane Arm. Others are there with him, giving the tight smile of fellowship, but not talking. Though he works hard as anyone else, and plants more trees than anyone else, in his mind he is considering and discarding apologies. His thought process is sluggish with guilt.

Bloodroot is surrounded by dense forest as a result of a tree planting tradition which dates back to the start of the colony. The habitat itself is interwoven with endless treeways, thick spirals of alternating woodland and paved road, so that there is no predominance of human constructions. Avoiding the mistakes of Earth and Nightshade, avoiding the insidiousness of land conquest, the colony is built on the principle of land collaboration and ecological integration. Buzzwords from his education. From what Fin has read, he would say the problem of Earth was greed and energy source choices, but who the hell knows? They had the same geothermal energy and nearly the same solar energy that Bloodroot uses.

Fin returns home. Entering the house is no problem; it's going out that drives him crazy.

He tinkers with the printer until it clicks back into the job he set it, making a new firing pin for his oldest handgun. Only then does he wash himself. The shower sputters out when he is covered in soap, then comes back ice cold, startling him, and he bangs his head.

He is washing the grease off when a call comes in.

"Hello?"

"Am I speaking to Rasheed Fin?" asks an officious voice.

"Yep."

"Hold for Director Unwin." A few clicks. While waiting, Fin realises that he is standing straighter. Gerald Unwin is his boss – or, would be. No, is. Fin is suspended, but still employed.

"How're you doing, son?" asks Unwin.

"I'm fine. Just finished planting. Keeping busy."

"Where do you plant?"

"Beltane."

"Ah, I do Innocenti. So, you're okay?"

Fin stops to swallow. "I'm fine."

"Good. I want you to come and see me."

"Yes, sir. When?"

"Right now."

Really? They finally decided to fire him? "Sir, can I ask what it's about? I don't think it's fair to bring me in without warning, without preparation. I—"

"Fin, just get your ass in here. I'll send a car." Unwin cuts the connection.

Fin exhales. His heart skips and slows, skips and slows. He heads for the wardrobe. He hasn't been at work for a year and all his clothes are out of fashion. If they're terminating him, he wants to have some dignity. No time to do anything about his hair, but he shaves and cuts his fingernails.

He yells in the direction of upstairs. "Mother, I'm going out. Don't let anyone into my room, I'm working on something."

"Rasheed, don't forget to eat before you leave." Her voice floats down like a prophecy.

"Yes, Mother," says Fin, barely attending to what he says. He is trying to decide whether to go out armed or not. He has no job, so technically he won't be authorised to carry weapons. And if they're finally pulling the trigger on Fin's dismissal, they might confiscate his guns. He goes without.

On the room door, the last thing he sees before leaving, is a painting of a boy walking across a desert with mud-cracked ground as far as the eye can see. He is facing away from the viewer and seems an incidental figure, with the mud-cracks being the focus. It is the only artistic object in a room full of technological bric-a-brac.

He hears the car engine and looks outside. It's like a pod, seating only one. Fin bets the AI doesn't talk. He zips to the door and stands there for a moment, forcing his hand to move to the handle. *Do it*. He manages to shove the door open.

Enough hesitating.

He squeezes his eyes shut, holds his breath and stumbles outside.

Unwin is an older man with beady eyes and a thinning pate. He is still most of the time but can launch from stillness into incandescent rage, a reaction that can disappear as quickly as it starts. Fin is glad to have worn a suit even if the suit is threadbare. He feels uncomfortable in the unfamiliar office. Unwin used to have an office with an abundance of wood and leather, resins and oils soothing visitors. This was concrete, glass and plastics. Fin can't help interpreting it as emblematic of a sterile, hardened heart.

There's another man in the room, thin, leaning on the white wall, rolled up sleeves, about the same age as Unwin but seems more cheerful. There are no introductions, and the thin man doesn't say hello or offer a hand.

"What's your health like, Rasheed?" asks Unwin.

"I'm keeping fit," says Fin. He flashes to the push-ups he failed to complete but tamps the memory down.

"Good. I want you to listen to this."

This is Captain Michelle "Shell" Campion of the starship *Ragtime*. I'm code 4717, repeat: 4717. Contaminant on board, possible contagion. Passengers still in Ragtime Dreamstate. Do not send shuttles for passengers until you hear further. Campion out.

"Where's it from?" asks Fin.

"Earth." Unwin studies Fin's face. "What do you think?"

Fin squints. "I think we should be hearing from the AI, not a human. Don't the Earth AIs fly interstellar missions?"

"They do," says Unwin. "We're thinking it's failed and Campion took over."

"Ship AIs don't fail, as far as I know, but I'll take your word for it," Fin says. "If that's the case, they didn't follow protocol, so they have measles."

"No; '4717' isn't the code for contamination," says the thin man.

Fin swivels his chair to face him. "What's it code for?"

"Untimely deaths. Multiple untimely deaths."

"Untimely death from disease. Like measles."

"Maybe."

"I'm sorry, who are you?" Fin looks from Unwin to the thin man.

"Sebel Malaika. Space Command. I'm friends with Gerald." He smiles.

Fin nods and wonders again why he is here. "How experienced is Campion?"

"This is her first interstellar," says Malaika.

Fin kisses his teeth. "She might have made mistakes with the code."

"Maybe, but unlikely. That message is on repeat, and it's a broadcast. We think the 'contagion' part of the speech is for others, but the code is for us. She wants to discourage tourists."

"Or she's panicked and made a mistake with the code," says Fin.

"Either way, we can't risk bringing exotic diseases to Bloodroot. We don't want to become another Nightshade," says Unwin.

"It wasn't disease that did in Nightshade." Fin leans back in his chair. "Why am I here? I'm suspended."

Unwin says, "We're considering you for an assignment. We want you to go up there."

"You what?"

"Don't get excited. This is fact finding only. No repatriation involved. No fighting, no shooting," says Unwin. "Definitely no pyrotechnics."

"We want to send you up in a shuttle. You have a look around, talk to Campion. If everything's okay we come and get the passengers on your signal," says Malaika.

"I'm a repatriator, not a spaceman," says Fin. When they mentioned an assignment, he thought they meant doing an IFC dive to mine for incriminating data, which Fin is good at, and has been doing on the sly as a favour to colleagues. He does not want to fly off into the Brink. "I don't like space."

"You've been to space twice," says Unwin.

"As a tourist, boss, and I hated it. The first was when I was in school and the second was to impress a girl. I didn't get good grades in astronomy and I didn't get the girl."

"This time you'll be just like a tourist with extra duties. You'll go with a partner who will fly the shuttle, dock with the *Ragtime* and help with protocol."

"Protocol," says Fin.

"You're not good with protocol," says Unwin.

"Shouldn't this be a government thing? Don't they have departments for this?" says Fin. "This isn't our ... my department. I have to wonder why they're entrusting something like this to a private company."

"Optics. Nobody in government wants to be responsible for releasing a plague on the colony. Better if 'rogue contractors' can be blamed. You wanted to get back into investigations, right? To repatriations? This is how.

You solve this, you get full reinstatement, back pay and exoneration."

I can't be exonerated when I'm guilty, thinks Fin. But getting his job back …

"You're sending me because if I make a mess, you can say it's because I've been away for a year," says Fin. "And I'm already tainted."

Unwin raises his eyebrows. "They do say after some years detectives become paranoid."

"But is it true?"

Unwin nods.

"I can't just go into space. My mum—"

"Don't be absurd."

"How much time do I have before—"

"Call your mother because you are not going home. You need training and there isn't much time."

In the spaceport, the first thing Fin notices are the rows of space shuttles that are poised to get passengers from the *Ragtime*. They run engine tests in series to maintain readiness.

For the next few days someone follows him about with a clipboard, testing his limits. They are used to younger postulants, and while Fin isn't significantly older, he is more tired, more depleted.

He tries, he pushes his body further than he has ever done, and he does want this. Nothing is more important than getting his job back because he doesn't know what he will do otherwise. He has stared into a gun muzzle a few times over the last year, and not to run a cleaning rod through or check the performance of his printer. Without challenge, his brain has gone to mush, his equipment, like his clothes, out of date.

He does not bond with his trainer. He wants to see her as an enemy to be defeated rather than a guide with the same objective. He knows this is unhelpful, but he can't help himself.

Dear Respected One,
I know how you must feel about me, and it can't be worse than I feel about myself.
It wasn't my fault.

No. Too whiny, not taking responsibility. He is responsible and it was his fault.

Time to rejoin the training.

In the evenings, when both his body and mind are tired from being taxed to the limit, Fin studies what information they have on Michelle Campion. Comes from a space-faring family, three generations of what Earth people call astronauts. The profile contains a standard image, which is Campion, face and shoulders, in a half-turn towards the camera, smiling. She has brown hair, brown eyes, and the kind of facial creases that make people trust. Or fall in love. This is a publicity photo, though, and she would have been given specific instructions. Her training and flight records are sterile figures. Data from Earth tends to come in bursts bounced from bridge to bridge. It is expensive, tightly controlled, and there is no room for embellishment. The records are routine and don't shed light on why this rookie is flying an interstellar without AI.

Fin disconnects his IFC from the terminal and tries to sleep.

Fin hates space: the cramped living quarters, the weird food, the toilets with their grasping tubes, the forced proximity to others, the smells. This persists despite the best efforts of the spacewoman in charge of training him.

"Stop fighting it. Work with the limitations," she says.

Fin shakes his head like a toddler refusing food. "I'm only taking this mission to get back to what I really do."

"Yes, you're an investigator. I know that. But you aren't one right now, so start to think like a spaceman, hey?"

"I'll never be a spaceman."

"You are aware that there are people who live in space all the time, right?"

"Good for them."

"Uh-huh. At least tell me you're going to trim that hair down to size. That's not going to fit in a helmet."

A few days to the end of the week, Malaika summons Fin. He has documents on his desk that Fin surmises are results.

"You drink?" asks Malaika.

Fin shakes his head. "My family is of The Book. Alcohol isn't permitted."

Malaika pours himself a drink. "Your boss told me a story about you."

Fin groans.

"Relax, it's not the one you think, although I have heard that one too." Malaika sips his drink. "Unwin says when he first met you it was in a class of twenty. He was there to introduce you all to criminology studies. He came in with a beaker full of urine. He stuck a finger in and put a finger in his mouth. Then he placed the beaker in front of the first student and told each of them to taste and pass on."

"I remember."

"He said you were the only one who didn't taste the piss."

"Mr Unwin dipped one finger in the urine and tasted a different finger, sir."

"Yes. He does this every year. When you didn't fall for it, he thought you had promise. He still thinks that."

"I failed the spaceflight training, didn't I?" says Fin.

"Woefully. Except on intuitive thought, where you failed marginally."

Fin sighs. He had really thought this would get him back to work. "I'll pack my things."

"I'm still sending you," says Malaika. He drains his glass.

"I don't understand. Why?"

"Because of promise. Unwin trusts that promise and I trust Unwin. Also, I pick people for work based on their strengths, not their weaknesses. You can adjust for weakness, but no adjustment will bring strength where there is none. At most, you get mediocrity. Congratulations, son, you're going to Bloodroot's first investigation in space. Don't fuck it up."

"Thank you, sir."

The car stops and the Artificial emerges.

"Salvo!" says Fin.

"It's good to see you, Rasheed Fin."

Unlike many Artificials, Salvo looks inhuman. No real attempt at verisimilitude, but he is a superficially male, bald android. He has a face and eyes, eyelids that blink, but he is clearly not human. These models are classified as equipment, mainly, and Fin has had him for six years.

"I have a job and I need an assistant because apparently I cannot be trusted to follow procedure. Tell me, are you rated for space?"

"Not yet, but there is a station where I can be updated," says Salvo.

"Absolutely splendid."

In the end, it takes ten days because of problems on the runway on day seven and a fuel line malfunction on day eight. Nothing explodes, though.

Fin calls his mother every night.

They clear Bloodroot's gs in eight minutes, leaving six hours to dock with the *Ragtime* – precise work that Fin is glad to leave to the untiring, undistracted Salvo.

Chapter Three

Ragtime: Shell, Fin

Shell dips, then thrusts herself upwards into the cupola, the most fore position on the *Ragtime*. The sun is in the right position to cast light over Bloodroot, blue-green, with an atmospheric force field. Weird that there was a time when humankind thought only one planet in the universe could support life. Weirder still was when they thought the Earth flat.

The cupola trip is illogical. She knows Bloodroot is sending someone and she wants to see the shuttle; to do that she'd have to use the external cameras, of course. She somersaults and kicks back down into the bridge. She runs checks for an hour and a half. A ship like *Ragtime* needs taking care of, and without the Master AI Shell has to make sure the systems are functioning – a task which has to be done by her and the various maintainer bots who take orders. The last thing she checks is the passenger quarters. That's a lot of real estate to keep sweet.

Shell is running on the treadmill when the call comes in on the radio, relayed by her IFC.

"*Ragtime*, come in. This is space shuttle *Equivalence*."

"This is Ragtime One. Over."

"Informing you of abortive six-hour dock. Now attempting two-day rendezvous with *Ragtime*."

Male voice, no sign of panic.

"Is *Equivalence* compromised? Over."

"Negative. All systems optimal. *Ragtime* failed docking protocol. Prep for manual protocols in forty-six hours, please. Acknowledge."

"Acknowledged. Over."

"Thank you, *Ragtime*. Over and out."

Failed?

Of course, Bloodroot sent an investigation team but doesn't know how compromised the AI is. That they didn't send a health team shows they got Shell's message. They are also keeping comms to the bare minimum, not knowing what lies on board.

She takes off the "gravity" harness that pushes her into the surface of the treadmill and towels off.

Why did the rendezvous fail? Shell's first thought is that it has to be something she missed. She queries the logs.

The *Equivalence* started messaging their protocol to the *Ragtime* as soon as they cleared atmosphere. Mission Control would have sent the rendezvous data to the *Ragtime* before launch, expecting the AI to sync. The *Ragtime* had to have acknowledged and agreed before the Bloodroot team set off. From the logs, the *Equivalence* started transmitting telemetry at Insertion Altitude, 220km. It started the Hohmann transfer into a phasing orbit that would have brought it up to the *Ragtime*'s 420km. The *Equivalence* fired engines, triggering the short rendezvous as agreed, then tried to accelerate to match the *Ragtime*.

Inexplicably, the *Ragtime* stopped responding to the data. Shell knows it heard the data because the *Ragtime* sped up, actively thwarting the possibility of the *Equivalence* ever achieving the six-hour dock.

There are pages of the *Equivalence* sending queries from the phasing orbit, as if the ship was repeatedly saying:

Are you there, Ragtime?

Are you there, Ragtime?

Are you there, Ragtime?

What the hell is going on?

Shell's unease worsens, moving like flood water tendrils. But that is a luxury. The ship still needs to be run. Shell pushes into the next node, moving aft. Most of the walls in all directions are full of attached storage behind netting, but on occasion Shell encounters arachnobots giving way, hanging on by grab rails, noting her, probing her IFC. She stares back as if it is a contest, and when she tires she heads for the science labs to check on the experiments. Not to go in, just to check the door.

Shell straps herself into the vertical sleeping bag and rests for seven hours because she knows that whatever happens, she needs her wits, and a rested brain functions better. All the yammering of her thoughts fades away as she works her phantom worry beads. She dreams of being on Earth, of being a child, of playing with her brother, her younger brother, on a swing. A few yards away her mother looks on with that vague smile she wears. She has a book from which she looks up every few minutes to be sure the kids are safe, regular as a cuckoo clock. Shell is trying to go higher than her brother. She cannot remember her brother's name in the dream and feels embarrassed about it. She wants to get off the swing and ask her mother, but she also wants to go higher. Shell is happy and wakes up abruptly, instinctively sure an alarm has gone off. She's wrong.

She feels a breeze against her right forearm and looks down.

There is a wolf right outside her sleeping pod, nose centimetres from her skin, hackles up, ears flickering. The breeze is the rhythmic breathing that matches the rise and fall of the wolf's belly.

Shell screams and recoils as much as she can. The wolf looks up into her eyes and launches away, floating as if it has lived in low gravity all its life. It flows aft. Shell releases herself from the sleeping bag but stays in the pod, hanging on to a rail, peeping out.

"Ragtime," says Shell, looking from fore to aft and back again.

"Captain."

"What is a wolf doing on board?"

"Captain, can you repeat your request, please?"

Damn. Backup AI. Simple instructions, simple queries.

"Ragtime, playback corridor cams, five minutes."

"Yes, Captain."

Nothing. Empty passageways, some floating lint, sickly jaundiced low-power light.

"Ragtime, get a medbot over here."

"Yes, Captain."

Nightmare?

Seizure?

Hallucination?

Am I ill?

Just what I need.

Fin

Fin watches Salvo and maintains comms with Campion. She sounds so contained and controlled that if not for the background file Fin would have thought her an Artificial. Salvo stares intently at the crosshairs from the periscope camera, trying to align for docking with the *Ragtime*. The distance counters rapidly fall to zero.

"Contact," says Salvo. "Confirm capture, please."

"Capture confirmed," says Campion.

"You should be on your way to the hatch," says Salvo to Fin.

Fin half expects something to go wrong, but the hatch opens, and there she is framed in the circular airlock.

They shake hands as is customary. Quarantine on both sides guarantees contagion-freedom. Small, dry hand, firm grip, fleeting. All business. Fin scrambles a bit and soon floats aboard the *Ragtime*, with Salvo scant seconds behind him. The ship smells of nothing. They must have excellent cleaning bots.

Campion seems to clock Salvo as an Artificial right away and focuses on Fin. He does the same to her. She's small, maybe five-four, five-five, but seems to have a strong frame, brown hair all tucked back, brown eyes like her photo; but enlivened, she is filled with anxiety-fuelled intensity. Fin wonders what she sees when she looks at him. Brown-skinned colonial?

"So, you guys are cops," Campion says.

"I'm a contractor," says Fin.

"And I belong to him," says Salvo, deadpan.

"No, he doesn't. But he works with me," says Fin.

"Okay. Have you done this before?" A note is creeping into her voice that Fin does not care for.

"Many times," says Fin. "On Bloodroot. With aliens."

"Let me get this straight. You have never investigated a killing on board a large spacecraft?"

"*Any* spacecraft, really. But don't worry. The principle is the same, except all your culprits are locked in here. With murder, some things never change: means, motive, opportunity." Fin shifts his weight as best as he can manage. "Tell us what happened. In your own words."

Shell looks from Fin to Salvo and back.

"The master AI failed . . . "

Chapter Four

Ragtime: Shell

Ten Days Earlier ...

"Campion, wake up. Wake up, Campion."

A cool mist, sprayed on her eyelids to dissolve the rheum. She does not know where she is, but the panic in her mind cannot translate to motion because she is without sensation, and paralysed.

Not totally, though. After the eye gunk is moisturised, Shell finds she can move her eyelids.

"Campion, open your eyes."

The hell is this repetitive voice?

She opens her eyes.

An image of a kindly older woman, blonde, familiar, larger than life, winking at her, filling Shell's entire visual field.

Feeling returns. Her mouth is dry and holds a metallic taste, with soreness down the throat when she tries to swallow. She feels tubes going into both arms and one into her bladder. She begins to remember.

I'm in space.

The giant face is her mother's, as is the voice prompting her – choices that Shell made for her emergence from sleep.

I'm on the Ragtime.

"Where are my worry beads?" she says, but not really because she can't move her mouth yet.

Her mother's projected face disappears, replaced by a display of her most recent blood results, then her blood gases.

"Captain, I'm awake," says Campion. She remembers more. She is first mate, and this is her first long-haul. The Captain does not respond. She remembers he likes to be called Ragtime.

"Ragtime, I'm awake."

There are bands around her limbs, myostimulators to maintain muscle tone during interstellar travel. Weight simulators would have been applied by the maintenance bots to stave off osteoporosis, physiotherapy to maintain nimbleness, and some kind of moisturising routine for the skin.

Shell can now move her fingers, so she mimes the movement of her worry bead meditation. The Captain, Ragtime, still hasn't answered, which is concerning.

"Ragtime, alternative protocol. Untether me."

If the Captain is non-functional, Shell has a lot of work ahead of her. The first bots arrive to detach her from life support. She starts with the first awake physio and TENS machines and sips of fluid through a straw. She spits some out to confirm artificial gravity. Confirmed.

Her first long-haul flight, her first voyage with MaxGalactix, and already the ship malfunctions. She should have gone to NASA.

"This is a recording for ... Michelle Campion. It will require you to respond to prompts. Do you understand?"

"Yes."

"To help you recover from the disorientation of Dreamstate, Ragtime produced this recording to tell you where you are, so that as soon as you can walk, you'll be able to find your way around. The *Ragtime* is composed of a stem made up of an integrated truss structure. There are two toruses aft, and a cupola with temporary crew quarters fore. Between them, on the outside, a solar array. Can you see the graphic?"

"Yes."

It turns like a ghost in Shell's visual field, transparent, insect-like, solar panels like wings.

"Thank you. You are in Torus 1, in one of the passenger pods. Your position should be glowing."

"It is."

"Thank you. The entire ship is modular so that the parts can come apart and be used on other designs after decommissioning. The toruses are composed of pods like the one you're in. The truss is composed of nodes, numbered zero to seven. The cupola is on Node 0. To get to the cupola, you would exit your pod, exit the torus through a spoke to the truss, then follow the fore directional arrows through each node till you get to zero. If the node number is increasing, you're going aft, the wrong way. It's a straight shot, so you can't miss it. The route should be glowing on your graphic."

"It is."

"Thank you. Airlocks and docking ports are off Node 1, as are temporary crew quarters. You would have seen these when you embarked. There are two nodes off Node 5: Node M, starboard, medical bay, and Node E, port, the experimental wing. You are forbidden from entering Experimental. Do you understand?"

"Yes."

"Thank you. Waste disposal is off Node 6. I'm told to warn you not to dispose of waste out of the airlock. Acknowledge."

"Acknowledged."

"Thank you. For power ... "

Shell tunes out. She knows this information because she overlearned it on Earth. Power is bioreactor, fuel cells and those solar panels. Limited solid fuel for engine burns. The subroutine requires her verbal responses, so she goes through the motions. Something to do with Legal, no doubt. She puffs her cheeks and blows air out of pursed lips.

Gonna be a long disembark ...

Day fourteen.

Shell can walk without support, and jog for short

periods. She clearly does not have Bridge Unreality Syndrome. The x-ray comparison shows one of her incisors as worn down since she went to sleep. Bruxism.

She stands in her pod now, finally ready to take charge, tilting and cracking her neck like a boxer.

"Ragtime, can you hear me?"

"Yes, Campion." Why is he calling her that? Doesn't he remember?

"In seed time learn, in harvest, teach ... "

"I don't understand, Campion."

That would be too easy, of course. "Ragtime, am I cleared by medical?"

"Yes, Campion."

"Activate my IFC."

"Activated."

"I'm taking control."

"Yes, Captain."

Holy fuck.

The entire display is flashing red. Not a few items – everything. Outside the pod, emergency lights are on. The maintenance bots are active. Artificial gravity is on, so count that blessing. Shell's IFC searches and finds a socket into a terminal, and she starts running checks that turn the red to amber and most others to green. Her left hand works worry beads that are not there.

Many of the problems have already been dealt with by maintenance bots, but they require acknowledgement from Captain: A small leak in the water recirculation. A sensor array knocked askew by space junk or a micrometeoroid, fixed by the Big Dumb Arm and the extra-vehicular bots. It looks less diarrhoea-inducing after a while. Shell finds herself wondering what happened to the primary AI.

"Ragtime, how long since Captain went down?"

"You are Captain."

Stupid.

Secondary AI is basic and has trouble recognising individuals. It sees roles; therefore, "Captain" means whoever the captain is at any given time, otherwise it will develop an internal conflict.

"Ragtime, how long since you have been active?"

"Five hundred and sixteen hours."

Three weeks. So, one week before I woke up.

"How long since the ship stopped?"

"The ship is still in motion."

God, this is tedious.

"Are we at destination?"

"Yes. Stable elliptical orbit around the colony Bloodroot."

Thank fuck for that. "How long have we been in orbit?"

"Five hundred and sixteen hours."

So the primary AI piloted the *Ragtime* to destination, then shut down. Why?

Shell makes a quick check of the passengers before a planned diagnostic debug of the AI …

What the hell?

"Ragtime, I'm only showing 969 passengers!"

"Correct."

That isn't right.

*

Don't lose 'em; don't break 'em.

The *Ragtime* is like a small town with most of the citizens asleep. The robots are active always, except when they shut down for servicing. Each passenger is in their own pod, similar to Shell's. Rather than trust sensors, she manually checks and finds thirty-one passengers missing. The pods are not only empty, they are clean – as clean as the day Shell first arrived on the ship a decade earlier. A thousand pods is a lot to check personally, and it takes twenty-two hours, but she can handle boredom. If she couldn't, she wouldn't have the job. Repetitive tasks are the norm in space and calming in a crisis.

Double-checking to be sure the empty pods have the same numbers as those in the sensor readings, Shell finds that all thirty-one unaccounted-for pod vacancies match. The occupants of the other pods are as peaceful as stoned university students.

Shell sticks her head into one of the empty pods and inhales. Something chemical, maybe disinfectant? A ghost of a smell. In her visual field, one of the flashing amber lights is waste disposal.

"Ragtime, are there video feeds from the empty pods?"

"Not available."

"What? Check again."

"No files found for empty pods, Captain."

"Feeds for occupied pods?"

"All accounted for."

There. The detail that tells Shell something or somebody

is deliberately giving her a bad day. Her skin crawls, and whatever sense of safety she has begins to fray.

The disposal unit is thirty minutes away. As soon as Shell enters, she sees the problem.

The entire space is filled with the chopped-up bodies of passengers.

She has no memory of how she passed from aft, where the passenger torus is, to fore, Node 1, the bridge, where the waking crew is meant to hang out. Shell has seen the dead before, but not like this. She feels the panic rising like a living thing inside her, bubbling up, starving her of oxygen. She breathes fast, holding on to a handrail and hanging in the low gravity. Nobody trained her for this. Astronaut training anticipates everything one can reasonably expect to come across. A killing spree is not reasonable. A murderer on board is not reasonable.

And the murderer is still on the ship.

Shell can see the dismembered bodies with her eyes closed. It's the tattoo that bothers her, a patch of skin with a picture intact – a fairy, artfully rendered, surrounded by clouds, hearts and feathers – the layers of cut skin showing subcutaneous fat in a marinade of congealed blood. She gags. The fairy, with veined wings, her tiny naked body revealed through the transparent membranes.

Shell's mouth and throat feel itchy, paper-dry. It is a few seconds before she realises her breath is raspy.

What the hell, Campion? Contain this.

She runs her beads, controls her breath, counts. She

focuses on the smoothness and the moment, getting from one to the next. She closes her eyes.

You trained for this.

Not mass mutilation; not defiled corpses.

You trained for the unexpected. You trained to be responsible.

When her body adjusts and her mind stops running in all directions, she speaks.

"Ragtime, seal bridge."

"Yes, Captain."

Chapter Five

Ragtime: Fin, Salvo

"And that's when you recorded the message?" asks Fin.

"Affirmative."

Fin can feel her thinking, "these primitive colonials". Earthfolk often mistakenly see Bloodroot as agrarian because they do not wear their technology on their sleeve. At the edge of his awareness, he is cognisant of his and her IFCs synchronising public data about themselves.

"That seems like enough for now," says Fin.

"I'll show you to your pods and where you can stash your stuff. Please meet me in the bridge in fifteen minutes."

The bridge, if you can call it that, is in Node 1, and Salvo is already there when Fin arrives. Campion is in the cupola watching the sun go down on Bloodroot. Fin wonders why Campion would need to view it right now. The *Ragtime* literally passes it every ninety minutes. The tugbots stow away gear from the *Equivalence*, berthed to the *Ragtime* like a tick. A spherical floatbot trails them – internal comm facilitator. In the bridge, Campion seems calmer, certainly friendlier.

"Captain, just to summarise what I've understood," says Salvo. "The *Ragtime* is a passenger ship. You have a standard AI, a software captain, that takes the ship from Earth orbit, through several bridges, to this point in Bloodroot's orbit. You woke up to find that, for some reason, the AI has gone silent and thirty-one of the passengers are dead, dismembered. Is that about right?"

"Yes."

Fin notices Campion makes a funny hand gesture; must be unconscious, rolling thumb over index finger repetitively.

"You've been running the ship alone?" Fin says.

"With the bots and the backup basic AI, yes. I've been doing the minimum to keep the boat afloat to avoid contamination of the scene."

"Will you show us around?" asks Fin.

"First things first. I need to know that you both understand that I am the captain. For all of our sakes, I need you to do what I say when I say it," says Campion.

"Yes, Captain," says Salvo.

"Well, hang on a second ... Captain. What if you're the murderer?"

She thinks for a moment. "Then I'd steal your shuttle and escape to Bloodroot. I'd find a way to disappear."

Fin can't tell if she's joking. "I'm a repatriator. You wouldn't get far."

"I don't know what a repatriator is," says Campion.

"I find people who don't want to be found," says Fin. "Especially aliens."

"Fine. How do you propose to vet me?" she asks.

"We won't," says Salvo.

"You'll remain a person of interest until we finish the investigation," says Fin.

"What does that mean? You'll lock me up in the brig?"

"You have a brig?"

"Figure of speech. Will you lock me up?"

"No, but we'll need to know where you'll be at all times," says Fin.

"Where am I going to go?"

Fin smiles, or at least thinks he is smiling. "Can we get that tour now?"

"Not yet. We need a schedule," says Campion.

"What now?"

"You haven't been listening." She gestures all around her. "Big ship; need maintenance. We all have to chip in or we crash into Bloodroot. I have been running this alone, and there aren't any extant protocols for the eventuality of mass murder, so I've had to improvise. I'm correcting work details, adjusting to your presence."

"We will be honoured to help," says Salvo.

"Glad to hear it. I'll get your work plans to you as soon as I can. Let's go."

Fin throws his hands up and mouths "honoured?" to Salvo, mock annoyed.

This far from the airlock, the sensory texture has

returned. Always that smell of rubber and ozone, the sound of humming machinery, the subtle vibrations.

Service bots scuttle out of the way like small animals in a forest. Campion launches from the grab rail of each node and propels all the way through to the next node. Fin and Salvo follow.

They emerge in a corridor labelled Node 6, where there is more space and nothing is tethered to the wall for storage. Campion somersaults and faces them, finally. Fin collides with her gently. She does not wear perfume. Fin hates low grav.

"We are off the main truss in the aft spokes leading into the aft torus, which is a passenger area."

After fifteen minutes they open a hatch, which Campion flies through and waves Fin and Salvo into. She seals the hatch and launches to grab rails directly opposite which she signals them to emulate.

When they are secure, she says, "Ragtime."

"Captain," says the disembodied voice.

"Spin Torus 2."

"Yes, Captain. How fast?"

Campion looks at Fin with contempt. "Better make it four RPM. We have beginners here."

Once the rotation rate is further cut down to two RPM – Fin cannot tolerate any higher because of nausea and dizziness – they have artificial gravity.

"You can get to either of the toruses from the truss by the spokes; there is no direct route from one torus to another that excludes the truss. This is the passenger area.

Each torus has five hundred and fifty pods for them to sleep in."

With gravity, there is a better sense of up and down. Walking is welcome, and room is welcome. Trust the company to leave the shittiest areas for crew. They look at an empty pod first. It's rectangular, maybe five-by-ten feet, white, clinical, dominated by the bed, which Campion calls a cradle, and the inert medbot fixed to the wall. The temperature in the pod is noticeably cooler.

"Do you freeze them for the trip?" asks Fin.

"No, that would kill them. We cool them to slow their metabolism. We tube feed, catheterise and wipe them. Or rather, the bots do. We anaesthetise them for the journey and insert them into the Ragtime Dreamstate."

Campion takes them to an occupied pod. There are red indicator lights on the outside. The pod has no window, but a large monitor takes up space outside. Campion punches in an override and they look in.

"Obviously, we lock the pods. Passengers are exposed and vulnerable," says Campion.

"Who has authorisation to enter the pods once occupied?" asks Fin.

"Me. The Captain, the original captain. The rescue robots can override anything in the event of a catastrophic event."

"Could I open it from the outside?" asks Fin.

"Try it."

"Salvo's much stronger."

"Salvo can try it."

"I've seen the specs, Captain. I don't need to try," says Salvo.

"Can we see the ones in which the occupants were killed?" says Fin.

They look at five. There is nothing remarkable about the pods. Clean. Empty, save inert medbots. The doors have not been damaged.

"May we see the bodies, Captain?" asks Salvo.

Like any large spacecraft, the *Ragtime* has several refrigerators, some truly huge. Campion had ordered a makeshift morgue and, from the looks of it, the bots improvised by merging smaller spaces. The body parts have not been assembled, just stored in the most convenient positions. It seems disrespectful to Fin, but these are not reflective beings. They do as they're told, to whatever extent subtlety is added to their instructions. Campion instructs the *Ragtime* to construct paper-polymer surgical gloves and masks for Salvo and Fin using their observed dimensions. Artificials can't get diseases, but they can store pathogens like any object, and the protection is for Campion, Fin and the hundreds of sleeping passengers.

"How do we do this?" asks Fin.

"Start with the heads," says Salvo. "Arrange them on the floor tiles. As many as you can find."

"You know what you are doing?" asks Campion.

"This is why I was sent," says Salvo.

"All right. I'll leave you to it. I can spare two mobile med units. Will that suffice?" Campion is on the way out of the door as if she is not really listening for the response.

"For now," says Salvo.

"How will we reach you if we need to?" says Fin.

Campion points to the floating orb. "Speak to these. The *Ragtime* will not respond to your voices as it does not know you. The Captain would have learned, but this … anyway. Yes."

The work turns bloody quickly as the ice melts from Fin's and Salvo's body heat. The bots arrive and station themselves where Campion stood before, and Salvo's IFC syncs with theirs. His eyes glaze over and Fin looks away. He digs out the head of a green-haired teenager that seems frozen solid, the kid's mouth open in a silent agony.

Salvo

Salvo snaps off his awareness from the task of assembling mutilated bodies. A fraction of him prepares to review his previous contact with Rasheed Fin.

Six years ago, they met, Salvo a shining new construct off the assembly line, Fin a talented rookie. Five years ago, they worked their first case: Grey haze. Dozens of people reporting a dust storm in the north. Grey dust, as if from a desert, visibility down to two inches or so. The trouble was, none of the cameras or Artificials saw any problem. There was no haze, but the humans were seeing one. They gave the case to Fin not because it was an easy case to cut his teeth on, but because nobody wanted it. Fin had smiled throughout. He had six thousand people tested for infections, especially encephalitis. When that turned up nothing, he interviewed them and gained permission for IFC dives. He perused five and came out prematurely.

"I know where it is."

He led Salvo right to the Lamber and repatriated it without fuss. In two days, the fog had cleared from all but the most chronic associates of the alien. In a year, nobody remembered the incident.

A year after everyone forgot, there were house fires in Feline Oracle. Nobody thought anything of it – as in, nobody thought they were arson jobs. And they weren't. Not really. Apathy fires, where the house owners just left stoves and lanterns and electrical appliances on for too long; whenever the owners were found alive, they were always in a catatonic stupor. Most of them choked to death on fumes, their corpses burned. Salvo could not work out Fin's algorithm. He plotted the fires on a map, stared at it, and said, "Let's take a ride." They drove straight to a nest of four Lambers linked to a "queen" and repatriated them all. Fin's reputation grew.

Then, the serial killer in Ciscoburg and the choreomania in Dolapo's Pass. Fin solved them all and made it look easy; he had just enough intuition mixed with his logic. Six years they have known each other, five of those working cases together. Fin's last case, the one that got him into trouble … Salvo was not involved. He had a human partner.

Salvo wants to believe that if he had been there, Fin would not have been suspended.

Looking at him now, Salvo can tell that Fin has lost a softness, a light-heartedness. Time will tell whether this will help or hurt matters … time will tell.

Salvo replaces a liver …

Chapter Six

Space Station Lagos: Lawrence

Lawrence Biz appends his digital signature to seventeen documents before taking a break by throwing food to carp in the outdoor rock pool from his bench. They slip towards the bits of nourishment lazily, like courtesans unimpressed with a suitor's gift. He's overfed them. Lawrence smiles. He's indulgent to fish like he is to his daughter.

The simulated sunlight and birdsong are convincing today, especially to someone who has lived with the real thing. It makes him wonder if he's been away from planets too long. He does nine more documents before dipping into the fish food again. At least the fish are real. The plaque says *Cyprinus rubrofuscus*, which is Chinese carp, or koi. These ones are first-generation from Earth and twenty-two years old – about as old as Lawrence's daughter, Joké. He returns to the boring work. Though they are legal documents, amendments to by-laws and eyes-only acknowledgements, he does not read before signing. They can't change them without his authorisation, although he is never consulted on the actual changes. Ceremonial guy.

He is meant to be here with Joké, but she doesn't show. This is not unusual for her, and the reason he brought fish food with him. He finds himself renewed by the carp. Cheaper than a massage, easier than therapy. He gets a notification for a meeting with Beko. Odiferous Beko. The only thing Lawrence finds more boring than a meeting with Beko is document ratification.

This meeting invitation seems more insistent than others, making Lawrence wonder what the problem is. The sky has not fallen, or he would have heard about it. The integrity is good, the miners aren't on strike, otherwise, the news feed would have told him. Lagos is not at war with anyone – not that they ever have been, but you never know. So far, war has been restricted to the home planet, Earth. No wars in the Brink, and all the systems would like to keep it that way. No huffing and puffing, no brinksmanship, no posturing; remarkable for Homo sapiens, really. If only they behaved that way on Earth. Lawrence has attended the congresses, and he agrees with their wishes broadly, but he knows that war is one of those inevitabilities like cancer or an asteroid strike. Most Lagosians don't feel that way, but most Lagosians have never left the space station.

His IFC pulses with the need to respond, but Lawrence hesitates. He watches the carp and, when the urge comes upon him, feeds them from the bag. Not many people come to this level any more, and the signage is in Yoruba and English. Most of the people on Lagos are spaceborn, Generations of the Brink. The Earth language Yoruba is still prevalent, along with French, Arabic, Cantonese and Mandarin. Lawrence himself speaks Yoruba, pestered by parents who half-remembered and supplemented their knowledge with network feeds. Lawrence is the only one of his family to have visited Lagos – the original Lagos, in Nigeria, on Earth – where they laughed at his space-learned Yoruba and took him to parties and clubs every night of the week he spent there. Lawrence tells people he's from Earth, but it isn't true.

Lawrence grew up in the Waikiki system, on a planet called Skeem.

As a child, Lawrence flips the pages fast, searching the pictures, not the text. He comes to a diagram of the solar system, with planets diagrammatically circling the sun, full page, in colour. Should be elliptical, but he's not choosy. He rips the page out and replaces the book on the shelf. He folds the paper carefully and pockets it, then sprints for the back of the library, running his torch beam across the spines of books, hoping that something will catch his eye, though nothing does this time. He kills the torchlight.

He works his way out of the toilet window and lands on the grass.

Light returns, and he thinks the impact switched the torch on again, but it's not his torch.

"Anything broken?" asks the uniformed guard.

Lawrence shakes his head.

"Let's go ask your parents why they permitted you to be out of the house after dark, shall we?"

His parents, of course, have no idea that Lawrence has been stealing out at night, breaking into the library and building a personal astronomy resource centre in a derelict car on their street. He has books, journals, hand-written notes and posters ripped from texts.

Getting caught turns out to be a good thing. The librarian says he ought to be encouraged, not punished. His father, a rickshaw driver, disagrees. They both have their way, and Lawrence fills out application forms while sitting on bruised, welt-covered buttocks.

He ends up with a special scholarship to a space academy on Earth, and when he graduates he immediately joins NASA after rebuffing three private firms. He's fast-tracked to interstellar work. This starts his career, which ends in Space Station Lagos in politics.

Lawrence signals Joké one last time without much hope. The girl is capricious at the best of times, and he has never been able to keep track of her. He waits five minutes, then rises, leaving the fish food for whoever comes to the bench after him. Some kids who are too young to be unsupervised hang out on this segment from time to time. Lawrence does not think they know who he is. He heads for the lift and calls up the IFC to signal his intention to be at the meeting. It promptly informs him that he is five minutes late, and the quorum is waiting for him to arrive before they start. Lawrence does not hurry.

Things weren't always thus. He took this post ten years past and he was by inches marginalised, although deep down he wants to step down and retire. Leadership was and is a mistake. He knows it's something they want, but a stubborn streak makes him refuse to quit until they come out and say it.

The meeting, the entire government of Lagos. Lawrence, the governor: an entirely ceremonial position for an entirely ceremonial person. Beko, a substantial woman and a woman of substance, the true power, at the head of the table. She calls herself the Secretary, which is vague enough. Lawrence likes her and is especially attentive when she speaks, mindful of the paradox. She is dismissive of him. Everybody is dismissive of him, so he does not take it personal.

"Good, we can start," Beko says.

"Sorry I'm late," says Lawrence, but he's not sorry.

"Lagos, no minutes," says Beko.

"Yes, Secretary Beko," responds the space station.

Beko clears her throat. "The last ship to traverse the bridge was the *Ragtime*, bound for Bloodroot. A minor concern around here is that the Captain has not sent confirmation of arrival. Today we intercepted a message from the acting captain, Michelle Campion, to Earth."

"Campion?" says Lawrence. "Shell Campion? I knew her when she was a child." As soon as he speaks, he regrets it. Beko looks at him as if wondering why he still exists. Lawrence remembers a bright child who played with rockets and Buzz Aldrin action figures.

"As I was saying before His Excellency interrupted me," says Beko. "We have a situation here."

"I don't understand," says Ibidun Awe. "We do not own the *Ragtime*." She is always daft. Pretty, ambitious, but stupid.

Beko, long-suffering saint. "Look at our charter. The Bridge Operational Standards say our job is not complete until the ship AI gives the all-clear. The ship comes through the bridge, gets maintenance at the space station and goes on to its planetary destination, at which point it gives the signal, and we get paid. Did none of you know this?"

Lawrence does, but he feels it is more important to be in harmony with the room, so he arranges his face into surprise, like everyone else apart from Beko.

"How can we be responsible for all that? The ship could encounter any number of ... incidents before arrival," says Silas. Tall, thin, eager to please Beko, always polite to Lawrence in the old Yoruba way. He'll go far.

"The problem is none of you reads," says Beko. "Or at least you don't read what matters. The wording of the contract has not mattered until now because the transport has always worked. The real reason it's worded like that is because we, the owners of the bridge and space station, *own* all the space beyond it. Notionally. On paper. This is how we guarantee that the items we manufacture – the ark-ships, the Einstein-Rosen bridge components, the Dyson swarm modules, the ship drones, all of it – are safe; we underwrite any loss in our space."

Some guy pipes up. Shittu? Shitta? "So the Colonial Authorities—"

"Are subordinate to us, yes, but are also our responsibility in some ways. You will not believe the shit I had to eat when Nightshade failed."

"I still can't tell Nightshade from Bloodroot," says Ibidun.

"Bloodroot is flat and Nightshade is dead," says Silas.

A rote simplification, although, like all such mental shortcuts, it contains a scaffolding of truth. The powers that be may like to dismiss it, but Lawrence would not classify Nightshade as failed. Dealt a mortal blow, yes; dying, but not dead. It follows the standard protocol for settling, an Earthnorm model: Establish safety, build habitats, mine materials, use them to build industry and structures of renown. Bloodroot came later and the first settlers were from Nightshade, not Earth. What most people don't know, or care about, is that the main difference between Bloodroot and Nightshade is philosophical. The colonists of Bloodroot wanted to work in ecological harmony with the planet, and such a group would find Earthnorm antithetical. Bloodroot *grows* its habitats using biopolymer substructures and has very few high-rises, hence flat. Nightshade's biosphere is poisoned, hence dead.

"All you need to know is that the *Ragtime*'s distress is our distress. I'm not saying we have to fix its problems and find out why thirty-one of its passengers are dead. We just have to get the AI to send the all-clear message, then it's Bloodroot's problem."

"Isn't it already Bloodroot's problem? They sent a team to investigate." Ibidun again.

"It isn't yet Bloodroot's problem, but they don't know that. I'd like us to be in and out of this before any questions are asked." Beko licks her lips, tongue darting out rapidly, like a reptile.

Silas says, "Ma'am, in and out of what? What are you saying we should do?"

"We're sending a team to fix the AI's Pentagram, or, failing that, to rig it so that it sends a completion message. We will do this quickly and quietly, in the Lagos way. Naija no dey carry last."

She stands, signalling the end of the meeting. Everyone else follows suit.

Lawrence is the last person to leave the conference room. He adopts the befuddled elder expression and immediately becomes invisible. He takes fifteen minutes to think. He is so still the motion sensors think the room empty and switch the lights off. He remembers Shell. Delightful child, inquisitive, funny. The only thing her father would talk about, even though he had two older boys and one younger son. Lawrence and Haldene Campion had solidified the bridge protocols and structure in their twenties, owning the Brink. They were relativity explorers, fearful but unwavering in their belief that humanity could and should spread to the cosmos and that they should be the agents of this.

"There is nothing quite like a daughter," Haldene was fond of saying.

Lawrence agrees with the sentiment.

Now Haldene is gone and Lawrence is an impotent bureaucrat and young Campion is in trouble on her first flight into interstellar space.

He rises and the lights come on.

"Nobody needs me here, anyway," he says to himself.

He gets Awe to fuel a shuttle for him. Awe is Beko's man, married to Ibidun though much smarter, and his job on many occasions is to keep Lawrence from interfering with the running of Lagos. Otherwise, his team services the Lagos AI.

"Who's flying you, sir?" asks Awe.

"The on-board AI and I can do it together," says Lawrence.

"But—"

"Listen, you are young. When you get to my age you start to wonder if you were ever alive in the first place. I need to do this myself. Glory days. You understand."

"But—"

"Awe. Think. If I'm out there in the Brink, how much trouble can I cause Beko here? I can't interfere with any Lagos things if I'm in space."

Especially if I crash and freeze in space.

The end of an inconvenience.

"Yes, sir." You can almost hear the cogs turn.

"And I want you to feed the carp on level five, pond eight."

"Yes, sir."

"Fit me for an EVA suit as well. I may be a bit thicker than the last time."

They give Lawrence the *Decisive*, which isn't bad. It's sturdy, not new, not fast, a bit like him. He waits in a lounge while it fuels and runs self-tests.

He files a flight path to one of the outer asteroid mines. *Fuck. Space food.* Okay. Lawrence hasn't been in space for seven years. He lives on the outer layer of the station – the best gravity. Even as he sulks, he can feel the old instincts returning. In the Brink you just make do, because the Brink hates humans.

"What are you doing, Dad? Where are you going?"

He turns to see Joké, a smile that breaks the heart, posture that is doe-like at times. She looks fragile though she isn't. She barely displaces air, as if her solidity is an argument between existence and ephemera.

"I've been calling you all day."

She squeezes his neck. "Umm, I know. I was ignoring your calls. I saw an interesting mould growth in the mezzanine between four and five on my way to see you. I tried to communicate with it. I read it poetry. Where are you going?"

"I have to help out a friend. The daughter of a friend. There's a thing on Bloodroot. I can't let that young lady deal with it on her own."

"What friend? What young lady, and is she cute?"

"Joké!"

"I'm kidding. But I'm asking for me, not you. Hmm. I'm not really kidding, then."

"I'm going because her father would do the same for me."

She plops down beside him. "Good man. I'm coming with."

"You are not."

"You need my help, old man. You wheeze when you climb three steps."

"We have no steps."

"Tomato, tomahto."

"I'm not going to countenance—"

"Hah! I know you know you've lost when you break out the big words. Action Governor! Let us proceed."

The Yoruba say, "If you're gonna eat a frog, eat one that has eggs," which means, if you're going to do something unpleasant, you might as well go large. He hates it when she calls him Action Governor.

The *Decisive* AI contacts him and soon it is time to countdown.

Once more into the Brink.

Chapter Seven

Ragtime: Fin, Shell, Fin

Fin and Salvo make good time. They have, between them, arranged seventeen bodies on the floor, side-by-side. They use Node M, which is roomier than other spaces on the *Ragtime* and designed for medical procedures. Blood everywhere. Fin is acclimatising to the gore, able to accept the feel of dead human flesh, but he expects nightmares. He has seen bodies before in his line of work, but this is far more than he has ever seen at one time. He knows from study that there are such things as mass murder and war, but Bloodroot has experienced neither. A part of him that he resents revels in this, catalogues the data relentlessly, sifts through Shell's account looking for flaws and considers the entire affair valuable experience. That part of Fin is like Salvo and his kin.

Fin looks up as the door slides open. It closes. Opens. Closes.

Opens.

A small bot, barely six inches tall, crawls through the door, smearing blood, scuttling towards Fin, and clamps on to his boot with a hook. Fin stares at it and flicks his leg, but to no avail. He drops the head he is holding with a wet *thunk!* and kicks out, but the bot holds on. Salvo continues his own work.

"Hey, what the ... Salvo, get this off me," says Fin.

Before Salvo can react, the door opens again, and a larger bot launches into the sick bay, springing and latching on to Fin's right hand with six punctures. Minor pain. He finds it heavy and struggles to hold his arm up. The bot fires a tentacle at the wall, anchors it, and pulls Fin towards the spot.

Salvo moves to help, but a wall-mounted medbot seizes the Artificial's arm and clamps him against a different wall.

"This is wrong," says Salvo.

"No shit," says Fin.

The medbot injects the Artificial with something, but there is no effect.

Bots stream in the open door now, splitting between Fin and Salvo, each latching on to a different part of the body or a different bot. The detached part of Fin admires how the bots take turns in a strict algorithm deciding on first human, then Artificial. Is this how those passengers died? Was the carnage logical? He finds it difficult to stand under the weight.

"Salvo, what can we—" Fin screams in agony. One of the bots drills into his leg. Blood spurts out of the wound and mingles with the puddle on the floor. Fin looks to the comm orb. "Campion!"

"Rasheed Fin, send an IFC distress call," says Salvo. The bots drill into him as well, trying to take the Artificial apart. His bland face shows no sign of distress.

Fin sweats and hyperventilates from the pain. He sends an all-points call from his IFC.

A sturdier bot than any of the others wheels into the room and swings an arm, smashing Fin in the chest, taking his breath away. Is he going to die in this place, cut up like the others?

A drill excavates Salvo's side. He does not show pain or confusion.

"This is not right," Salvo repeats.

The bot at Fin's foot starts sawing at the level of the ankle joint. Fin strains against his bonds but the bots hold fast.

"Campion, fuck you, get over here! We're dying!"

The comms orb stays in place, impassive.

Fin sends an IFC distress call again, then he takes a gamble. *Fuck this, we're going to die anyway.* He sends a remote signal to his supply pack and detonates a fraction of the ordnance. He is too far away to know if it works.

Shell

Shell feels the explosion and shudders. She darts out of her sleeping bag and runs into a cloud of debris in the microgravity.

"Ragtime, what just happened?"

"Repeat command."

"Was there an explosion?"

No answer.

Messages pop up on her IFC and she swims through the cloud, aiming aft, for Node M. They've been trying to reach her.

"Rasheed Fin, come back," says Shell, propelling herself with grab rails.

No response. What's going on?

"Salvo, Salvo, come in," says Shell.

"Captain," says Salvo.

"I'm on my way. What's your status?"

"The bots are taking us apart. Fin is unconscious, bleeding and about to lose a limb."

66

"Understood," says Shell. She can't move any faster.
"Ragtime, Ragtime."

"Yes, Captain."

"Reboot all bots now!" *Please do it.*

"Rebooting."

Fin

Salvo finishes the suturing on Fin's leg. It's numb and Fin feels only the tugging, but no pain. He's also got an IV line dripping synthetic blood into his veins. Almost finished. He's not even dizzy any more.

Campion seems confused. Her hands are smeared with blood from taking the inert bots off Salvo and Fin. The constructs lie in a mess on the floor. Campion stands at the edge of one of the pools of blood. She's in loose trousers and a white tee shirt with the MaxGalactix logo over her left chest. She has not packed her hair back, so it seems informal compared to before. There is no guilt in her body language, but Fin doesn't rule anything out.

Campion says, "When you sent the distress signal, what happened? Tell it to me again."

"Nothing to tell. They ignored it," says Fin.

Salvo says, "The normal protocol—"

"I know the normal protocol," says Campion.

"Even I felt the urge to drop what I was doing and assist Fin when I received the signal," says Salvo.

"Salvo, I get it. All constructs are required to respond to expressed human distress by lending assistance. I know my bots are broken. I'm trying to figure out how and why."

"Did you programme them?" asks Fin.

"No. They came pre-loaded, and that's beyond my expertise."

Fin snorts. "How do we know you're telling the truth?"

"I don't know. Because I said so?"

"Where the hell have you been anyway?"

"Sleeping."

Fin sputters. "What? How could you—?"

"Captain, what Fin is trying to say is we needed your help," says Salvo. He finishes dressing Fin's wound. Fin finds the interaction odd. The Artificial has never finished Fin's sentences before. This is not the time for odd behaviour from constructs. Or humans, for that matter.

"I know what he's trying to say," says Campion, eyes on Fin. "He wants to know if I set the bots on you both."

"Is that unreasonable? The bots attacked us, and you control the bots," says Fin. Her face is a beautiful blank and Fin cannot get a read.

"You tried to blow up my ship," says Campion. "You endangered my passengers."

"If I tried to blow up the ship, we wouldn't be standing here," says Fin.

"Yes, we would," says Salvo. "We don't have enough explosive material to destroy the ship. We can't even breach—"

"Shut up, you," says Fin. He pulls out the IV line, which has finished anyway, and steps into Campion's personal space. "I want your IFC logs."

"Not without a warrant," says Campion.

"'War-rant'?"

"Legal authorisation. It means a judge who has jurisdiction must look at the facts and order me, on pain of imprisonment, to give up the last line of privacy humans have. Or maybe you do things differently in the colonies." Just short of a sneer that time.

Salvo moves between them. "I'm sure there's a middle ground to be—"

"No, fine." Fin steps around Salvo, back into Campion's face. "I'll get a war-rant. Salvo, escort *Captain* Campion to her quarters and keep guard."

"Am I under arrest?" asks Campion.

"If you want to be. Tell the ship AI to obey us."

"No. You'll need a court order for that." Campion looks up. "Ragtime, unlimited comm use for Rasheed Fin."

Fin looks to Salvo. "What's a court order?"

"You can't arrest Campion, Fin," says Malaika.

"I have to—"

"You can't arrest her. Lagos will have our heads, and nobody wants aggro with them."

"I want a war-rant, sir. She could be a murderer."

"Is she?"

"Probably not, but I haven't ruled her out yet."

"You can't arrest her. Didn't the Artificial tell you this?"

"How am I supposed to fix this case if she won't cooperate?"

Malaika exhales, long-suffering. "Luckily for me, I don't care, because it's not my job. It's your job, therefore you are the one who needs to know. Negotiate, cajole, beg, but fulfil your mission. Understand, Fin, we don't want to become another Nightshade. The *Ragtime* cargo has experts in many fields and a boost to genetic diversity that we are keen to integrate into Bloodroot."

Fin misses hunting aliens. "I hate working with humans."

"The way I heard it, humans hate working with you, Fin. Get it done. Mission Control out."

At least he's had a lot of practice apologising.

Salvo and Campion have not moved. She is doing that thing with her fingers again.

"I'm sorry, Captain Campion," says Fin. "I really am. Can we start over?"

For a moment she does not react, then she nods. "Ragtime, cool temperature five degrees C."

"What do we do about this?" Fin points to the blood seeping out from under the lab door.

"You two will go in and count the heads, as planned. It'll be messy work, especially without the bots, which will need individual debugging."

"Why were you asleep, Captain? We're in the middle of a crisis," says Fin.

"Because if I don't rest, I'll make a mistake and *Ragtime* will crash into Bloodroot. You investigate. I'll try and keep us alive, otherwise it won't matter." She softens her tone and Fin supposes that is as conciliatory as it gets with her.

When they're finished, both Salvo and Fin are covered in blood again. Fin's muscles hum with fatigue and the two of them sit together on the floor, backs to the wall, admiring their handiwork. The bodies are no longer a jumble of parts. They have order, although it still looks like a wild chainsaw ripped through a lawn party.

"Well, that's not right," says Fin. They checked three times, recounting.

"Maybe the bots left some parts elsewhere?" says Salvo.

Fin talks to the sphere. "Campion."

Campion's voice is tinny. "Campion here. Go ahead."

"We don't have enough bodies."

Chapter Eight

Ragtime: Shell

Shell has a two-hour sleep deficit. She scheduled it, but cannot relax because of the investigators and her fury at them trying to arrest her. She cannot decide if they are incompetent or hyper efficient. She checks the systems, forcing back the emotional detritus of the day. Orbit stable, atmospheric oxygen and carbon dioxide acceptable, bioreactor in balance. Microbial counts are somewhat high, but the breakdown shows the cluster is around the bodies, so this does not alarm Shell. Some microbes can cause corrosion, and it's theoretically possible for food contamination to occur, but it's low probability and Shell has some higher-order problems. There are displays that are faulty, and since the bots are glitchy Shell has to fix them herself. Boring work, but lifesaving. She completes worksheets for Salvo and Rasheed Fin. She does not know if Salvo needs rest, but she treats them as a human and schedules in breaks. She misses the damn AI captain.

"Ragtime."

"Yes, Captain."

"*In seed time learn ...*"

"I don't understand the command, Captain."

Still not working.

Shell emerges from her sleeping pod and heads to the gym, starting her workout with running, planning to move to the weight machine, but Fin calls to tell her there aren't enough bodies.

"What does that mean?" says Shell. That sinking feeling of dread.

"You have thirty-one passengers missing. We don't have thirty-one bodies."

"I'm coming."

"We were expecting a hundred and twenty-four limbs," says Salvo. "Sixty-two arms, sixty-two legs, thirty-one heads, thirty-one torsos.'

"We estimate that you're missing two and a half people," says Fin.

"'And a half'?" says Shell.

"There are ten missing limbs, two missing heads. We are two legs short of a third full body. Two and a half people unaccounted for."

What the hell? She looks at the laid-out bodies and wishes she could get in a shuttle and run away, or at least sleep. Her throat goes dry again and she keeps flashing back to the tangled mess when she found them, but she is the captain and she will comport herself as such. She has a distinct sensation of being watched by her father and feels the urge to turn around, but she does not. If there are missing parts, they have to be somewhere. The robots must have taken them and dropped them by mistake. There will be microbe spikes in the locations as the meat rots. Meat. *I'm calling human remains meat now.*

They sit together on the floor like errant schoolboys, and the Artificial is matching Fin's body language. It's subtle, but Shell never misses that kind of thing, designed to build trust and rapport between them. She wonders if it is software coded or a trait that emerged in the whole soup of machine quasi-autonomy that characterises the constructs.

"What do you think?" asks Shell.

"It's too early and there's not enough information to think," says Fin. "But we can make observations. We have a ship where everyone was asleep. The robots and Ragtime were working and animated until three weeks ago. Two weeks ago, you woke to find the passengers already dead. The bodies are piled up in a most dramatic way. If we had not counted the body parts, we would have assumed, by subtraction, that they were all there."

"What conclusions do you draw from that?" asks Shell.

"None, just theories. The body parts were piled for emotional reaction, for horror, by the killer or killers," says Fin.

"But the bodies were piled by the robots," says Shell.

"Yes. And most likely, the robots did the actual cutting of the bodies. But let's assume, for the sake of my theory, that the killer knew what the bots would do with the bodies, that they would see bodies as waste and try to stuff them into the disposal unit."

"Why?" asks Shell.

"In my career, I've found it useful to ignore why until I know how, Captain," says Fin. "They didn't want us to know about the missing parts, is my guess. If they are parts."

"What do you mean?"

"Isn't it obvious?" Fin looks from Shell to Salvo. "There might be two wakeful people in the *Ragtime*. We can't assume they are dead, although they might be."

"You think the killers are walking about on my ship?" asks Shell. She wonders about fitting a search-and-destroy into her work schedule. She is not in a forgiving state of mind.

"Maybe. But maybe the killers are dead," says Fin.

"I don't understand," says Shell.

"There may be two people still alive on the ship, or there may be one, last-person-standing-type situation. Or there may be none. We cannot rule out the possibility of murder-suicide," says Fin. "Right now, everything is possible."

"Okay, okay, this is all interesting, but what should we do?"

Salvo says, "It makes sense to try to establish the location of the missing parts."

"People, Salvo. We call them people," says Fin. "But, yeah."

"All right, we search," says Shell. "Ragtime."

"Yes, Captain."

"Organic matter search on board, excluding passengers in pods, excluding bioreactor, excluding this room, excluding Node E."

"What if what we're looking for is in Node E?" asks Fin.

"It's not in Node E," says Shell. "Ragtime, commence search."

"Yes, Captain."

"Have you rested?" asks Shell. She faces both of them but makes eye contact with Fin. He seems lost in thought, contemplative. There must have been a reason Bloodroot chose him for the mission. Maybe he's not entirely useless.

Fin seems to come back to himself. "No, but I will."

"Do it now. I don't want you making mistakes with the work detail," says Shell.

"Organic matter located," says Ragtime.

"Where?" asks Shell.

"I cannot say, Captain. It is in motion."

In motion? Maybe they have found the killer. Good. Oh, *that would be so good. And bad.*

"On screen, Ragtime," says Shell. She fires up her IFC display and the video appears. She broadcasts it to Salvo and Fin.

"What in the name of all the Heresies ...?" says Fin.

It's the wolf, the same one that Shell woke up to, loping down the walkway with limbs showing a slight splay in the rotational gravity, snout low, unperturbed. At least the ship and the others can see it too, meaning it is real, not a hallucination, and that it is a real problem.

"I've seen it before," says Shell.

"And you didn't think to mention a pet wolf loose on your ship?" says Fin. He sounds incredulous, and Shell can't blame him.

"It does rather change the parameters of our work, Captain," says Salvo.

"I thought it was just in my mind. Astronauts . . . space-people, as you call us . . . we don't like to admit when our minds play tricks on us. Sometimes it means we don't get to go into the Brink any more. Sometimes it means extensive testing. I don't have the time for that here."

"Captain, I disagree. This is the precise time we need to know if you're going crazy," says Fin.

"Well, I'm not, so it's academic," says Shell.

Fin shakes his head. "We don't know that, and it isn't academic. It means something else might be wrong with you as we speak, and you'd hide it."

"You're working yourself up to another apology, repatriator."

"And you're working yourself up to more dead passengers. I don't want to be dead. Don't endanger us, Captain."

"Can I just point out that we have a wolf on board and we have to capture it?" says Salvo.

"Do you think it savaged the passengers?" asks Shell.

"Negative. No bite marks, no shredding, no tearing. Just cutting," says Salvo. "The robots did the cutting. But we need to isolate the wolf so that it does not interfere with the search for the body p— the missing people."

"Fine. Let's go get the wolf," says Shell.

"That sounds like a good idea. Where are your weapons?" asks Fin.

Shell blinks. "Weapons?"

The cowboys brought weapons, of course – something that would never have occurred to Shell. There is no conflict in spacecrafts; at least, not among crew. There's a lot of tension, sometimes sexual, and being alone in space, especially when the Earth is no longer visible outside the cupola, brings its own stresses.

Space wants to kill you always, Shell. Never forget that.

It is insane to bring weapons into such an environment, where the psychological meaning of a thing is enhanced after ten days. Back in ancient history, Shell knows of a time when cosmonauts were issued with firearms, for killing bears and wolves after the space capsule returned to Earth. At least, that's what the public was told when the information leaked. Even now, stalking through the *Ragtime*, looking for a wolf, Shell's attention is focused on the guns that Fin and Salvo have, pointed forwards as they listen for the pad of lupine motion, inching in an aft direction towards Node 3. The bizarre thing, if you discount the wolf itself as something bizarre, is there are no droppings. Shell tries not to think of the most obvious – but also, at this time, most irrelevant – question: where has it come from? Her training is to always identify the task at hand, which is to find and neutralise the predator in the corridors. They can answer the "where" forensically. Fin's way of thinking is catching.

"I think I can smell it," says Fin.

So can Shell. She recognises the scent from the last time they met. What she hasn't said is that the wolf may not be a threat. It didn't do anything but breathe on her, did it? But she needs it captured. It is, at the very least, a puzzlement, a distraction, and at most it's an agent of harm. It needs to be isolated where it cannot affect the work or the investigation.

They arrive at Torus 2, and there it is. It stops when it sees them, or smells them. It does not growl; it just charges. Something hypnotic about a seventy-five-kilo predator charging without any signs of rage. Fin sets his shoulders and raises his handgun, legs slightly apart, one in front of the other. Shell knows how to fire a gun, knows an expert when she sees one. When the shot comes, it still startles Shell, with the vibration in the enclosed space and the muzzle flash with the delayed smell. The wolf is unharmed and keeps coming, closing the distance.

"Did you miss?" asks Salvo, who is behind Fin.

"No," said Fin, not defensive, not disturbed, stating fact. He fires again, and this time Shell can see where it hits the wolf just beneath the neck. The animal slows slightly but keeps coming. Five metres.

Shell's hands tighten around the adjustable spanner she chose. Salvo pulls Fin behind him and moves to meet the wolf. Two metres.

"Ragtime, kill rotation," says Shell.

All of them are thrown into microgravity and rise like birthday balloons. The wolf's momentum keeps it coming, but now uncontrolled and uncertain of itself.

"Out of the way, Salvo," says Shell, in her element, feet hooked on rails. She swings with all her might and feels the satisfying connection of tool with head. The wolf does not whimper or cry out, but Shell feels something give, like a skull caving in. The impact changes the animal's direction and introduces a spin. It also sprays blood droplets in a spiral that follows the head. Salvo avoids the open jaws and gets on its back, sinking the spanner into its windpipe and pulling like an old painting of Samson. Splayed out, they can see the wolf is a he. It struggles still.

Fin looks comical in the zero grav, but he manages to get the muzzle of his weapon against the skull and pull the trigger.

The wolf goes still, but they all exist within the snowstorm of its body fluids and fur.

Fin stabs the inert wolf in the gut and saws up towards the head. Gravity is back. Behind them lies a messy passageway which remains messy because nobody trusts the bots and water is too limited to be used for clean-up without careful consideration. He lays down the blade – a hunting knife with an elaborate worked handle – and sticks both hands into the belly wound. He pulls the edges apart, and both he and Shell gasp. Salvo stays silent.

The wolf's innards are synthetic. There is blood surrounding ruptured cabling and some components that still pulse with electric light.

"This . . . is not what I expected," says Fin. "I mean, the wolf was unexpected, but . . . "

Salvo opens the mouth and looks at the teeth, then he examines the wound. He sticks his hands deep inside and comes up with faux intestines, which he cuts open with Fin's knife.

"What are you looking for?" says Shell.

"I'm checking what it has had to eat," says Salvo. "We started out looking for body parts, remember?"

"Do they eat?" asks Fin.

"I do," says Salvo.

"Ragtime, reactivate cleaning bots and direct them here," says Shell.

"Yes, Captain."

To Fin and Salvo, she says, "We need to regroup. We haven't found the missing body parts, and this canine just adds confusion. We're going to the bridge. I think better there."

Ragtime scours for more organic matter but has not turned anything up yet. Shell is in the cupola waiting for sunrise on Bloodroot. It grounds her in something familiar, and it slows her racing heart better than the worry beads.

"One of the passengers must have brought it on board," says Fin.

Shell shakes her head and drops down into the bridge node. "No."

"How do you know?" he asks.

"Because we checked luggage, which is vetted, and each passenger's allowance is extremely limited. There are absolutely no electronics allowed, only Interface Chips and mechanicals related to prosthetics and disability. Luggage is scanned. It wasn't there."

"There was skin and blood in its gut," says Salvo. "Human skin and blood. Or at least, human-seeming."

"What do you mean?" says Shell.

"I'd have to get it to a lab to confirm," says the Artificial, "but I think the skin was the kind of simulated integument that I have."

"By the Thousand Heresies, are you saying there might be an Artificial on board that is unaccounted for?" says Fin. "A wounded one?"

"Or dead," says Shell.

Salvo shakes his head. "Not the conclusion I would draw. We don't know when it 'ate'. It could be before the *Ragtime*. Was any of the passengers an Artificial, Captain?"

"I don't know. On Earth, in some countries you don't have to declare. Artificials have full personhood. To ask is ... offensive. There were some Artificials when I came on board. I don't know if they went to Dreamstate or returned to Earth."

"So let's retrace the steps and find out what he ate," says Fin.

"Ragtime, video feed of the wolf's path," says Shell.

"Unavailable, Captain."

What?

"Try again."

"No files found."

"Ragtime, video files of our fight on IFC screens."

"No files found."

Shell's disquiet returns. "This is what happened the last time, when the wolf licked my hand or something while I slept. No recording."

"That means someone or some entity decided the video should not be kept. The footage of the wolf is deliberately being kept from the record because it makes someone vulnerable," says Fin. "Perhaps the wolf belongs to the killer."

"Interesting theory," says Shell.

"It scans," says Fin.

"Not if someone illegally brought the wolf along, a pet, and wanted to hide it. It's an offence, yes, and one that carries a hefty fine, and maybe even some jail time. A lot of these folks are rich and don't think rules apply to them."

"You're missing the part where it was combat ready," says Fin. "It took two shots without slowing down."

"It did slow down, actually. And like I said, rich folks. Pets can have self-defence modes to protect—"

"How did this person modify the *Ragtime*'s AI?" Fin leans away from Shell – a bad sign. "The person could hide the wolf from being recorded. Such a person could also manipulate the instructions for the bots."

"Captain," says Ragtime.

"Yes," says Shell.

"Warning."

84

Shell had seen flashing in her peripheral vision but she'd been too riled up by Rasheed Fin to focus on it. She expands the alarm.

"Oh, fuck."

Proximity alert.

Chapter Nine

Ragtime: Shell

Breathe, calm down. Remember your training, Shell. Breathe.

You wanted to be captain. This is how you captain a ship.

Now, then.

Fin is quiet this time, and even Salvo manages to look expectant.

"Ragtime, open channel to approaching vessel," says Shell.

"Yes, Captain. Channel open."

"Unidentified vessel, you are approaching the starship *Ragtime*. Reverse engines and correct course to avoid collision. Please acknowledge."

"Ragtime, this is the shuttle *Decisive*. Michelle, is that you?" A familiar voice.

"Uncle Larry?" says Shell.

"Shelley! Hey, send me the docking protocol. I'll see you in a second."

Fin is signalling for speech.

"Stand by, Decisive." Shell turns to Fin. "What?"

"You can't let him on board."

"Do we have to go through this authority thing again? Because I am tired of it."

"Captain, the *Ragtime* is a crime scene. You can't just invite anybody in before Salvo and I have cleared it. It's contamination." Damn it if Fin doesn't sound reasonable this time.

"Fin. Rasheed. No disrespect, but you're a shitty spaceman. I need help with the ship and you and your shiny Artificial are not pulling your weight. Uncle Larry—"

"'Uncle Larry'?"

"Lawrence Biz. He was my father's friend. The point is, he's an experienced astronaut. I need someone else who can carry water when we can't trust the robots, and you don't look like space is your natural habitat. I need him, all right? So we all don't die of something routine like carbon monoxide poisoning."

Leaving unspoken what both of them know, the fact that an ally balances things out. Fin has Salvo; Shell now has Uncle Larry.

"Is this your girl?" asks Larry. "Wow."

He is a huge, muscular man taking up space to the side of Shell's father.

"This is Michelle, yes," says Haldene.

Larry settles into a crouch, one hand on the rug. Shell still has to look up at him.

87

"Hi," he says. "I'm your uncle Larry."

Shell looks to Haldene, who shakes his head. "He ain't your uncle, baby."

"How old are you, Michelle?"

"Nine, but ten in the fall."

Larry laughs. "Ten in the fall. You know, your dad only talks about you when he's not talking about flying?"

"Are you an astronaut too?"

"I am."

"Have you ever seen aliens?"

"If I had, I wouldn't be able to talk about it, darlin'."

"So you have."

Larry looks to Haldene, who just raises an eyebrow. "I told you she was smart."

"Yeah, but everybody says that about their kids, even the ones as dumb as a rock."

Shell's belly warms whenever her father's eye is on her.

"Crosshairs aligned, Ragtime. Eleven metres. All thrusters inhibited."

"Roger that, Decisive. Target at centre," says Shell.

The *Decisive* had to descend to a phasing orbit, then perform a bielliptic transfer. It caught up to the *Ragtime*, taking three hours and giving Shell a headache. AI would normally do this. The transfer went well, although the *Ragtime* changed attitude twice. At least it didn't speed up like when the *Equivalence* tried to dock the first time.

"Contact. Capture."

"Confirmed."

The external cam shows the *Decisive* tacked on to the *Ragtime*.

"Fin, do it," says Shell.

"Do what? I'm waiting at the hatch."

"The manual locks. We discussed this."

"Manual locks. Right."

She does a quick systems check, turns and propels herself out of the cupola. Shell heads for the fore airlock. She ignores the equipment lock and joins Fin beside the crew lock.

Larry is older. The face is more lined, the hair has more grey and there's some slump to the posture; more round, less muscle. That smile, though. Unmistakable. Shell pushes past Fin and hugs Larry. She feels inexplicably sad and thinks it's because he reminds her of Haldene.

"Hey, Shelley."

"Hey, Uncle Larry."

There's a woman behind him. Fin seems to have frozen after the post-docking handshake. Hell is he looking at?

"This is my daughter, Joké," says Larry.

Even neutralised in an EVA suit, Joké is distracting. Her eyes seem ever-so-slightly larger than usual. Dark brown skin, mouth quick to smile, taller than Shell. Joké looks at Fin briefly, then turns back to Shell without saying a word.

"Do you want to brief us?" says Larry.

Shell leads Larry and Joké to Node 1. Fin keeps up his weird stare, but he and Salvo move aft.

"Keep in touch," says Shell.

"I need to speak with you," says Fin. He's looking at her in a way that mirrors her own feelings: like, Who's this child commanding the ship, and does she know what she's doing? Joké, behind Larry, wears an amused smile. Difficult to read, that one.

Shell breaks off with Fin, not missing the look Larry exchanges with Joké.

They both hold grab rails.

"What?" asks Shell.

"That spaceman. Spaceperson. Joké. She's not human."

"So? You have an Artificial." Shell tries to keep cool at this information. Many reasons this could be the case.

"She's not an Artificial – she's an alien, a Lamber."

Shell glances back at the woman beside Larry. "What about him?"

"He's human. All the way."

"How do you know this?"

"It's my job to know, Captain. There are signs I can pick up. I'm a repatriator."

Low voice now. "Is she impersonating the real girl?"

"No, Lambers wouldn't do that. She seems to be a hybrid, which I haven't seen before. I didn't even know it was possible." He seems to be in physical pain.

"Okay, so, say she's half-Lamber. Hell, full. What makes ... is this a danger to us?"

"'Us'? We're on the same side now?"

"Fin, how is her being on board a problem?"

"I don't know. Lambers are—"

The world shakes as the entire ship judders.

Fin goes green. "What—?"

Shell holds up her hand. "Ragtime. Diagnostics."

"All systems optimal, Captain."

"Then why—"

Everything shudders, and the vibration increases in frequency. Alarms go off. Gravity disengages and the five of them fly around like rag dolls. The micrograv saves them from injury. Metals groan from mechanical stresses.

"Ragtime, what the hell is going on?"

The sense of up-down disappears. Bits and pieces not secured properly float around and a screwdriver misses Shell's eye by inches. Alarms now insistent, loud, red alerts on the IFC.

Shell has hold of a grab rail, as have Joké and Larry. Fin is panicked. Shell waits till he rotates then launches and clutches him from behind. "Calm down, Fin. Go limp. Like swimming. Go limp."

She allows the momentum to take them both to the other side and places his hand on free rails.

Shell accesses the external cameras on her IFC. Maybe a collision of some kind? Meteoroid? But no proximity alert. The feed comes in, and she cannot believe what she sees. The stern node, Node 7, is in the process of detaching from the *Ragtime*. The planet Bloodroot, instead of being calm in one orientation, rotates around the camera crazily, meaning the ship is in a spin. The last restraint snaps, and the node is free. Which means—

"Brace! Atmospheric leak in—"

The hurricane hits, sucking at them all with gale forces.

Shell yells above the howling depressurisation. "Ragtime, seal Node 6!"

Node 7, along with a pair of solar arrays, tilts, smashes against the stump and spins away off the frame of the camera. No possibility of recapture. Debris, robots and air still discharge from Node 6. And liquid. *Fuck.*

"Salvo, get in the *Equivalence*. Larry, the *Decisive*. I need some thrusts to stop this spin. Joké?"

"Captain?" Calm, this one. Unpanicked.

"Help Mr Fin into an EVA suit, please."

Ragtime is not answering queries, but Shell still receives telemetry on her IFC. The ship is still depressurising and power has fallen, but that's understandable in the context of solar panel loss. Joké is now helping Shell into her own suit even though the atmosphere is still breathable. Shell wants no surprises. She and Joké move aft. They could have used the portable breathers, but if parts of the ship are going to start spontaneously snapping off, she wants to be ready.

Pressurised suits make movement slow and cumbersome. There is no space to move side to side, and Shell has Joké to her back – someone she does not know. Larry knows her, is her father, maybe, if she's not an alien. She'll be fine. Shell can hear her own breathing: raspy, loud, hint of a wheeze.

A bar swings from the ceiling and smashes her in the centre of her visor. Not a bar. A robot arm. A second arm falls as the first rises. A third prepares to strike.

"Arachnobots," says Shell into the comm. "Fall back."

Penetrating a space suit is difficult. The suits are like armour – they *are* armour, but they are built for outside, not inside the ship. Shell is not in pain, but she cannot manoeuvre and can't get to the robot, which is latched to a spot above her, swinging its arms, one of which wraps around her and begins to squeeze. Doesn't hurt, but she feels it. How long will the suit hold? Joké tries to peel the arm off, but she makes no progress.

"Captain," says Fin over the comm. "Hold still."

Gunshot. The first arm splinters at the point of articulation with the ceiling, raining down alloy chips and hard plastic. For the other two, Shell is aware of the explosive bullets before they disintegrate. She turns like a woman made of balloons. Fin is holding a gun in one hand and his helmet in the other. He is out of the top half of the EVA suit and says something she can't hear. She waves.

To Joké, she says, "Come on. Let's go."

"Captain," says Joké on the radio.

"Yes."

"Now that we're alone on the comm, I have a question."

"Go ahead."

"What is ahead that we are, ah, going to?"

Weird construction. Weird girl. "Aft to manually close the penultimate node and assess damage."

"But, um, you're the one with Ragtime access."

"What's your point?"

"The captain can't go. It's too dangerous. If you die, everyone dies. Nobody else can do what you do, and though you have a really nice ass that I don't mind staring at along this journey, you, ah, need to send someone else."

"I—"

"What? You need someone five-eleven and gorgeous, you say? Okay, you twisted my arm, Captain. I'll go." Joké squeezes past. "Um, I'll relay information back."

She moves faster than Shell is able to, so there's that. And Joké is right.

Shell looks at the time, takes a scheduled sip of water, then checks on the passengers. *Don't break 'em; don't lose 'em.* Stable. At her feet, maintenance bots clean up but are frustrated with the microgravity. Each fragment reminds her of the broken ship and the broken mission.

Her comm lights up. "Ragtime, this is the *Equivalence*. Come in." Salvo.

"Ragtime, over."

"Equivalence ready for burn."

"Thank you. Wait for my mark. Decisive, come in."

"Decisive standing by for burn, over."

"All right. Let's sort this spin out ... "

Chapter Ten

Decisive: Lawrence

While correcting the *Ragtime*'s spin, Lawrence leaves most of the precision work to the AI and lets his mind drift. Little Michelle. Look at her captaining a ship.

Other memories come back. Lawrence alone in a ship. He looks at the screens showing the colony planet. *Long time no see*.

Decades earlier, Lawrence did some work on Bloodroot as a survey pilot. He expected to map the limits of the inhabitable region of the planet. At the time he thought he wanted to join a fleet, but it was not to be; Bloodroot toned down its space programme. That didn't mean there wasn't work to be done planetside, however.

"You're going to it alone," his CO had said.

That was back when Bloodroot was more dependent on Lagos. Old tech propulsion, it took three hundred days to reach Bloodroot from the space station, and Lawrence took a twin-engine plane, parts printed and assembled, and flew free, beaming images and environmental information back.

Long lonely flights. Lots of ice in the poles. Weather checks. Rations. More flights. Cold nights. Conflicts with pack canines and biting insects and dermatophytoses. Hyperkinetic creeper vines reaching for his plane along the equator. Unfamiliar indigenous species mixed with carelessly introduced terrestrial ones. Failed, abandoned outposts. An ancient meteor crater that took him four hours to fly around. Reading. Refuelling. The unending desolation of deserts and tundra alike. Waterlogged islands on which he could not land. Alone on plateau regions of mountain ranges. Scratching his name on a rockface using a diamond-tipped tool from Lagos. Because the arrival of humans interrupted local evolution in the Greater Arboreal Sea, he encountered resentful hominids who hurled shit at him. He forgave them. Losing track of time. Watching earthquakes and orogeny, landscape changing as fast as waves on the sea. He saw the bones of the first explorers and the preserved, frozen bodies of waves of rescue teams. Once his path crossed that of another surveyor and they spent a slow night together and exchanged tips, body fluids and narcochemistry.

Bloodroot forgot him, and perhaps Lawrence forgot himself, because when he got back to civilisation looking to find a replacement component for his plane, there were no longer any survey trips being sponsored. Nobody missed him, nobody fought for his return. Hal was already dead. He had people somewhere, but he had no contact even before he went off-station. Nobody cared. Lawrence thought he was stuck on Bloodroot until the end of time.

Or the end of his new mission.

He flew some desultory missions after that, but all he really wanted to do was lie down and die. No, what he wanted was for Hal to be alive. Since that was never going to happen, he laid roots on Lagos.

And here he was, with Hal's daughter. Perhaps, as they say, Hal lives on in her.

Chapter Eleven

Ragtime: Fin

Fin discards the helmet and pulls himself with grab rails into the cupola. The spin has stabilised along with his nausea. Salvo and *Uncle* Larry must have done it. He tries to find a channel to Bloodroot to give a report, but all he gets in his visual field is a "busy" bar.

He gathers his thoughts and puts the facts together as he knows them.

The *Ragtime* left Earth on schedule, stopped over at Space Station Lagos for a service, then made its way to Bloodroot's orbit. Campion wakes up to find the AI infantilised and thirty-one passengers dead, cut up and disposed of by the ship's bots. Someone's artificial wolf roamed the *Ragtime*'s passageways, now neutralised. Fin and Salvo, counting the body parts, found two and a half humans missing. Mild friction with Campion, but Fin is used to that. Then the *Decisive* turns up with Uncle

Larry and his Lamber daughter Joké. Then the ship kind of breaks up without warning.

They need to work on the facts of the matter, the time-line, then, when all the known players are understood, find out motive. Fin needs to know the identities of all the victims and their positions in the passenger pods, and then dive into their IFCs.

The break off of Node 7 is convenient for the killer. It distracts from investigation to something primal: survival. In survival mode, the human doesn't default to detective work. Fin is afraid he'll miss something in this tumult of survival. Plus, it's space. The Brink. He might die for real. This kind of shit, Fin knows on an instinctive, molecular level, is coming his way like a fucking asteroid or heart attack or something. This is how he dies. In space. With strangers and robots and suffocation.

Static and random sentences coming from the open channel. Joké mumbling to herself.

"Nobody soothed his nightmares when he was a child."

Who is she talking about? Fin likes the woman, but she seems ... out there. But so what? So was he, according to his colleagues on Bloodroot. They thought him some kind of wunderkind from his first cases. Which is why he fucked up the last one. Hubris.

He reloads his gun and settles back down and waits near the crew lock. He crouches in Node 1 so that he can see as many directions as possible. Up, into the cupola, aft to the opening of Node 2, and fore into the crew area, the docking area and the airlocks.

Esteemed Ones,

I apologise. There are no words to express how sorry I am, and because of my mistake a life has been snuffed out.

I know this letter is abrupt, but I have reason to believe my life is in danger and I do not want to die without you knowing that—

No. It doesn't work. It places a burden on them, a burden to listen and a burden to forgive because he might die. If they are to forgive, it must be freely. It must not be emotional blackmail, if they are vulnerable to such.

Take stock. None of this shit means Campion is innocent, but it does seem like excessively elaborate efforts at misdirection. Fin can't see it. Technically, though, she is still the only viable suspect.

Careful. Don't be spellbound by the super-competent astronaut.

Is that it? Deep down Fin doesn't want her to be guilty?

Easier if she is. He and Salvo can go home, Fin back to repatriation or maybe just regular investigations. Crimes of passion, premeditated crimes, crimes of stupidity, of which there are many.

But they have to survive first, and that prospect isn't looking good. Fin doesn't want this tug of war diluting priorities.

"Equivalence, come back," says Fin.

"Go head, Ragtime Two," says Salvo.

"I'm Ragtime Two?"

"She *is* the captain."

"Fine. Heretic. How is your mission?"

"Almost accomplished."

"Will I distract you?"

"No. I can split my attention. What do you need?"

"As long as we're alive, let's remember why we are here. Anything further on the wolf?"

"I ran a trace on the parts. Most appear to be proprietary, but those that aren't are from MaxGalactix."

"Who owns MaxGalactix?"

"Someone called Yan Maxwell—"

"Why ... where have I heard that name?" asks Fin.

"From the list of murdered passengers. Yan Maxwell was on the passenger manifest and is one of the people we put back together."

Shit.

"Did the wolf—"

"No, Ragtime Two, the wolf did not kill Maxwell or any of the other passengers."

"You know this because ... "

"I have already covered this. Wound pattern. The wolf did not kill anybody on the *Ragtime*. Nothing human in his belly. The robots did the killing."

"Malfunction?"

"Robots don't malfunction that way. They were programmed to kill. Reprogrammed."

Maybe.

"Send me what you have on Maxwell," says Fin.

"Doing it now."

"And find—"

"Links between Maxwell and any other passengers. In progress."

"Good man." Oops. "Equivalence, was that offensive?"

"No." Was there a delay?

"Ragtime Two out."

Something vibrates heavily and Fin braces, hands against two walls, expecting to be turned upside down but disappointed. The *Ragtime* settles like an upset stomach, although the lights flicker. Fucking space. *Fucking spaceships.*

Indistinct chatter on the radio.

One of those cleaner bots comes slithering by, and Fin tenses, but it just … cleans. Fin still wants to shoot it just on general principle. How many are there on board?

He'll go crazy if he ponders that. Instead, he goes back to what he knows. Data. Salvo has some information on Yan Maxwell shared, and a few candidates with links. Fin goes through the linked people first. Tenuous links at best, statistical anomalies, too far removed to be anything useful. He's their employer, although with several intermediaries in between. He's the wealthiest man in the Sol system. Indirectly, he employs everybody.

Video files play on Fin's IFC.

A young Maxwell funding the first successful mining of an asteroid, piggybacked on someone else's pipedream. Some bright spark tried to turn a space rock into a spaceship by coring it out, building life support inside and attaching propulsion systems. Ten years of failure. When the instigator moved on, Maxwell examined what was left with a moving R & D craft. He found hyperconductors, iridium, piezoelectrics, unknowns, unknowns, unknowns, all of which he ferried to Earth. He had to fight off a lawsuit from the pipedreamer, but soon became pretty much the richest person in the solar system – which, if explorers are to be believed, means the richest person in the galaxy. Adjusted. The rise of MaxGalactix.

The first discovery was a freebie, scavenged from the cast-off of another enterprise. He sent robot ships far and wide – even, it is rumoured, into the Oort Cloud, beyond Earth's nearest bridge. And it all flows back to Earth for analysis, conversion, empowerment of humanity. Geologists suddenly in higher demand than they have ever been; rock nerds to rock stars in one generation.

And Maxwell? Shrank from view as his star rose. No scandals, no children, no drama. True, impossible to make that much money without pissing someone off, but Maxwell seems to have done it. Or paid off his enemies and scrubbed public records.

Sixty-three years old at time of death. Some plaque in his carotid artery that might have got him within two or so decades. Massive amount of fat in the greater omentum. Heart encased in fat that must have rendered him breathless. Lungs healthy, no soot spots. Brain pristine. Polyp in rectum, but benign, unimportant. Curiously, one ingrown toenail that must have hurt given the inflammation around it. He could have had it sorted out surgically in less than an hour. Why did he leave it?

Why the fuck are you dead, Maxwell?

Fin pulls up a conceptual map of the passenger place-ment. Marking the diagram with the thirty-one dead shows most of the bodies on Torus 2, clustered around Maxwell, as if he is patient zero and the murder contagion spread from him to the pods adjacent. He was the target. Great. So many reasons for anyone to want to murder the richest man in existence. Fin rubs his eyes and dismisses the display.

"Fin, come in." Shell.

"Captain?"

"The *Equivalence* and the *Decisive* are going to stop thrusting now. You'll need to help remove the manual locks from the hatch. Can you do that?"

"Yes."

"Thanks. Uncle Larry will talk you through it."

"Affirmative."

"What?"

"I thought that's what you say in . . . never mind. When are you coming back this way?"

"After I've inspected the passenger sections. Why?"

"I have some news on the investigation."

"I do not care. Do you even understand our situation? We need to get planetside, to safety, and soon."

"I appreciate—"

"Get off the comm unless it's an emergency. Larry will need the channel open. Out."

Fin must be starting to like her because he isn't even angry.

He is barely irritated.

Chapter Twelve

Ragtime: Joké

Joké has a better EVA suit than anything they have on the *Ragtime* – companies are cheap – but it's still hard going. Her muscles are screaming with the exertion of it all, microgravity be damned. If not for the fluid and temperature balance of the suit, she would be drenched in sweat.

Grab the next rail, propel forwards, try not to bounce off anything. Travel from node to node down the truss, try not to get confused by the turn off to the spokes of the torus.

She is vigilant of robots, but they scramble about ignoring her, seeming to have their own mission. She sees a flash of her father crossing her visual field, running, saying words she cannot hear. That's not now, so it must be later. She stops.

"Decisive, come back," she says.

"Joké?"

"Hmm?"

"What is it, baby?"

"Action Governor!"

Lawrence sighs over the comm. "Is there a point to this?"

"Mmm, no, just checking on you."

"Mission accomplished. Shutdown protocols in place. *Equivalence* goes first, then me."

"Mm-hmm, sounds good." Joké ducks under a series of dangling cables that look like jungle vines; then she sees a man, sad, trudging, linked to the Us. "Nobody soothed his nightmares when he was a child."

"What, darling?"

"Nothing, governor. Odabo."

A clear glowing arrow pointing aft, but an intersection, and different arrows – one pointing to Node M, the other to Node E. The first nodes without a number. There's also a one-foot cut-out of Snoopy plastered to the wall.

"Captain," says Joké.

"Go."

"Ahh, what's in Node E?"

"Node E is the wrong direction. The leak is aft."

"Mmm, and I'm going aft, but what's in Node E?"

"Experimental. I don't know. They don't tell us. It's sealed and I'll never know. It's automated. All I do is check the door."

"Ooh. I like shiny, experimental things."

"Are you getting distracted?"

"Uuuhh, no. Out."

She pledges to check out Node E on her way back

106

because it gives her an uneasy feeling. With external microphones she can hear a whistling sound, the rushing of air through a small aperture. She pushes, flies through the air, feels a pull. Debris and loose objects move in the same direction. She is at the end, but not in danger, she doesn't think. A shutter has slid down to form a seal, but it is incomplete. The door stopped about a foot from the end, and atmosphere rushes away, along with whatever objects will fit the space. Globules of grey-green fluid float in the air like a snowstorm, and she hopes that's not something from the waste system. Joké's body moves from momentum and air current, but her spacesuit won't fit through, so she's not worried.

"Captain."

"Go."

"Some kind of emergency door has come down, but ... " She describes the scene.

"Are you anchored?" asks Shell.

"Uh-huh."

"Can you see the emergency fire extinguisher?"

"Uh-huh ... yeah."

"Next to that, you'll see a panel labelled 'control'."

"I do."

"Open it, you'll see something that looks like a winch handle. Turn it clockwise until the gap closes. Joké, we all depend on you being able to close that shutter."

"Go away now, Captain."

Joké sips water. The panel is where Shell said it would be, but the EVA gauntlet is too cumbersome to manipulate the latches. She takes off the top part of her suit. The air tastes like burnt rubber, but it's breathable as it rushes out into the cosmos.

The handle is cold.

Joké pushes clockwise. The gap doesn't seem to change, and it's hard. Fine. She pushes harder and this makes maybe an inch of difference.

"Fuck, this is not going to be unicorns and rose petals, is it?"

She pushes, sometimes with two hands, but the swirling droplets land on her; one or two to start with, then she glistens with it. At least it's not foul smelling, but she loses her grip.

"Suboptimal."

She knows what's about to happen before it does, she sees it, and is calm. She loses her moorings, what anchors her in place, and is pulled towards the gap. Too late, she realises she has taken off the suit that would have stopped her from squeezing through and kept her alive.

Joké is sucked out, banging her head and torso, spinning, into the cold blackness of space.

She is in the Us, the nothingness and everything, the universe around her, all of spacetime open to her. Joyous.

"Ahh ... this place. You guys ... "

Others in the Us greet her in the Lamber way. Her mind is not nimble enough to take their form, but she can slip into and out of the Us at times. Her body can slip.

They want her to stay, her human biology attractive to

them, sustaining in some undefined way. They bob around her, tentacles everywhere, entangled. She has, in the past, spent aeons with them before returning to her point in the time stream.

Her mother is in the Us somewhere, and it is likely that Joké has met her. But Lambers don't do personhood in quite the same way as humans, and Joké's flesh has always been a barrier to integration.

She opens spacetime and inserts herself back into the *Ragtime*.

This time she's ready and gives it all her might. She wipes her hands on herself to keep the palms dry. Stubborn though it is, the winch submits to her determination. The gap closes. Pressurisation should start to build up again if life support isn't damaged.

Body aching, Joké allows herself to drift, to float free. To rest.

It is only when she sees globules of blood in the air that she realises she is bleeding from somewhere.

"Captain?"

"Go ahead."

"Your hole is plugged." Joké giggles.

"Joké, check carbon dioxide levels. Are you getting CO_2 narcosis?"

"Naaah. It's the thought of hole-plugging. Besides, I took my suit off."

"Why?"

"I did a spacewalk … it doesn't matter. There is one

other thing." She touches her head and the hand comes away bloody.

"Go on."

"I might have a small skull fracture."

Joké loses consciousness.

Chapter Thirteen

Lagos Bridge: Awe, Beko

Awe settles into the seat and takes a deep breath. He is brewing a headache and would rather be doing anything else. The iced tea he brought along stands on the table in front of him, untouched.

"Connect IFC, Lagos," he says.

"Connected. Are you comfortable?"

"Yes, thank you." He knows the AI's personality changes depending on whose IFC connects, but he finds her voice pleasant, lulling even. "I want to review the *Ragtime* service, please."

"Of course."

"What was the bridge path from Earth?"

"Point of origin, Earth; then Daedalus, Crucial, Waikiki, Corazon, Brighton, Goldsmith, Oya, Harvest, Shango, Lagos. From Lagos to near-planet orbit on Bloodroot."

"Were there any complaints, cautions, notifications or sneezes from any of the other bridges?"

"None."

"Not even Shango? They whine about everything."

"Not this time."

"Interesting. All right, show me the arrival."

"Do you want the raw data, or do you need visual accompaniment as well?"

"Visuals, from the convergence. Panoptical view, please."

"Onset on my mark. Mark."

Awe steeples his hands.

It starts in empty space – or, rather, space without human-made objects. Bridges are not permanent structures. A signal arrives from the nearest bridge – in this case, Shango – and Space Station Lagos bounces the signal to the Dyson swarm around the star.

Awe observes eight of the Dyson elements break off, fully charged, and occupy the bridge zone. They form a crude circle and each forges links with the adjacent element. This takes hours but Lagos AI has sped it up for Awe.

Once they have claimed relativistic space, the tunnel forms between Lagos and Shango. A communications satellite slips through first, as a test. When it arrives on the Lagos side, an all-clear signal is transmitted.

The circle becomes opaque with light, and after five hours the starship *Ragtime* emerges. Lagos is its final hop. Awe thinks it's ugly, with no streamlines. It looks like an insect, with the solar arrays looking like wings. A dragonfly, maybe. Awe has never seen an actual dragonfly, but photos and videos bring the picture home. He thinks the ships they build on Lagos are better-looking.

"Lagos, Lagos, this is Ragtime. All systems nominal," says the ship AI.

"Ragtime, this is Space Station Lagos. How was your flight?"

"Uneventful."

"And your cargo?"

"Asleep, intact."

"Good to hear, Ragtime. Please transmit telemetry for comparison and power down for servicing."

"Will do, Lagos Bridge. See you on the other side."

Awe knows the interaction did not go like that and that Lagos dramatised it for his benefit. AIs talk to each other in binary and hexadecimal bursts of information over fractions of seconds.

The *Ragtime* goes dark while a flock of robot ships converges on it. They replace fuel cells, repair the micrometeorite damage on the outer Whipple shielding of the hull, replace panels, replace stuffing, run integrity tests, check the air quality, look for any relativistic travel side effects, and they check the integrity of Omega Protocol for last-resort safety.

There is one anomaly, but Awe chalks it up to instrument error. One of the passengers' vital signs seems to read wakefulness, but a rescan shows all asleep.

Four days later, the *Ragtime* is spanking new, charged up, ready to soldier on to the colony Bloodroot, a mere fortnight away.

"Happy trails, Ragtime," says Lagos.

"Stay reliable, Lagos," says Ragtime.

The servicing-robot ships withdraw like a school of fish who spot a shark, and Ragtime fires engines, orients itself and heads for Bloodroot, ahead of schedule.

The video stops.

Awe rubs his chin.

"Are you happy with what you saw?" says Lagos.

"Yes, I am," says Awe. "But I want to see it again."

Beko

Secretary Beko is silent for the first few minutes, attending to documents; then she looks up, sharp, birdlike. "Well?"

"It went like it's supposed to, like clockwork. Nothing missed, no shortcuts taken, nothing damaged left unreplaced. The gate dismantled, Dyson elements returned to the solar swarm without attrition. All the drones and bots returned to base, accounted for, and returned to routine construction in the dry docks. The whole process left me thinking of the Philosopher's Axe."

"What?"

"You know the saying. You buy an axe, the handle breaks, you replace it, then years later the head gets damaged, so you replace that too. At that point, do you still have the original axe?"

"Is this ... meant to be funny or to provoke reflection on my part, Awe?"

"I'm sorry, Madam Secretary. I misspoke."

She exhales heavily. "Send three ships to Bloodroot."

"Yes, Ma'am."

"Where's the old dodderer?"

"He . . . ah . . . the governor went to the mines, Ma'am."

"Why? To do what?"

"An inspection tour, Ma'am. He gets bored. You said to keep him out of your way. The mines are out of the way."

"Awe."

"Yes, Ma'am?"

"Is he going to be talking to miners while out there?"

"I—"

"The moment after you leave this room, I'll be speaking to the representatives of miners about their conditions. It's delicate work. I don't want Lawrence Biz fucking it up. Recall him immediately."

"Yes, Ma'am."

Except the *Decisive* is out of range of comms, which is impossible. There are deep-space relays between the space station and the mining belt. They have to have them for safety.

Awe queries the governor's IFC location. Not found. No joy looking for the *Decisive*'s beacon either.

Where the blazes is the old man?

Awe systematically queries the personnel of each mine and unless one of them is lying, the governor never went to the mines in the first place.

You old goat, did you fuck me?

Awe puts out a quiet alert using only the IFC hardware code. It won't raise any alarms, but every ship AI, every scan-capable robot and Lagos herself will be on the lookout for him.

Awe tries to locate Joké. She's nowhere to be found either, but that's not unusual. Lagos often records conflicts, exceptions and errors when it comes to her IFC location. Been like that since she was a child. It doesn't mean anything.

Shit.

Shit.

He updates the mission profile for the three ships on their way to the *Ragtime*: Look out for the governor. If you find him, bring him home. Alive.

Shit.

Awe calls his wife, Ibidun, to let her know he won't be home. He settles in for a long night of waiting and sifting through data.

Chapter Fourteen

Ragtime: Shell

Laid out in sick bay, in Node M, Shell acknowledges that Joké is good-looking, but the girl is uncooperative. The service bots have cleaned up all the blood from the autopsies, and there's no visible gore, but Shell thinks she can smell a whiff of the abattoir on the air. Must be her imagination, though. It'll take time and therapy to get this trauma out of her mind, but only if they make it out alive.

"I'm fine," says Joké, attempting to get up.

"Stay where you are," says Larry.

"I fainted, Father. It was hard work, hmm?" says Joké.

Fin lounges at the door, staring, silent, but Salvo steps forward. "I've been analysing the telemetry from your suit. What it tells me doesn't make sense."

"What do you mean?" says Shell.

"It says half the suit went outside," says Salvo. "And it is still there."

"Oh, that," says Joké.

"Did you throw a suit out?" asks Shell.

"Uh-uh, I didn't. I got flung out the airlock."

"How did you get back?" says Fin.

Joké raises her head and locks eyes with Fin. "You know how."

Shell says, "Will someone please explain to me what's going on here?"

"Lambers can slip between realities and back," says Fin. "She left her suit behind in space when she moved."

Shell looks to Larry who avoids her eyes, a conversation for another time. "So we're down a space suit."

"Mmm, but we're up one life – me," says Joké. "And I did stop the leak."

"One of the leaks. There are still some minor ones, but the one you blocked was the largest. Good job," says Shell. "I have bad news, so if Joké's all right, then I'd like to go to the bridge."

Each of them hangs off whatever they can find. Shell floats at the opening of the cupola because, well, she feels stronger there. Joké beside Uncle Larry, Salvo at Fin's side – IFCs synced, no doubt. Shell feels the loneliness of leadership but struggles to keep her body language neutral, which is less than they need. The crew, such as it is, needs inspiration, not neutrality, but it's the best Shell can muster at this time.

"On Earth there used to be this soothsayer, the Delphian Oracle. Supposedly it spouted glossolalia, gibberish, and the seekers of wisdom took away whatever message they wanted to hear guided by projections of their own subconscious. I don't know if that's true or not, but I do know that whatever oracle we choose to consult will tell us we are cursed."

Joké says, "Umm—"

"Shut up. Let me finish," says Shell, not unkindly. "The breaking off of Node 7 cost us atmosphere, but when it detached, it bounced off the hull twice before disappearing. Among other things, it broke off the long-range antenna. Half of the backup was attached to the terminal segment."

"So we can't contact Bloodroot?" asks Fin. Seems alarmed.

"We can't contact Bloodroot. On Earth we have a satellite array, but the space programme on the colonies is . . . rudimentary. That's not all. That wetness all over Joké was bioreactor fluid. It has sprung a significant leak."

This is non-trivial because the algae make oxygen, food and energy for the ship. Combined with solar thermal fuel, the bioreactor fluid flows on the outside in transparent channels to trap sunlight, then all round the ship.

"I've run some numbers and had Salvo check them. In the current circumstances we have one hundred and thirty hours of life support left."

"Five days and change," says Larry, unperturbed. Which makes sense for a pioneer pilot whose life could have ended at any time during any number of his missions.

"So let's get all of us down to Bloodroot," says Fin.

"Don't be daft, son," says Larry.

"What? What do you mean?" asks Fin. He looks from Larry to Shell and back.

"The *Ragtime* is not a planetside ship," says Shell. "It was built in orbit and designed to park in orbit. It's less a large ship than a small, travelling space station. You need shuttles to evacuate. For shuttles, you need mission control. For mission control, you need—"

"Long-range transmitter, yes, I got it." Fin frowns. "So we take one of the docked shuttles, fly down to the surface and radio them. We don't even need to land. We just need to get in range and transmit a mayday."

"I agree," says Lawrence. "It's a two-hour mission at most."

Shell nods. "It'll have to be the *Equivalence*. The *Decisive* has no landing gear to speak of. It's for space station capture, not atmosphere or terra firma."

"There might be a problem with propellant," says Salvo. "Fin and I were only meant to fly here and back. After the various burns that we used to stop the *Ragtime*'s rotation, there won't be enough fuel to take us back, even when you take into consideration that we will glide a lot of the way. Slowing down for re-entry takes fuel."

"I'm kicking myself for that. Ragtime was unreliable. I had to use the shuttles to stop the spin." Shell swallows. "Uncle Larry? Ideas?"

"Fuel from the *Decisive* to the *Equivalence*?" says Lawrence.

"In zero grav, at 7.67 kilometres per sec?" says Salvo.

121

"You have very little solid propellant and depend mostly on ion thrust. It does not seem wise, Governor Biz."

"It'll make a pretty fireball," says Joké. She seems amused at the prospect.

"Retrofit the *Equivalence* for ion thrust?" says Larry.

"In five days with unreliable bots and no specialist engineers? Plus, ion engines won't work in atmosphere. You know that," says Shell.

"What about the passengers?" asks Fin.

"What do you mean?" says Shell. "I'm open to all ideas."

"These colony ships tend to be experts in something or the other, right? Why don't we go through the manifest and find engineers and rocket scientists to figure out our refuelling problem and AI experts to fix Ragtime. We can wake them up."

"Good idea, but you can't just wake up and get to full functioning, Fin. It takes about two weeks. I repeat, we have five days. You've got muscle atrophy, biochemical changes, all kinds of adjustments the body has to make. Plus, they're cooled down to keep metabolism down. When they wake up, they'll use more oxygen and require more nutrients. Each additional person we wake reduces the survival time with no guarantee that they'll give us the silver bullet we're looking for." She sighs. "We're not going to be getting help from those quarters."

"Do we have the humanpower and expertise to fit the *Decisive* with landing gear?" asks Lawrence.

"No," says Shell.

"One way trip, then. I fly to Bloodroot, broadcast a mayday, then glide to the ground."

"No," says Shell. "Because when you say glide, you mean crash, and we're not doing that. Everybody lives. I'm not losing any more, especially not you. Tell him, Joké."

"He's a grown-ass man. He can decide for himself if he wants to volunteer to go splat on the north face of a mountain on Bloodroot. Action Governor!"

Larry groans. "There's a time and place, Joké . . ."

"Hey, tick-tock everybody. Why am I the only one panicking?" says Fin.

"We're all panicking, rest assured. We're astronauts. They trained us not to show it," says Shell. "All right. Can we fix the backup antenna or build a new one?"

"I can run through options," says Salvo.

"Good. I have worksheets for everybody else. The backup AI is kind of malfunctioning too, and we can't trust the robots. Maintenance is more important than ever."

"What are you going to do?" asks Fin.

"I'm going to sleep for four hours, then I'm going to fix the reactor leak. Right now it's plugged, so it won't get worse. You'll find sleep schedules on your sheets as well."

"Umm, I don't rest like you do," says Joké.

"Joké, if you can survive outside a spaceship is there a chance you can . . . I mean, can your kind . . . we need someone on Bloodroot," says Shell.

"I'm exploring options, Captain. I have to figure it out," says Joké. "I've never been to Bloodroot. I have no mental anchor there."

"Whatever that means. Do whatever you can," says Shell. "I'll see you all in four hours."

Shell meditates.

The distractions come, but she is expecting them. She hangs in her sleeping bag, right hand flipping phantom beads one after the other. She has an EVA suit in her quarters with her, prepped, just in case something happens while she sleeps, and she ordered the same for the rest of the crew. Crew. That's amusing. A found crew, like a found family.

She thinks of her father all the time now, what he would think if he knew she had fucked up her first commission. She would say it wasn't her fault, but words like that just bounced off Haldene Campion. There is no fault; there is only duty, sacred or near enough. There is only crushing responsibility.

Maybe it is true that she is too young, too inexperienced for this – whatever "this" is. Uncle Larry didn't seem to have any problems obeying her commands, though. Didn't call her aside to chide her or question her choices, isn't giving her shit. If he's calm about it, surely that's some kind of endorsement? Or perhaps he's too old to know better.

She yawns. She is tired, but none of her tricks is helping her sleep. She briefly contemplates drugging herself but discards the idea. Sedatives can affect cognition for days, even after a single dose, and she needs clear thought. That's the whole point of sleeping in the first place.

She is so glad that her brothers will not hear of this until it is too late. She'll either be dead or the crisis will be over and she'll have a tale to tell.

A year before take-off from Florida, Shell was at the end of a relationship. It is not dead, but dying, just as doomed as the *Ragtime*, winding down. Fred Singer-Ward. They had been together for three years, and Shell loved him. Maybe he loved her. He certainly said he did.

Fred was fun, quick to laugh, accepting of the media and government as purveyors of fine truths, close to his parents, loyal. People flocked to him all the time because he was that kind of guy. Shell has a different relationship with people, and that created a paradox. Nobody flocks to Shell because she knows things and lets people know that she knows. She and Fred were opposite poles of a magnet: stronger together, but, when it came to interacting with others, confusing. They came for Fred and left because of Shell. It wasn't a problem at first, Fred being willing and able to smooth troubled waters, but the closer Shell got to the end of her training, the more intense she was. It's difficult to understand if you're on the outside, and perhaps it was her mistake to date someone ... uninitiated, but the sex was good, the conversation better, and she needed a break from understanding radiation shielding.

"You don't have to say everything you know, Shell," Fred said. They were driving home from a disastrous dinner. "You don't have anything to prove."

Yeah, she did. She'd had to prove herself from a very young age. To everyone. Fuck them.

"Fred, the Dark Side of the moon isn't dark. I thought everyone knew this."

"I didn't," said Fred.

Don't say it. Don't say it. Don't.

"Well, then you're an idiot. We're in a solar system. How could that possibly be the case?"

Shouldn't have said that.

Shell apologised, but in retrospect that was the moment the relationship ended. They stumbled on for another year, fulfilling the bare minimum of interaction required. Conversation died, so did the sex, but neither Fred nor she could pull the trigger.

Ultimately, it fizzled, going out with a whimper rather than bang. It still hurt when he stopped calling, or when she saw him with someone else. Tara, her name was. Nice girl, no dark secrets, shame about the hair.

Shell did what she always does and threw herself into work. Whenever anyone asked about That Guy, she changed the subject.

When the Operations Officer of MaxGalactix US called her in, she hadn't spoken to another human outside the training for six weeks straight, not even her brothers.

"What are your plans?" he asked.

"Well, I'll know in two months if I qualify for—"

"You're going to qualify. What are your plans?"

"I was thinking NASA."

"Why?"

"Sheer breadth of experience. Resources. Vision."

He laughed at that. "You'll run tests for a few months,

then you'll go into orbit, run more tests there, come back, they'll consider you for Mars, pass you over, then accept you, but by then you'll have a hard-on for interstellar work. Not that you don't have it now, but you need to know an acceptable outlet – a sublimation of your erection, so to speak. You follow?"

"I have no idea what you're talking about, sir."

"I'm saying you'll go in there with a dues-paying mentality, thinking you ought to do your time, let those with seniority travel to the stars first. People like your father. Old-timers who respected the chain and expect to be respected in turn, am I right? I'm sure you learned that with mother's milk."

Shell says nothing. Why is this guy being disgusting?

"I can send you to the stars in six months, guaranteed."

"Is this a test?"

"No test, although if we did, I'm sure you'd ace it. I've seen your record."

"What are you asking me to do?"

"Finish your studies, then commit to a trip to one of the colonies under the MaxGalactix banner. Don't think the prep will be easy. We'll stretch your considerable intellect and discipline to the limits of your sanity. What will really annoy you is you'll never get to use what you learn. You'll be Second Mate to the AI. You won't have to do anything at all. You'll be backup, but that just means you'll sleep for like ten years and wake up on the other side."

"Unless the AI fails."

"Ship AIs don't fail. It's never happened. In some

commonwealths they have been granted personhood without voting rights. In the UK they're thinking of giving them citizenship status. Theoretically, a ship can become an individual. It'll never happen, but it shows their degree of confidence that the technology is near-human."

"Humans fail, sir."

"They do, don't they? That's why we use AI for the interstellar work. Better than human."

The motto of one company that manufactures them.

But here Shell is, on the *Ragtime*, with AI failure, and human casualties. Historic. A moment in time that will live in infamy. Her name, eternally linked with her father, will be ... the family name, Campion, will always be associated with this.

When she sold her stuff for practically nothing, Fred asked her if she was coming back.

"I don't know," she had said. That wasn't entirely true. She could not imagine being back on Earth after a mission that would be effectively a twenty-year round trip, with the relativity weirdness altering her ageing. She could not see a future for herself in space, either. Did that mean she would settle in a colony? Did she precognitively not expect to survive?

Her hands work the imaginary beads faster.

She hopes Salvo can come up with a workable solution. They need not just call-making but telemetry information, otherwise the shuttles would not be able to rendezvous safely.

She has never felt a keener sense of her own mortality,

but she isn't terrified. Astronauts circled the globe without their pulse or blood pressure changing. Shell read all the telemetry from the Apollo missions as a child, and she knows Neil Armstrong's pulse better than her own. Her IFC glows with her own vital signs. She cycles through the rest of her crew and sees Fin struggling with tachycardia. She wonders if they're going to have to sedate him.

Finally, exhausted, she sleeps.

Chapter Fifteen

Ragtime: Fin

"We're due a fifteen-minute break," says Fin. "Right about now."

"Mmm," says Joké.

Fin and Joké have merged tasks. They are inventorying the dry-food packages which are stowed on the walls. She stops, hand hooked into one of the net holes, and she turns to him. They are inches apart and Fin can smell her.

"Are you going to stop?"

Joké wags a finger from side to side. No.

"Why not?"

"Do you know what a zeitgeber is?" she asks. She hasn't bound her hair, so her braids float about in the microgravity. Each braid seems an independent, living thing and Fin can't stop staring. Free-floating long hair doesn't seem like the right thing to do, but what does he know?

"The cutting edge?"

"Uh-uh, that's zeit*geist*. Zeitgeber is what helps humans maintain circadian rhythms. Biorhythms. Light-dark, sleep-wake cycles. Cortisol and shit. You follow?"

"Not really. Sort of."

She checks something off the list she has. "When you're planetside, the sun helps you do that. In space, it's not so reliable. Work schedules help maintain those rhythms and stop us from going nuts. Without proper rhythms, the crew is prone to mistakes. That's why she's giving us this work."

"So Shell's wasting our time?"

"It's not a waste of time. She's being a good captain."

"But you don't want to obey her schedule."

"That's different. This is a worksheet for humans. I'm not entirely that. I require less sleep."

"You like her," says Fin.

"I like everybody," says Joké. "Shell gets those cute little creases on her forehead when she disagrees with you. Sure, I like her."

"Nobody likes everybody," says Fin. "Some people are shitty."

She sucks her teeth. "Some people are just more difficult to accept than others, and you shouldn't dislike someone because of their weakness, rather enjoy them for their strengths. Now, Rasheed Fin, what shall we do with your fifteen minutes?"

Fin isn't exactly sure how it becomes lovemaking, but it does. Fifteen minutes is not quite enough. The logistics and contortions required are considerable but overcome.

Standing room only.

"What do you do on Lagos?" asks Fin. He can't stop looking at her.

"Um, anything I want. My father's the governor, don't you know?" She laughs.

"And so . . . ?"

"So I bless the ships being built in the dry dock. I play with the children. I flirt with the university students. I, uh, follow my father around when I'm not ignoring him. I read old and new books. I stare through telescopes at distant nebulae. I pose for the artists. I visit the markets when New Yam comes in. A bit of everything." She sighs.

"You're like a space princess, then. Royalty. And you miss it."

"I do." Joké kisses him. "You tell me something about yourself. Why repatriation? We don't have that profession on Lagos."

"It's a job."

"No, I mean why do it at all?"

"It was before my time, but when things were still precarious and everybody thought Bloodroot would fail in a year or two, the Lambers used to make folks lazy and stuporous. Lambers were never content to just attach to one person. It would grow to six, sometimes all the way to sixty, and that's a lot of people checked out of the workforce. The pioneers realised they had to neutralise them in some way, but on the other hand wanted to be in harmony with them, with nature in general. They managed to communicate, and repatriation was the result. It works for both sides."

Joké stands in the weightlessness, eyes out of focus and maybe her lines are not as distinct as they should be. Fin reaches out to touch her because he is not exactly sure she is there.

But she's back.

"What are you doing?" asks Fin.

"I tried to reach Bloodroot. I didn't think it would work, but I had to try."

"And?"

"I was right. It didn't work."

"Why?"

"I've never been to Bloodroot. I don't know anybody there. I am not linked to places, Rasheed, I'm linked to people, to consciousnesses. I can find my father wherever he goes. But I can't go to a place where I don't know anyone."

"It was worth a try," says Fin. "And you know me. I'm from Bloodroot."

"I suppose. I think I need to be alone, to try something else. Leave. You have places to be, thoughts to think, hmm?"

"Okay." He withdraws, reluctant, holding her hand until he can't any more.

Salvo is still in the bridge, floating on air. Fin emerges alone, although he has the sense that someone was outside.

133

Not Salvo, but maybe Larry. Heresies, but that would be creepy. Larry looks like the kind of person to shoot anyone who even looks at his daughter. Maybe. Or maybe it was Shell outside, checking on the crew.

"What have you come up with," says Fin.

"Not a lot," says Salvo. "There's hope, but we're going to need a spacewalk. I need to know the specific damage, what's left, what can be used as raw material for repair, what needs to be discarded."

"All right, but that's going to be dangerous. The AI is still out of commission."

"Do you know how ship AIs are built?"

"Let's say I don't."

"Conceptually, it's built to resemble the human brain."

"Let's say I don't know anything about that either."

"You have two brains, conceptually. One is an automatic brain that deals with breathing, heartbeat, digestion, all the neural functions that you don't think about. Then you have the new brain, the neocortex, which lies on the automatic brain like a blanket. Your humanity lies here – your morality, your refinement. Do you follow?"

"Just about."

"If you have a bad accident and go into a coma, the neocortex is out of action and your automatic functions continue. Does that make sense?"

"Yes."

"The *Ragtime* is similar. The innermost part of a Pentagram is the automatic functions. Layered onto that is the 'personality'. What's happening now is that all the functions that give the AI its personality are gone. The automatic AI, the last backup, is still working. It's coded in Pentagram hardware. It is rudimentary and obeys instructions."

"Shell's instructions."

"Yes."

"But what about the robots?" asks Fin.

"The AI instructs the robots; so if it is out of commission, the robots will be too."

Fin is confused. "But they're not. They're trying to kill us."

"Not exactly. They seem to be trying to impede us, which is not the same thing."

"Impede us from what?" More important, Fin thinks, why?

Shell drifts in, kicks herself in the direction of the cupola and watches planetrise. Fin may have heard a sigh. She drops back down.

She faces Salvo. "You said something about a spacewalk?"

They all watch the feed from the external camera. There is still debris stuck to the hull, and the stump of the long-range antenna is present, but no dish.

"This really isn't the time for EVA," says Shell. "The ship is too twitchy for my liking."

"I'll do it," says Lawrence. Does he sound cheerful?

Shell looks to Joké with slightly raised eyebrows, as if to say, Are you cool with this? Joké doesn't respond. To Fin she seems oddly unconcerned about her father's welfare, but theirs isn't a typical relationship.

"It makes sense, Action Governor," says Joké. She drops a head on his shoulder. "You've probably clocked more spacewalk hours than all of us combined."

"You can see some of the free panels are from the interstellar shielding. They had to have gone first before the section broke away," says Salvo.

"You want me to bring all that shit in?" asks Larry.

"No, just tell me what's out there."

The camera has limits, as does the Big Dumb Arm. Salvo is right.

While the others work out the exact path of the EVA, Fin goes to the water dispenser. Larry is standing in front of it, arms crossed. As he gets closer, Fin hopes the man will move, but he does not. Fin wonders if the man knows what he was doing with Joké. Awkward.

"I need to get some water," says Fin.

"Need," says Larry. "Or want?"

"Need."

Larry nods but doesn't move. "You know water is essential ... and precious."

"I agree."

Larry nods again and propels himself away. "I'm glad we had this talk."

Fin dry-swallows, no longer thirsty.

*

Fin retreats to his pod and tries to put together what he

knows, because he's fine with Salvo doing all the space survival shit, and maybe they die in five days anyway, but he still has a case to solve, or at least a report to begin. If he dies, he wants something to survive, even if forensically. He has, in the pod, a foot clearance to his sides, less in front and back. Above, a lot more, but that's because it's the exit. Everything is close. And hot. The microgravity means there's no cross vent. The spacesuit Shell mandated stands there like a bad conscience.

He daydreams about Joké pressed against him and is surprised at the longing this produces. It is strangely easy to feel close to her. She's fey and batshit, but maybe that's a plus.

He goes through the files that Salvo sent. The links of some passengers to Yan Maxwell are tenuous, and, to make matters worse, each one of them is still alive and in longsleep. It's one thing to wake up and commit nefariousness; to get back to sleep is another matter. It's impossible without external help.

Dreamstate isn't really sleep. Passengers are anaesthetised at hypothermic temperatures. Fed nutrients, blood and urine monitored, any illness swiftly treated. Theoretically, one could wake from this state, or be woken, because that's just a matter of changing the balance of anaesthetics, removing certain tubes and physiotherapy. Fin personalises the murderer into a silhouette. This person wakes, commandeers the medbots to apply physio, is up in two weeks, finds Maxwell, kills him. But what about the twenty-nine-odd others? Why kill them?

But say that happens – how does this person get back to sleep? We know he can programme the bots. They could put him back to sleep and the crew of the *Ragtime* are none the wiser.

Nah, the person isn't asleep; someone or something is causing the ship and its bots to malfunction, and those two phenomena are related. That is, unless these problems have been scheduled, programmed to happen at this time, in this place. Or unless the killer isn't human and doesn't require anaesthetics or Dreamstate. Is Ragtime itself the killer? If personhood can be contemplated, why not malfunctioning personhood? Humans have killed each other from the start. Uncomfortable thought, though. A murdership reduces the probability of survival considerably.

They really need to find those missing bodies. Body parts.

They have the raw data from all the IFCs, which is just a file dump right now since Salvo has to work on survival. Usually, like Shell insisted, nobody alive has to reveal IFC data, but the deceased data can be mined under certain circumstances. Murder is one such circumstance – or, it should be. Fin is not sure.

He muses that they haven't even thought about jurisdiction. Convention dictates that crimes committed in space be judged by the laws of the place of origin of the criminal. It'll be a nightmare, but luckily one that does not concern Fin. He dictates out a preliminary progress report in his IFC, sets it to send as soon as a transmission pathway is available. It's full of conjecture, but they'll see what he was thinking and follow the threads.

That done, he pulls out of the pod and into the bridge, pulls down a flat velcroed surface as a table, and lays out collected fragments from the destroyed robots. Explosive bullets seemed to do the trick. The robots in question were not hardened for combat. He checks the stash of rounds and sends a note and a CAD file dump to Salvo to get the printer working on more.

Don't we need all the power and materials for survival?

What he means, of course, is the humans do, not him.

It doesn't help us to breathe and eat if robots are going to slit our throats while we sleep.

All right.

One other thing: I need to do an IFC dive.

Now?

After the antenna thing.

I'll keep it in mind.

Chapter Sixteen

Ragtime: Shell

In the spartan cosiness of her sleeping bag, Shell wakes from a dream about blood-drenched fairies and Fred, her fiancé, her *previous* fiancé, asking her, "Why go to space?" "Because it is there." Shell quoting Kennedy quoting Mallory. She has had that speech memorised since she was twelve, to the delight of her father. It was her party trick to deliver it in JFK's exact cadence and diction.

Shell remembers a conversation about Bloodroot, about the efficiency of ferrying new colonists and the practicality of having a geostationary space station with space elevator. She distinctly remembers being told this was on the cards.

But the present remains the present. Sparse satellite density compared to Earth's Sat Constellations, and no global transmitter coverage or Deep Space Network like Earth. Just some provincial colony bullshit.

"Ragtime," she says.

"Captain."

"Status?"

"Nominal, Captain."

Yeah, but it said that before parts of the ship broke off.

She undoes her sleeping bag and rises from her pod. She has missed two exercise slots and feels apprehensive. Not that she can develop osteoporosis in four days and some hours.

Fucking ship. Fucking *Ragtime*.

"Captain?" It's Salvo.

"Go ahead."

"I have proposals to show you."

"Stand by. I'm coming."

In the bridge, Salvo floats in front of Shell. He tracks her approach and looks inhuman in the gloom. His bald head is too symmetrical, his skin too perfect. His makers were not concerned with him passing.

The light is not as bright as usual. The *Ragtime* is power saving, and the temperature is half a Celsius lower than normal, though that would cause humans to expend more energy upping their body temp. While hunger won't send the ship crashing into Bloodroot, energy loss might.

In his left hand, Salvo holds the comms orb.

"I've modified this into a minisat. It's not going to extend radio range but it'll broadcast a distress call for us. We can deploy it through the equipment lock or during a spacewalk by hand."

"And Bloodroot will pick this up?" Shell asks.

"Maybe, but it's unlikely. But someone else might. It's not a solution; it's a probability raiser."

"But we lose comms in *Ragtime*?"

"We won't have uninterrupted communication, yes, but there are other comm orbs. Does that matter?"

Shell doesn't know, but she goes along. "Tell me what else you got."

"May I link to your IFC?"

No. "Yes."

A hologram: a long-range, high-gain antenna. "Your EVA will have to build this outside. We can make the parts with what we have on board and outside, but it'll have to be cold-welded to the existing stump."

Shell goes on the comm. "Uncle Larry, come back."

"Here, over."

"Can you use an ion beam welder?"

"Sure can."

"On an EVA?"

"Never done it before, but I'd like to try."

"Okay. Out." She looks at Salvo. "We're building it."

Takes too long.

Even with all hands and Salvo's crisp, precise and unaffected instructions, with Joké scavenging, Larry's experience, Shell's determination and Fin's ... well, and Fin. Larry works in his spacesuit gloves – he's going to need the dexterity practice. They all sweat, and they're all using more oxygen than Shell would like. It takes up what is left of the first day.

142

Larry wants to don his suit and jump right out, but Shell stops him. Two-hour mandatory rest. Fucking cowboy.

Shell has a constant, low-grade headache. Not enough to need a painkiller, but it's there. Niggling. Will it go away, will it get worse?

She leaves the bridge for the main truss. She works her way to the first torus and inspects the passenger pods herself. Most are fine. She doesn't look at the empty ones, the ones for the dead. One door bothers her. It looks different from a distance, but not radically so. It's got a dot, which, close up, looks like a smudge.

"Ragtime, lighting increase, fifteen per cent."

The corridor becomes brighter. It's not a smudge. It's a hole.

The hell is that?

Shell pushes closer and holds a handrail, inches nearer. Paint layer peeled away, no flecks on the floor, but they would have floated away in the microgravity and collected at air vents. No hesitation marks – maybe not a tooled hole? But how could anything get through the alloys without tools? The hole is an inch across, the walls corrugated. As much as she wants to, Shell resists sticking a finger in there. She looks through and can see the pod interior but not much else. Maybe a wall.

"Ragtime, status of pod 308."

"Status nominal."

"Bullshit."

"Repeat command, please."

"Seal integrity on pod 308."

"Seal integrity nominal."

"Ragtime, is there a hole in the door of pod 308?"

Silence. This is nonsense. The ship can't just decide not to respond. Shell feels disquiet starting at the edges of her being, like something pulling at a loose thread of sanity. She will not unravel, though. Or, she will unravel on her own time.

Rest on your own time, Mission Specialist.

Yes, Commander.

"Ragtime, is the passenger in 308 still alive?"

"Affirmative."

Yeah, right. I'm going to need more than that.

"Respiratory rate?"

"Twelve per minute."

"Blood pressure?"

"110/72."

"Pulse?"

"Sixty."

She looks at the hole. Was it there before? Is it machine-drilled? She rolls her phantom beads.

"Ragtime, replay video, last twenty-four hours." She gives the code and a video file shows the spot she is examining. "Speed up. Times sixteen. Double. Double."

It isn't clear enough to see if the hole was already there, but no person came through the corridor in the entire runtime.

"Ragtime, open pod 308."

"Cannot comply. Action forbidden."

"What?"

144

Silence.

"Ragtime, this is Captain Michelle Campion. Acknowledge."

"Acknowledged."

"Open pod 308."

"Cannot comply. Action forbidden."

"Open pod 309."

"Cannot comply. Action forbidden."

"What is—"

She is interrupted by the shrill tones of an alarm.

Chapter Seventeen

Ragtime: Lawrence

An alarm, flashing lights.

Lawrence rises to investigate.

Twenty minutes earlier, silence, tranquillity and stale warm air – the complements of enforced rest. It's not truly silent, of course, but you learn to cancel out the hum. True silence would be alarming. Lawrence knows of an experimental engine used in a spaceship once that was utterly without sound. The crew didn't go crazy, not exactly, but the anxiety levels were through the roof. The engineers had to pipe a low-volume engine vibration through speakers.

Lawrence thinks of his time at Goldsmith Bridge, twenty Earth-years back, drifting in space close to that failed colony – TransAx? TramsNack? – ion drive dead due to faulty power cells from Goldsmith, the cheap bastards. Lawrence is alone in a dead ship, the deep-space skiff *Shuttlebug*. Life support is working. This isn't the worst situation he has ever been in, so while he is afraid, he isn't panicked. He looks at the darkness and the stars penetrating it. Haldene Campion is somewhere bullying technicians into sending replacement power cells. This was to have been Hal's mission, but he developed a viral infection.

Perception shift. The walls of the *Shuttlebug* seem to expand outward, even though the air smells the same: canned. Shit, this is one of those deep-space disorientation experiences. He's had them before. He places a helmet on his head and takes a shot of oxygen just because he can. He has no idea if it'll help.

Some booze? If only he had some. Maybe he should inhale some hydrazine from the short thrusters. It has to be some form of disorientation. He makes a note of it.

"Shuttlebug, mark onset."

"Of what?"

"Of . . . call it medical manifestation."

"Diagnosis?"

"No diagnosis."

"Then it can't be medical."

"Shut up. Who wrote your code, anyway?"

"Someone better than the one who wrote yours."

"Blasphemy. I'm shutting you down."

"What's wrong, Larry?"

"Perceptual abnormality, specifically depth and light."

"Take a sip of water and I'll keep track. Close your eyes."

"Ok." Lawrence waits for the lights behind his eyes to

reorient him. He's heard of IFCs that work even when your eyes are closed. How would people with such IFCs rest? "Shuttlebug, tell me a story."

"I am not your mother."

"Fuck you, Shuttlebug."

"You don't mean that."

"How do you know?"

"Skin conductance, heart rate, blink rate, respiratory rate – none of these changed. You are relaxed, Lawrence. Which brings me to a question."

"I don't look at you that way, buddy. It would never work. I'm never anywhere long enough, you're a ship . . . "

"Will you just listen? You volunteered for this mission."

"I lost a bet with Hal, but, yeah, I volunteered."

"And you knew the probe surveys were hostile."

"Yes."

"And you knew the odds were that you wouldn't find anything."

"Yes."

"And you came anyway? Why? Humans are supposed to self-preserve."

"Depends on how you define self. What I do, what Haldene Campion does, is for the survival of humanity. This is self-preservation, but on a group scale. The whole of humanity is more important than any individual, than me."

Shuttlebug is silent so Lawrence opens his eyes. He is no longer on the ship, or in space. He is in a cafeteria – familiar, from his childhood, a place he feels safe and happy.

No, not a place; a day, one particular day. He remembers it. It's the day that makes him feel happy. Rice and peas. Curried goat. The goat was overcooked and underspiced to cater to all tastes in the school, which meant that Yorubas like Lawrence had to either endure or bring their own spices in a baggie. Jenna Masters, who Lawrence has spent the summer writing love notes to, walks into the cafeteria, up to where he is eating, and kisses him on the lips in front of everyone. She sits next to him, looking uncomfortable but defiant. This is the first time he feels what he defines as love. He has measured every subsequent feeling by this.

"It was also the fact of puberty, Lawrence," says someone behind him.

Jenna. Older, but still with dimpled cheeks and a toothy smile. Long limbed. Twinkle in her eyes.

"You're—"

"No, I just made myself look like her."

"I'm hypoxic, aren't I? Ran out of air, finally. Never thought I would die in the Brink, though." He is more contemplative than sad.

"You're not hypoxic. I felt you out here, I felt your loneliness. I came because the emptiness in you called."

"Are you the AI fucking with me? Shuttlebug, I will vandalise your Pentagram as soon as—"

Jenna shakes her head.

"Where are you?"

"We are everywhere. But you don't know that yet."

She grasps his hand and they step outside time. To this

149

day, he doesn't remember what happened next. He has impressions, emotions, but no images. He is happy, content, at peace.

Shuttlebug warns him of the approach of self-propelling fuel cells. He recovers, exits the vehicle to connect them up, discards the old ones, heads for stupid Goldsmith Station.

That night, and every night for the next week, he hears a baby crying while he sleeps.

It takes twelve days to return to Goldsmith. Hal Campion is there, worried sick, but handling it by hurling profanities at Lawrence. He gives as good as he gets, takes an actual shower, which is heaven, eats an actual warm meal, and plans to sleep for a week.

He hears crying, a baby again. He wonders, though. This sounds different. While the hallucinatory crying has been muffled, at a distance, this seems to be right in his quarters.

He turns on the light, and there's a baby on the floor.

"She's at least ten days old," says the medic.

"How do you know?" asks Lawrence.

"The umbilical stump has fallen off, for one thing."

"Whose is she?"

"Yours, Lawrence. DNA testing confirms it."

Huh.

Joké.

His heart.

She is like any human child, and she runs with the brats

in the space station, coming back filthy but always happy. Lawrence thinks she sometimes leaves to see her mother, but it's difficult to tell. She waits till he's asleep.

He wants Jenna, this Jenna, to visit him again, but she never does. He hopes she will and doesn't get close to anyone. He's superstitious. Joké may be telling her everything, or maybe she's always around, just one corner away from his dreams. Maybe there is something he is meant to do to be worthy? Maybe he was a one-night stand for a cosmic being.

Nobody asks him where the baby came from, which makes him suspect he is not the first to have had this experience. His superiors ask for an account, which he supplies. Hal knows and believes. Lawrence has the distinct impression it may have happened to him, without the accompanying baby.

"To alien sex!" Hal says, when he crashes metal mugs together.

"To Joké," says Lawrence.

On the *Ragtime*, Larry emerges from his pod, looking left and right. Should take an EVA suit – who knows if the air is venting again?

"Shell? Joké? Anyone?" he says.

"She's out of range," says Joké, floating towards him.

"What's the alarm about?"

"Um, no idea. Ragtime won't answer me."

"Let's go find out, then. We head aft."

"Action Governor! I'll take point."

She will never change.

"Fin, come in," says Lawrence.

"Yes, go ahead," says Fin.

"Stay in your pod. We're going to investigate the alarm."

"Weapons ready?"

"Fuck, yes. Keep Salvo with you. We need at least one pilot out of harm's way."

"Where's the captain?"

"I don't know. That's part of what we're going to investigate. Out."

Lawrence hates the situation. Joké knows to maintain silence as they work their way through each node. Ragtime may not be talking to them, but it's always listening, and always watching. Old-timey god. A god they cannot trust. Lawrence wants to be out in free space, flying or floating with an umbilical. None of this claustrophobic shit.

The alarm stops, just as suddenly as it started. The lights remain red but stop flashing.

Joké stops, looks back at him. *What should we do?*

The absence of alarms is somehow more frightening than their presence.

"Shell, come in." Maybe she's now in range.

"Uncle Larry?" Shell sounds like she's panting.

"Affirmative."

"Uncle Larry, retreat to the bridge, right now! Retreat!"

"Where are you?"

"Get the fuck back to the bridge. I'm working my way there. *Move.*"

"Daddy." He looks at Joké. *Oh, shit.*

Her forearm is covered in insects, heaving with their movement. He follows her arm to the grab rail, which is layered in the same bugs. The entire wall of Node 3 seethes with them. At first, he thinks they are flying insects, but some are just floating in the micrograv, no wings, legs flicking about.

"Daddy, um, what do I do?"

The comm comes alive. "Larry, why in hell are you stationary? Ragtime tells me you haven't moved."

"We seem to have a bug problem."

"Hmm. They're moving higher," says Joké.

"The bug problem means you should be moving away from there."

"Shut up, Shell, darling. Let me think."

He moves back a bit.

"Daddy!"

"Stay still, baby. I have an idea."

He knows he saw it on the way. He keeps moving along the panels until he sees the fire panel. He opens it and pulls free a hose, drags it with him.

"Close your eyes."

He blasts carbon dioxide onto Joké's arm, anchoring himself against the reaction forces that threaten to send him careering in the opposite direction. He inspects the arm: dusty, but clear of crawlies. The insects don't like it, though, and they seem agitated. Some of them have discovered Lawrence.

He grabs Joké by the waist and hurls her ahead of him, into Node 2. He follows after.

When they get to Node 1, they seal it manually since Ragtime won't listen to them. He checks for bites on Joké and himself. None that he can see.

The seal breaks, and Shell tumbles in. "Ragtime, seal bridge," she says.

"Captain, why are there insects on your ship?" Joké asks.

Shell catches her breath. "It's not just insects. That alarm was the experimental wing. Deep-space flights sometimes contain experiments in plant tropisms, micro-organism growth, insect survival, tumour behaviour and so on. There are some animals in suspended animation."

"Sure. I know about those. We usually leave them alone. They're supposed to be locked until the ship returns to Earth," says Lawrence.

"Yep. But Ragtime just opened all the locks."

How biblical.

We're fucked.

Chapter Eighteen

Lagos: Beko, Awe

"Lagos."

"Madam."

"Put me in touch with Awe."

"One moment . . . go ahead."

Awe sounds breathless. "Yes, Madam Secretary?"

"I need the old man. Where is he?"

"I'll get a message to him. What do you need him to do?"

"I asked you where he is."

Some dead air. Why is Awe hesitating?

"I don't know where he is, Madam Secretary."

"Did you recall him like I said?"

"He . . . ah . . . he wasn't at the mines, Madam."

"So where in the name of The Sixty Curses is he?"

"I don't even know where he went."

"Well, find out."

"That's what I'm trying to do."

"Out." So hard to get good help, although Awe is better than most. "Lagos."

"Yes, Madam Secretary."

"What ship did the governor take?"

"The *Decisive*."

"Are you in touch with the AI?"

"Negative."

"Send a probe to look for it."

"Yes, Madam."

There's no sleeping after that, so Beko works.

"Lagos, pull the Pouch from the *Ragtime* for me."

"On screen."

Every interstellar flight comes with something from Earth for Beko's eyes only. Most cannot be entrusted to electronics. They are, to a one, out of date by the time the ship arrives, but it helps her feel connected.

But, shit, here's a letter, and not one she was expecting.

Dear Madam Secretary,

My name is Toby Campion and I write on behalf of myself and my brother Hank. I'm a pilot, though I cannot tell you the work I'm involved with.

I'm writing to enquire about the Ragtime. *Our baby sister Michelle Campion is taking her first interstellar flight and we're all very excited. She is first mate, which is a tremendous honour for someone so young and just out of training.*

Could we ask that you look out for her? She's new to spaceflight and although she's probably the smartest person you've ever met, she sometimes underestimates the value of experience. We're proud of her, but we would feel much less anxious knowing you were providing overwatch.

   Sincerely,
   Hank and Toby Campion.

Beko puts the letter down. This *Ragtime* is proving to be a thorn.

"Lagos."

"Madam?"

"Give me everything you have on Michelle, Hank and Toby Campion. You may find some intersections with Governor Lawrence."

"Yes, Madam."

Beko looks at the time. She's lost four hours already, and she isn't even sleepy.

She keeps working.

The probe cannot contact the AI of the *Decisive*. The records and extrapolation of the last known trajectory show a vector towards Bloodroot.

Lawrence has gone after Michelle Campion, after the *Ragtime*. There can be no other deduction.

Awe

Awe had a call from her not too long ago, so he is surprised when the bell rings and the cameras show her outside, wearing her most irritated facial expression. Secretary Beko makes Awe uncomfortable, but this is normal. She makes everyone uncomfortable, and it doesn't make him feel weak. It's worse when she is in his space. She's been standing at the door too long.

"Come in, your ... ma'am."

"Thank you."

"Do you want some iced tea?"

"I do not."

Silence. Awe is hypervigilant about the mess in his workspace. It's about the same for anyone else in the Service, but Beko notoriously has a thing about cleanliness. Showers three times a day or something equally sacrilegious and water-expensive. But who's gonna tell her off? Not Awe.

She stares at him.

"Ma'am?"

"What bothers you about the *Ragtime* job?" she keeps

her face expressionless. Awe has read that old Yoruba kings did this, practised shielding their faces from emotional incontinence, so that the report of their generals could be objective and not swayed by the royal mood. It would work if he hadn't already seen her face before she came in.

"Nothing, Ma'am."

"Nothing."

Awe shakes his head, knowing this is the wrong answer but not having a right one for her. Holds the gaze, though. Not a punk.

"Take me through this, Awe."

"But we already ... okay. Lagos, review number seventeen, Ragtime service. Acknowledge."

"Good evening, Awe. Acknowledge." Lagos changed personalities again, most likely because of Secretary Beko. "Panopticon again?"

"Even so."

The lights change.

Awe and Beko seem to stand in space while the Dyson elements leave the star, form a ring, create the bridge, admit the test satellite and finally welcome the *Ragtime*.

"Lagos, Lagos, this is Ragtime. All systems nominal."

The exchange between Lagos and Ragtime continues, with Awe mouthing it exactly. He has listened to the recording so many times and the memorisation is accidental. Beko glances at him briefly, then refocuses.

They watch the robots repair and replace components. The scan anomaly and rescan correction, right on schedule—

"Stop," says Beko.

The image freezes.

"You said everything was normal," says Beko.

"It is."

Beko shakes her head. "Lagos, mark this spot."

"Marked."

"Continue at speed."

The rest is of no interest.

"Lagos, run again, at thirty-two times normal speed. Keep running until I tell you to stop."

"Aye-aye."

Awe is unable to follow anything, but Beko just sits there with unblinking eyes like an Artificial. He can't leave, he can't close his eyes. It's an endurance test for him.

"That's enough, Lagos. Stop."

"Yes, ma'am."

"Awe, is there an image of the *Ragtime*'s Pentagram?"

"Yes. Routine."

"Retrieve it. Go over it byte-by-byte if need be."

"What am I looking for?"

"You'll know it when you see it," says Beko. "Don't leave this room until you find it."

"Ma'am, if I may, what's wrong with the service?" asks Awe.

"Nothing. The service is perfect. An advertisement for our work that is sure to keep MaxGalactix coming back."

"Then what—"

"Someone was awake when Ragtime came through the bridge. They shut down as soon as the first scan happened.

To do that, the Pentagram had to have been involved. Humans don't just wake up. I'm willing to bet this has something to do with why the *Ragtime* has gone dark."

She swirls out and Awe calls his wife to say he'll be late. Again.

Beko seals her living quarters off, has a shower, lies in bed.

She can't sleep. Three of the Campion children in her thoughts plus the delinquent *Ragtime*. She wants to be rested before Awe brings her information, though.

"Lagos, pharmaceutical sleep, four hours, no interruptions. On my mark. Mark."

"Affirmative."

A sleep like death, a curtain of unawareness falling like an asteroid.

Chapter Nineteen

Ragtime: Shell

Shell sets all IFCs to receive the video footage from the experimental section, Node E. It's easier than explaining.

All is quiet and lit with blue light.

It is metal and plastic and glass, vaults, cabinets and conventional refrigerated compartments. In some way, it looks like the lock-box room of a bank. Sterile, straight to the point; a rectangular space with all walls covered in slots and sealed doors. It seems almost holy in its isolation.

Readings show different temperatures on each door as well as humidity and a few other numbers that didn't make much sense to anybody uninvolved with the programming.

This is not a room anybody enters – at least, not crew. This is an Earth compartment. It is stocked by Earth on Earth, and it is meant to be opened only when the vehicle returns to Earth.

Indicator lights on each door turn red, in a cascade that spreads from the centre outwards. Each opening is followed by a thunk as bolts within locks are slid back and magnetic seals are deactivated. Neither the lighting nor the surveillance camera fails. When one of the doors swings open, the shipwide alarm goes off.

The video feed dies, so abrupt that the IFCs send an after-image to all their owners.

"Do we have an inventory?" says Larry.

"We do not," says Shell. "Node E is usually none of our business."

"And we're sealed back here," says Joké. "Umm, not cool, I guess."

"Count your blessings, girl," says Shell. "We have functional airlocks on this side."

"We're killing ourselves?" asks Fin. "I'd like to go on record as wanting to try something else first."

"Nobody else is dying here. Not crew, not passengers," says Shell. "But we will use the airlock first. Salvo?"

"Captain?"

"Is the minisat ready?"

"It is."

"Okay, let's go to the equipment lock."

"You have to record the message we want it to broadcast."

Shell floats towards the device and Salvo activates it. He nods.

"*This is the starship* Ragtime *in low planetary orbit*

of Bloodroot. Our principal antenna is down and we have four days of life support left. There is also a risk of microbial contamination. We need urgent assistance or hundreds of souls on board will die."

The message marker has the Bloodroot date and time as well as a counter so that anyone listening will be able to tell how long ago the satellite was launched.

Salvo opens the equipment lock and places the sat inside. He reseals it. Fore of this position, the crewlock lies dormant. On the walls above the panels, the signatures of every mission specialist who has traversed the airlock before now. There are some thumbprints and photos. Two EVA suits stand attached to opposite walls. From there, Salvo moves to a glove-box arrangement so he can manipulate the sat with sealed gauntlets. He nods to Shell.

"Ragtime, open equipment lock," says Shell.

Nothing.

"Ragtime," says Shell.

"Captain," says Ragtime.

"Open equipment lock."

"I am forbidden from carrying out this instruction."

Motherfucker.

Shell manually opens the lock and Salvo pushes the minisat free. It floats away and is soon gone from view.

They return to the bridge.

"What's the plan here?" asks Lawrence.

"We need to hold this area, and we need to hold Toruses 1 and 2," says Shell.

"How? There are only five of us," says Fin. "Besides,

164

it's tactically suspect. You want to hold one area fore, then cross a no-man's-land, then hold another area aft. You split your forces creating an enemy sandwich. Can't do it with five. Can't and shouldn't."

"And we don't know what's out there," says Joké.

"We don't have five," says Salvo. "We have three at the most. The captain can't go out on field missions because she's the only one who can even marginally talk to the *Ragtime*, and it doesn't always listen. I can't go because as important as this biological spill is, building and re-attaching the high-gain antenna is more pressing. When I'm done, I'll need Lawrence."

"Superb," says Fin.

"We need data. A reconnoitre," says Shell. "Ragtime, do we have a drone?"

"There is no drone under your command, Captain," says Ragtime.

"I'll go," says Joké.

"I just got you back from becoming a meal for exotic insects," says Larry.

"Action Governor! None of them bit me, and I wasn't prepared. They caught me by surprise and I was more disgusted than harmed. I love what insects do for us, but I hate looking at them or having them creep all over me. I'm prepared now." Joké is smiling. Shell figures risk-taking is in the family DNA.

It can't be Fin. Too clumsy, too important for weapons synthesis.

The truth is, Shell would rather go herself, but Salvo's

point is valid, same as what Joké said before. If she dies or is incapacitated, nobody can command the *Ragtime*.

But Joké lost the EVA suit she was fitted for. Or half of it, at any rate.

"You'll need a new suit," says Shell.

While the others help refit Joké, Shell does a sweep of the cameras. None of them function except external hullcams, which are dull to watch since they show the Big Dumb Arm and service bots scrambling. Not exactly useful in this situation.

Ragtime agrees to unseal the bridge and Joké, after sharing a melodramatic kiss with Fin, slips through. When did that happen? The crew syncs with her suitcams this time, and Shell notices they are all starting to work like a team.

The node adjacent to the bridge is already coated with some moss-like substance. It looks different from just an hour earlier. The *Ragtime*'s walls are all invisible under this creeping plant-like thing, the cargo nets acting like a trellis in places. Joké lingers over a clump.

"Joké, don't. Advise rapid movement. Don't stop for anything."

"Yes, Captain."

Flying insects stop on Joké's helmet and slide off. Some might defy easy definition as they don't look like anything Shell has ever seen. There are spiders the size of kittens, but with no eyes. They scuttle out of the way when Joké approaches. The going is difficult because although she is flying from node to node, the moss obscures the handrails or the directions.

Shit, the directions.

"Joké, stop," says Shell.

"What is it?"

"Turn around, please. I want to see something."

Behind, a sea of grey-blue, but no grab rails. The moss grows fast.

"Joké, how are you going to make your way back? You have no breadcrumbs," says Shell. "Even Ragtime's cameras can't see you. Or maybe they can, but not in a visual electromagnetic spectrum."

"Umm … I have a great sense of direction, Captain. I'll be fine."

Shell isn't so sure. The lighting was already in power-saving mode because of the reactor leak. Now, covered in moss, the lights barely shine through. The gloom makes the *Ragtime* look more like a rainforest under the canopy. What is this gunk doing to the air filters? And what's the moss feeding on? Growing on? There's no soil or wood. The little Shell knows about the experimental organisms is that some of them are extremophile derivatives: they can live in difficult circumstances, which is the whole point. Human scientists need to know what can survive deep space. They need to know if this is something that can be genetically programmed into humans. Currently, deep-space travel involves hibernation, cooled temperature, slowed metabolism, that kind of thing. If humans can somehow be like the fungus that grows in nuclear reactors …

"Captain, can you see this?" says Joké.

A mound in the moss heaves sluggishly, like a velvet-covered animal.

"Avoid it," says Shell. Are the creatures consuming each other? "Joké, I need you to get to the toruses, first priority."

"Aye, Captain."

The camera shows other vegetation now, some flowering. Blob-like beings fling themselves at Joké and hang on to her suit before dropping away, disappointed. The passages are narrowed at hatches. The crew and service areas of the *Ragtime* weren't built to be pretty, and at the best of times they have rivets visible, bags of junk festooned, cables and ties and duct tape all over the place. The grey moss smooths everything out, like a soft-focus camera, a blanket of bluntness over reality. Cosy danger.

Joké flings herself into the next node and is blanketed in something scaly, slimy and muscular.

She screams out briefly, but the screen is covered in slime and blurry.

"Joké!" says Fin.

"I'm all right. The suit is holding, but I'm stuck. Something has me. I can't see what it is, but I think it's trying to pierce my suit. Or eat me. I can't figure which. Um, both?"

"Can you move at all?" asks Shell.

"Negative."

"Sit tight, I'm coming," says Shell. She turns to the others. "I don't want to hear any objections. Suit me up. Fin, weapon."

"What kind?" asks Fin. "What are we facing?"

"I have no idea, and I will find out when I get there. Give me whatever you have."

One of the storage bags attached to the walls contains an MCP suit, which is more manoeuvrable than a pressurised suit. This one is experimental but fully functional. Shell remembers being told to "take it for a spin a few times" back on Earth. It will protect from kinetic and radiant energy as well as inhalants.

Before anyone can object, Shell is out into the grey.

The MCP feels like every part of Shell's body is being squeezed by a boa constrictor. It makes her more aware of the microgravity. It's like a new and different force acting on her, but of course it isn't. She propels herself the normal way: grab rail to steady herself, then push off through the air to the next node. The grey moss layer between her gauntlet and the alloy feels disgusting, like rot. It comes off and forms puffs of powder.

The entire experience is like swimming down the throat of a giant.

She is passing one of the shapeless mounds when it bursts open and reaches for her from her left. It's one of the hauler bots and latches on to her. She cries out in surprise. It pulls her towards the wall, where a second one shakes free of the moss. She doesn't fight. She needs the firmness of the wall to push off against, so struggling would be a waste of energy. Both bots have cutting implements on their appendages: one mechanical like a saw, the other a fine laser. She doesn't wait to see how the suit will hold up. She fires at their appendages, which break off and fragment, scattering into a cloud. Their centre mass still functions, but it doesn't matter. Without limbs they are harmless units, and maybe Salvo can make something with their parts.

Shell keeps going aft, noting from her visor that the weapon stays hot; no air currents to take the heat away.

She can't see any signs, but Shell estimates that she's in Node 4, just before the hatch into the spoke for the first torus. She grabs a rail to stop herself moving when she spots a heaving mound with a boot poking out.

"Joké, is that you?" asks Shell.

"Aye, Captain," says Joké on the radio.

"How's your suit integrity?"

"No warning lights, Captain."

Joké is surrounded by tentacles and held fast. They come from three different sections of the *Ragtime*'s wall and, given their placement, are likely to be emerging from air vents. What are they growing on? The tentacles, once free of the grey moss, lack skin – or visible skin, at any rate. Shell can see muscles tensing and relaxing, fine blood vessels transporting blue liquid.

"I'll get you out of there," says Shell. "Don't move."

"Umm ... I can't."

Closer look. There are spines on the tentacles. Even so, Shell gets a grip, braces her feet against the body of the ship and pulls. The tentacles do not budge. Shell traces one to the point furthest away from Joké and closest to the wall. She arms her weapon and fires. The tentacle ruptures, but it spews something that aerosolises – black inky stuff that obscures vision and does who knows what else.

"That worked ... something gave," says Joké.

"Try to disengage. It has some kind of counter-measure," says Shell. She shoots the other two tentacles, and the same thing happens. The entire node will be full of the stuff. She grabs Joké's gauntlet and pulls her free.

"The bridge is that way," says Joké.

"I know. We're not going to the bridge."

Shell looks back. The blackness of the node is complete. She shines her powerful suit light at it, but it bounces off. "Ragtime, decrease atmospheric pressure on Node 7."

No response. No guarantee that the moss isn't blocking speakers.

"Lawrence, come back," she says.

"Lawrence here, Captain."

"Reporting. I have Joké, no injuries. We're continuing aft. Be advised, the robots are still in play."

"Acknowledged."

"Out."

"I'll go first," says Shell. "Keep a hand on my suit."

"Ooh, Captain."

"Try to be serious," says Shell. "And why didn't you just ... you know, get out of your suit the other way?"

"It doesn't work like that. It's somewhat unpredictable, my connection with the Lambers; you never know where you're going to end up, and, umm, I wasn't in danger yet. It was snug in the suit, but I had lots of air."

Joké's suit is covered in something, maybe a digestive slime? Thankfully it cannot digest the suit.

They fly past a quadruped hunched up, eating something. It eyes them and emits a low growl. Shell considers shooting it.

They get to the first spoke and manoeuvre into the first torus, which is clear of the moss.

"Ragtime, spin Torus 1." Shell isn't sure the ship will respond.

"Yes, Captain."

The sinking feeling, the brief nausea, as artificial gravity comes on.

"We need to check here and the second torus. I was here before the alarm went off and there were things here."

"What things?" asks Joké.

"I don't know. They were slithering things that slithered in my direction. They drilled through alloy. I didn't wait to see."

"So these . . . things can get through our suits?"

"Probably. If they can drill through walls."

"So why are we here?"

"Because I want to see. If we know what they are, how many of them there are, we can decide how to fight them. I also want to be sure the passengers are intact."

All round the passenger section, they don't encounter anything biological. The hole Shell saw before is still there, and Ragtime still does not allow entry into the pod. Just before Shell and Joké arrive at the point they entered, they see a much larger hole, maybe a foot across, cut into the floor. The edges are sharp and jagged, but regular.

"That looks like a problem," says Joké.

Shell gives the gun to Joké and gets prone.

"Whoa, don't stick your head in there," says Joké.

"It'll be okay," says Shell.

"No, come on. It will not be okay. The mission was to check if the passengers were intact. They are. You're the captain. We have to go back and regroup."

Shell hesitates.

"You don't go in such tunnels, Captain. That's just asking for your head to be cut off. You get drones to explore them, preferably the kind of drone with a lethal payload."

"You were there when I asked Ragtime. There are no drones."

"That's ... um ... not what Ragtime said. It said there are no drones *under your command*."

Shit, that's true. The constant stress is getting to Shell.

"I still have none to drop down this hole."

"Um, then Salvo can build one for you. Come on, Captain. You know I'm right."

She is.

"Fine. We check Torus 2, then we go back."

Torus 2 is full of robots. Medical, haulage, mechanic, exploratory, cleaner, general maintenance, all-purpose serpentine – everything except the gargantuan hull robot crane Big Dumb Arm, and that's because it's outside the *Ragtime*.

173

"No," says Shell.

"No," says Joké.

They make their way out and aft.

"We have to focus on what we can fix," says Shell. "Because we can't fix it all. We need to get the antenna running, but at the same time we need to clear these vermin from the ship. Dormant, they weren't an issue. Awake, they're using more energy and will factor into our calculations about how many days we have left. Awake, they're capable of mischief, by which I mean they might damage machinery, cause disease or kill us directly."

Fin says, "Why can't we just fix the antenna, find a hole to hide in, and wait for the cavalry?"

"Because we do not know if the cavalry is coming. Have you ever tried planning and executing a mission in three days? Maybe on Earth, or Space Station Lagos. But Bloodroot's space programme isn't designed for that. It's more a reception party for these kinds of missions than a constantly evolving exploration apparatus. In between colonist deliveries, it goes dormant. Plus, we're contaminated. We have no idea if their response will be to detonate us in orbit."

"Would they do that?" asks Larry. "Do they have that kind of missile tech?"

"I don't know. Any spaceship can be a missile if you pack it with enough explosives and send it on a collision course. But it's a colony. They have to be careful of outsiders," says Shell.

"You do realise the irony of using 'outsiders' in this context, right? All colonists everywhere are outsiders by definition," says Fin.

"The point is their reaction should be marked 'x' for unknown. I need you to print weapons and MCP suits for all of us."

Fin looks at Salvo, who nods.

"All right. You all have your tasks. Go. Lives are at stake."

They somersault and brachiate to the labs.

Shell holds Fin back.

"What is it?" he asks.

"I want to ask you something unethical."

Sudden interest in the eyes. "Go on."

"Hypothetically, if I ... if someone were to ask you, hypothetically, to lie to Bloodroot Mission Control, hypothetically, whether you deceived them or not, would you be obliged to report it?"

An expression that Shell did not expect darkens his face. Anguish, pain, weight.

"Hypothetically," he says. His voice is hoarse.

"Of course. I would never ask you to go against your ... ethics."

"I'd ... I'd have to first refuse, then report verbally and in writing."

"Even if you could save lives by lying to Bloodroot?"

"Enough with the hypotheticals. I know what you're asking. You want me to lie to about ending my investigation."

"No."

"Then what—?"

"I want you to tell the truth about your investigation, which I'll come back to. What I want you to lie about is the contamination. If we get the antenna back online, could you bring yourself to minimise the contamination from the opened science labs so that we can save nearly a thousand people?"

Fin swallows, more distressed than Shell would have expected.

"I'd still have to complete the investigation," says Fin.

"Your investigation is over."

"What do you mean?"

"I'm saying there is no longer a need to investigate. I am confessing."

"What?"

"I, Mission Specialist Michelle Campion, acting Captain of the starship *Ragtime*, confess to the murders of the passengers." She looks him right in the eyes. "I did it."

Chapter Twenty

Bloodroot: Mission Control

Once every lunar month, something Bloodroot colonists call a Scintillation occurs. A hundred or more Lambers flick in and out of existence in the city centre. It starts with two, then others join in. They float less than a foot above ground, teardrop-shaped glowing splotches of cytoplasm trailing tentacles.

Scintillations occur around the Lamber Tower, that focus of repatriation. It's not really a tower; it's an antenna of sorts, and, even though the entire colony piggybacks signals on it, the primary purpose is to link with the Lambers' homespace and send them packing through a portal. Scientists have said from what they can see it is not similar to bridge technology. Though Bloodrooters built it, they did so using specifications provided by the aliens. There are some hints that the entire structure is a resonator, and the antenna alone won't do the job. Where do they go? What happens to them when they get there? No answers.

If the settlement was planned, no way would the Tower be at the centre. But a colony can be a chaotic thing in the beginning. Ask Nightshade. The lore is that the structure predates its use as an antenna, and people naturally build houses in spirals around it. Alternating arcs of dwellings and tree boulevards, lessons learned from Earth, trying to work with the environment instead of conquering it.

The Tower is visible from Mission Control, although not a single person looks at it as they go about their business. The twinkling of the Scintillations doesn't turn heads in Mission Control, not even for a group as bored as The *Ragtime* Team.

They have a pool going while one of them, Demetrius Peole, throws balls of crumpled paper into a waste basket from ten feet. His failures dot the low-friction floor. After each shot, the wager changes. Everyone present knows that Demetrius misses one in ten shots and bets accordingly, which is boring and reduces the probability of any one person winning big.

The others keep busy by drawing staff portraits on copy paper, drinking coffee, performing dubious acrobatics, racing with wheeled office chairs, making origami, sipping sneaky alcoholic beverages in coffee mugs, pencil balancing, flirting, everything except what they are paid to do.

Since Peole has a supervisory role, nobody else worries about getting caught. Peole has a streak of fourteen baskets. A miss is imminent, but nobody seems brave enough to risk a wager.

Bayo Coker stands at the periphery of the basket action,

waiting. Peole notices him but throws first, then collects his winnings – chore tokens – before attending to the timid and quiet Coker.

"Yes? What may I help you with? You seem to have something on your mind. You have something on your mind, don't you?" asks Peole.

"I ... why aren't we ... doing anything?" asks Coker.

"We are. I am. Behold what I am doing." Peole points to the basket.

Coker is silent.

"You don't think this is good use of my time? I have degrees, you know. More than one. I can determine how best to use my time. I have expertise, dammit."

"We have a fleet of shuttles. We power them up, we run them through their tests, then we power them down again. Then we play crosswords. Meanwhile, there are passengers up there."

"I know this. But we don't do anything until we get the order."

"I'm worried about that."

"They have plenty of air, nourishment and fuel, Coker. They aren't going to die because of an investigation."

Coker inclines his head.

"What? Speak! Seven Curses, you are so reticent."

"The *Ragtime* has gone dark, sir."

"What do you mean?"

"All signals ceased. Not even a beacon."

"That's impossible."

"Sure, it's impossible, but—"

179

"Show me," says Peole. "If you've lost my starship . . ."

The data, or lack thereof, is correct. The *Ragtime* isn't there.

"Well, Shit and Heresies," says Peole. "I think I need to talk to someone in authority."

Unwin, the lead investigator, and Malaika, the chair of Bloodroot Mission Control, dismiss Peole.

"Do you still think Rasheed Fin was a good choice for this?" asks Malaika.

"It doesn't matter. He's the one on the spot. The Artificial should have been able to keep him in-protocol, so this might not have anything to do with our recovering repatriator," says Unwin. "No, the *Ragtime* might have faulty radios or have crashed into the Greater Arboreal Sea or drifted off into space."

"I'm worried. He wanted to arrest Campion. We should have let him."

"He had no evidence, no reason except his bruised pride. It would not have held up."

"Yes, but maybe she's killed them all." Malaika opens a communications channel. "Go to Fin's house. Search the house, interrogate his mother, see if anything has changed since he went to space. On Unwin's authority."

Unwin nods. "Authorised. What do we do now? You're the space guy."

"What's the precedent on a missing crime scene?"

"I have no idea. I have my law folks looking into it. It would seem obvious that the safety of the souls on board should be priority. We can arrest Campion when we find her."

Malaika rubs his eyes. "I had a dream about this, you know. I dreamt I was ready to send the shuttles up, but I couldn't find the *Ragtime*. It never arrived, and it was all my fault."

Unwin scoffs. "Standard anxiety dream, old chap. Nothing precognitive about it."

"I know. I'm just saying." Malaika sighs. "I'm a little concerned."

"There's a missing spacecraft with thousands of people on board. Concern is natural. Besides, you're always concerned. You are paid to be concerned."

"I mean, I'm bothered about what our role will seem to have been if this is a disaster. We left people in space."

"Quarantined. Not left."

"We should have brought them home."

"In hindsight. We use the information we have to make the decisions we can. Besides, we don't know. This Peole fellow might be flaky," says Unwin.

"Demetrius *is* flaky, but not in matters of space travel."

"What do we do?"

"We search. We turn every telescope on Bloodroot to the sky. We commandeer every satellite and scan for anything."

"And Lagos? What do we tell them?"

"Nothing."

"Malaika."

"My bailiwick, my responsibility. We tell them nothing

until we have hard facts. A debris field, a broadcast, something."

There are ten thousand registered objects orbiting the Earth and who knows how many unregistered. The space debris is a whole different matter, data about which Bloodroot doesn't have. On establishing the colonies, it was important to avoid the crowded sky of the homeworld, so the space programme is very specific. Enough satellites to ensure reasonable contact with Lagos, some entertainment, and the arrival and departure of colony starships. There are perhaps twenty satellites in Bloodroot's orbit. On Malaika's order, they all begin to look for the starship *Ragtime*.

Three officers go to Rasheed Fin's house, two of whom are Artificials.

They knock, IFCs spontaneously pinging, sending public data to any available open client. Nothing comes back. Nobody opens the door or answers.

"Isn't the mother supposed to be in?" asks one of the team.

"Yes."

"That meets the criteria for entering."

"Breaching now." The second officer remembers once this happened to him and an elderly person had died. He wonders if he will ever live it down. Did his hesitation kill her?

The door crashes inwards from the battering ram.

"Mrs Fin?"

The house is an exquisite mess. A stink hits the team first, but chocolate wrappers crinkle underfoot. Grime everywhere.

"This guy went into space?"

"We're going to find a body, aren't we?"

Dust on every surface. Dried food. Toilet unflushed.

"Rasheed, is that you?" says a voice from upstairs. "Don't forget to eat, baby."

"Mrs Fin?"

He sends two officers up. Rotten fruit in the kitchen, mould climbing the walls.

The officers call down. "Sir, you're going to want to see this."

"Software?" says Malaika.

"Wireframe Mother," says Unwin. "They're popular with traumatised people these days. And those who have lost their own family, like Fin."

"I looked him up before any of this," says Malaika. "Nothing has happened to his family."

"Sealed record, old son. His entire family died in one of those venting incidents that were common thirty years back. He was younger than three, and assigned to Wireframe. Obviously, he wasn't monitored."

"And we sent him into space without—"

"Oversight. Too late to cry about it now, hey?"

"I see," says Malaika, although his tone says he does not. "Thoughts?"

"In hindsight, I should have done more thorough mental health screening," says Unwin.

"No, I mean thoughts going forward."

"I have no fucking clue. I'm going to sit around and wait for your Malaika Magic to work. You bring them home; I'll take care of Fin."

Demetrius Peole swears at the back of Coker's head.

"I hope you're happy now, Coker. I hope you enjoy this work."

Coker is silent and watches the data streaming in from the satellites. If there is a hint of a smile on his face, Peole cannot tell, but he's sure the man is amused.

Chapter Twenty-one

Ragtime: Fin

Fin stares at Shell as if willing her to take back what she just said. She doesn't.

"You murdered the passengers," says Fin.

"I did," says Shell.

"Why?"

"What?"

"What was your motive for killing them?"

"Mental illness. Asthenisation."

"Asthenisation."

"Yes."

"What is—"

"Labile mood, altered sleep-wake patterns, territorial behaviour, hypoactivity, fatigue, attention and memory deficits. It's a space thing. Look it up."

"And—"

"I was territorial over the *Ragtime* and I didn't want them here, so I started killing the passengers."

"I—"

"I'll IFC-sign a confession, all right?"

Fin thinks of everything that has happened, and all of Shell's reactions, and he shakes his head. "You're lying."

"What does it matter? You have an out. Let's go home!"

"I can't."

"Why?" Her turn.

"I've lied before, and it very nearly destroyed me. My family tends to be inflexible and it destroyed my relationship with them. This is my second chance. *Ragtime* is my second chance. I can't risk it."

"I understand family expectations, Rasheed. I feel the weight of filial duty too."

"Not like mine."

"Trust me; like yours."

"If we survive, we must swap stories some time, Captain Campion."

"You are obligated to arrest me, Rasheed," says Shell.

"No. What I'll do is get Salvo to record your statement, Captain. When we get out of this, if you still want to be arrested, I'll do it. My investigation is still open. For now, do your job and get us planetside."

Years ago, they were relocators, enforcers of the agreement with the Lambers. At some point they started calling them repatriators, which is the name that stuck, which is what Fin is.

Waiting outside a building, waiting on confirmation, eating something fried, waiting while the treewall behind the structure sways in the wind bringing a tangy scent. Through the treewall, the next boulevard is not visible, but the lights from the houses seem to blink as the trees part, then close, like a gentle dance of tentative lovers.

Fin has a mouth ulcer right at the angle where his left cheek meets the gums, and he tongues it as if that would make it go away. He doesn't like waiting because he gets sugar cravings.

"I agree," says Duro, his partner on this escapade. Human. Salvo is overbooked or undergoing maintenance or some shit.

"With what? I didn't say anything."

"Exactly. You should have been."

"I'm not here to entertain you," says Fin.

"Talking to me can count as entertaining yourself, brother," says Duro.

"I don't need entertainment. I'm on the job."

"No, you are waiting for a signal confirmation. We can do our jobs when we know for sure the Lamber is in there."

"The waiting is the job," says Fin. "And the Lamber is there. I'm waiting for official acknowledgement of knowledge I already have." To discourage Duro from talking, Fin checks his weapon. Never used, it is only effective against Lambers, and since they are generally peaceful . . .

Fin has always wondered what happens to aliens when they're shot. He rises and squirrels into the back of the van where the techs are trying to pick up a signal that suggests Lambers.

"You are making me look bad, children," he says. "Really bad."

Cables everywhere, trailing from batteries, competing for end points in the back of receivers and transmitters, cobbled together, bunched in places, snaking free in others, getting underfoot no matter how careful Fin is. There are three techs in the back, listening to arcane outputs. Such is their focus that they don't acknowledge Fin's taunt. One of them sweats even though it's cold from the fans keeping the machines cool. Fuck 'em, wasting his life with their dilly-dallying.

"Call me when it's done," he says. He walks all the way through and opens the back doors of the van, steps into the night.

Fin has never been able to explain his talent for finding Lambers. It is an itch in his brain, a surge of blood across his scalp. It doesn't matter. He finds more than anyone else and sends them all back to wherever the fuck they come from. He's not much good at anything else. He's a better-than-average marksman, a passable investigator, and an indifferent scholar. He flirts with weapons manufacture because they fascinate him, particularly old Earth technology.

He walks towards the building. Even in the dark Fin can tell it's been recently constructed by people wanting what the Lambers have to give. Fin is immune and in quiet moments wonders what it feels like. An intoxication? Maybe that's why he can find them. In the skyline, to the west, the tower they taught Bloodroot how to build, the link to their homeworld. Nobody knows how it works, but then, they don't need to. How many people know how electricity works? Just need to know that it works and how to use it.

The door is closer now; Duro still in the van, thinking Fin is in the back. Doesn't matter. "Duro" means "wait" in Yoruba, so this is in line with the man's destiny.

His gait slows as he reaches the door; nerves, unknown number of people in there, no way to predict their reactions to interruption from their ecstasies. But Fin is young and invulnerable, unable to contemplate his own failure, death or oblivion. Non-existence is a myth. The wind whips his coat, and Fin takes it off, folds it carefully and lays it on the ground to the left of the door. It opens outwards, so he knocks first. Nothing happens. No sounds in the night, no lights, no animals shuffling. The wind again, but it blows between buildings, whistling and ghosting.

Fin fits a Locksmith on the door and waits. It cycles through several frequencies until it hits the right one. The door swings open and he enters. Gentle lute music plays, the remnants of cooking on the air, something spicy. No real lighting, everything dim, so dim. From his back pocket, enhancer glasses – good for getting around, but poor for Lambers. He'll have to remember to take them off. It's warm in here, from heating, cooking and the bodies of the addicted. He's on a hallway of some kind and he comes to the bottom of a stairwell. A figure lurches out of shadows under the stairs, and it heads for him and performs some kind of gesture between a bow and a duck. It repeats the action. And again. A robot, busted, no threat. Its lips move, but no sound comes out.

Fin takes the stairs, sensing the Lamber closer. A shuffle, and someone comes down the stairs, a human this time, saying nothing but staring at Fin. Blank face. Fin draws his other weapon, the rubber projectile one, and shoots the wall adjacent to the person. The ricochet hits the man in the foot, the second in the knee. Fin pulls the man behind him before he can cry out in pain. The sound, the air displacement, must attract attention of others unless they are too far down the Lamber hole.

His IFC buzzes. "Rasheed, where are you? I just heard a shot!"

Distraction. Fin kills notifications and climbs faster.

People coming for him in earnest now. He makes sure he is transmitting his authority as a repatriator to all IFCs within ten feet. The feet do not slow down.

"Stand down," he says. They do not.

He does fire warning shots into the stairs, but the dark, seething mass coming towards him seems even more inhuman. They're human enough when lit up by muzzle flash. Few of them cry out, even though everybody hit falls. There's a rage, a miasma of anger in the air, a sense of how-dare-you to all of them. Everybody is brave until they're hit by a rubber bullet. Fin steps over the incapacitated to make progress up the stairs.

At a landing, he comes to a short corridor with rooms off it. Training says to clear the rooms before advancing, don't leave an enemy at your back, but he knows the Lamber is not there. It's higher up. Fin goes higher.

Resistance thins out, sporadic confused addicts who don't even know what law enforcement means in an elastic universe. He can and does discourage them in a non-lethal way, but this has never been Fin's favourite thing. He hates hand-to-hand because he does not like to touch people, but the very hatred is what made him master the techniques, so that if he must do this it will take the shortest possible time.

All the hairs on Fin's body stand on end and he knows the Lamber is mere feet away. He runs out of stairs and there is one person blocking an entrance. This person is resolute, and Fin does not suppose she is a user. This is some kind of believer in ... what, freedom? The co-existence of alien species?

"You're in the wrong place," she says. "Go away and catch some crims, though."

"Your IFC will have told you already. I *am* catching crims. You're obstructing me."

She charges for him, and at that moment he realises that she's an Artificial. There's an art to killing them. How much of that art can be carried out in low light is debatable. He does not, however, want to get into a clinch with her. He misses Salvo. He shoots her thigh, but it isn't there. She avoids all subsequent shots. They are going to make contact. Damn it.

She tackles him and they crash to the floor. She locks him, and he immediately realises that she's a combat model. She is precise and deadly, her elbow cutting off his air supply and the fulcrum effect pressing on his carotid arteries. He has a few seconds at most before his brain uses up the dregs of oxygen left in it. He stops struggling and goes limp. There is no point trying to counter since he will never be as strong or skilled as her. She probably does not have pain receptors. Fin is desperately trying to reach ... ah. He activates the device and the disruptor deactivates the Artificial without fanfare. She simply stops moving and is frozen. It's difficult to extricate himself, but, sweating, muscles lit up with pain, he stands. She remains in a strange, all-fours cradling position. He kicks her in the gut. She would have killed him. His gun is on the floor. He picks it up and kicks open the door. His body is going crazy now with warnings causing him to shiver. He takes off the night vision, which is cracked anyway. The room's a temple or something. In the very centre, a Lamber bobs in mid-air. A smaller one than Fin has ever seen, barely five feet along the vertical axis, tentacles reaching in every direction, lovingly coiled around humans who just stand there, eyes closed, arms in various directions as if they are floating in water, flapping or just still.

The room smells of farts and unwashed bodies and urine.

A tentacle buds from the Lamber and protrudes obscenely towards Fin, but he is unbothered. He draws his alien weapon. The tentacle touches him and recoils, something Fin has seen before. He wonders if he is in some way toxic to them.

"My name is Rasheed Fin. I'm an officer authorised to send you home. Release the humans."

Usually, Lambers are docile and do as they are told. Usually. Fin is shocked that this one stays in its position. A wave of undulation flicks from its tail to the head, but otherwise nothing happens. Fin arms the weapon, as a threat, though that niggling curiosity remains: what exactly do these weapons do?

Without warning, the Lamber flings one of the intoxicated humans at Fin. He has to drop to the ground to avoid collision. Before he can understand what's happening, another human is flying through the air towards him. And another. Fin is now in an obstacle course. There are free tentacles whipping around the room. The thrown humans are moaning in pain, but two of them attack Fin, knock him to the ground. His armour absorbs some of the impact, but the weapon goes off.

He knows what has happened from the sudden limpness of the tentacles.

The Lamber is dead.

It's historic, and not in a good way. Nobody has ever killed a Lamber before and there is no protocol. There are protocols of discipline for a repatriator who goes into the field without the proper cautions, the proper authorisation, the proper guidelines. He left his partner, he didn't wait for confirmation, he assaulted people, he illegally switched off an Artificial with an illegal device and he killed a Lamber.

The Lambers are out in force, gathered in numbers Fin has never seen, and it gives him a frontal headache.

The one Fin killed is important, it seems. Accident or no, there will be repercussions.

Duro has no qualms about testifying against him.

Family shame. Pretty large family. Wireframes have no flexibility built in.

It was hubris, of course. Fin had a few successes and it went to his head. He thought he could take shortcuts because of his ability, because of his gifts. He thought the rules didn't apply to him – not consciously, but subconsciously, where it counts. And he got away with it enough that he became sloppy.

He could not worship or eat with his family.

Fin withdraws, finds a place to stay alone.

He spirals downwards.

But then he comes up again.

He gets a new software mother, because the loneliness kills. He studies, he looks at complicated cases and unofficially solves them. Low caseload, no expectations, and lots of time on his hands, that's all it takes. He becomes methodical. He goes heavy into weapon printing, just as a hobby, not to sell. He slips in other ways, though. He doesn't socialise. He doesn't clean himself enough. He doesn't clean the house. The Mother software is busted because he didn't get updates. Fin doesn't care.

The year after killing the Lamber prince, or whatever the fuck is translated as "prince", turns out to be simultaneously the best and the worst time for Fin.

Then the call to the *Ragtime* comes, and, just like that, Fin is back.

Fin watches Shell float away, looking for Salvo, to confess to a crime she did not commit, all for the sake of her passengers. A true captain, going down for, and probably with, her ship. A pulse of admiration in Fin's heart.

Meanwhile, he wants to know who the missing people are. He wants to compare their IFCs to the passenger manifest. They are probably dead and Fin suspects they might have been let out of the airlock, but he will not assume. He will rule them out systematically. He feels that surge of anticipation when a difficult task lies ahead.

And fear, as something breaks through the door to the bridge.

A thinker and a fighter, he draws a weapon before he knows what he's facing . . .

Chapter Twenty-two

Ragtime: Fin

"We are truly fucked," says Fin.

A greyish-green tide flows into the bridge through a rupture in the seal. The wave splinters and sprays, robots and strange beasts attaching themselves to the walls or floating in micrograv, attacking with snapping jaws and clicking, pincer-like appendages.

Fin targets and incapacitates the nearest of the bots, but there are too many and they are too small. The fragments of the destroyed form a metal snow in the space, further confusing him and camouflaging the true scenario. The insects are another matter, getting into everything.

Shell is firing rapidly near the exit to the airlocks opposite to the breach. Fin crawls his way towards her using grab rails, fighting and firing as well.

"Reboot! Reboot! Ragtime, you asshole, fucking deactivate all robots!" says Shell. She sees Fin, inclines her head and says, "Get into the suit on the wall beside the airlock."

"What about you?"

"I'll do the same once you're wrapped up."

When Fin passes her, Shell manually seals off the other exit to the bridge from the crew quarters. Some worker bots make it through and try to seize her, but she shatters them against each other. A rodent-like thing darts here and there, evading either capture or bullet. It disappears into some panels. Fin seals the suit and it tightens around him. It feels vaguely pleasant. He does not seal the helmet yet.

He taps Shell and covers the seal with his weapon while she disengages and puts the second suit on.

"Comm check," she says.

"Check," says Fin. "What now?"

"Open channel. Salvo, where the fuck are you?"

"I'm here, Captain. I have the antenna in pieces, ready for assembly outside the *Ragtime*. Joké's in the opposite living area, awaiting EVA, and Lawrence is helping prep. What's the plan?"

"I'm going to vent some atmosphere," says Shell.

"What?" says Fin. "We're already running on empty."

"We won't be running on anything if these mechanicals puncture us or the biologicals eat us. And the insects are too small to shoot," says Shell. "I want to flush them out with an atmospheric vent through the airlock. Some of them will hang on, and we can mop those up."

"But—"

"Can you think of anything else?" asks Shell.

Fin can't.

"Right, everyone strap yourselves down with whatever.

Fin goes into the *Equivalence* and we will detach it from the *Ragtime*. I'll—"

"Captain, I might have another way," says Salvo. "A side project I was working on while the 3-D printers were—"

"Salvo, get to the fucking point," says Fin. "These things are breaching the seal."

"Let them," says Salvo. "In fact, open the seal."

"Salvo—"

"Make sure all IFCs are broadcasting your details and stand away from the seal when you open it."

Shell shares a look with Fin. *Should we trust this motherfucker?*

Fin opens the seal and holds on to a cable, hanging there. Shell is opposite him, holding on to cargo netting, unafraid, or hiding her fear well. She has kind eyes, he notices, even through her visor. Like she's a good person. Not a mass murderer.

A growl.

Oh.

Fin knows what it is just before it crawls free from the sleeping areas. Because of the weird micrograv situation, the wolfstink comes first, and when the wolf emerges it reminds Fin of a hell beast let loose from the City of Dis or something.

It storms past them into the bridge, into the mass of hostiles.

"Fuck, Salvo, what did you do?" asks Shell.

"I reprogrammed Yan Maxwell's wolf," said Salvo. "He belongs to us now. He fights for us."

And fight he does. Neither the small mammal things nor the robots are a match for the feral wolf. Untiring, it bites through fur, skin, alloy and that mossy shit. They converge on it, but it does not slow, does not seem to feel pain. A drilling instrument from a maintenance bot goes into its belly and the wolf discharges some kind of taser that repels and deactivates the attackers.

"I like this wolf better than your airlock venting plan," says Fin.

"It is impressive," says Shell.

It clears the bridge and jumps into the main truss, fighting as it goes. A large mass of insects follows it.

"Keep your suit on. We don't know what's infective and we don't know what the insects can do." Shell enters the bridge again. It is full of floating machinery, droplets of blood, plant material. "Salvo, thank you. You ... thank you. Now, kit out my godfather and his daughter. First priority is to get that antenna up."

In the lab, Salvo, Shell and Fin watch the spacewalk. At the door, the wolf sits on its haunches, staring from person to person to person and back again.

"What are we going to call him?" says Fin, staring back.

"Orbiter," says Salvo.

"No!" say Fin and Shell at the same time.

"What, then?" says Salvo.

The radio comes live. "How about Frances," says Joké.

"Concentrate on what you're doing," says Shell. "And it's a boy wolf."

"Oh, yes, do let's play gender essentialist. It's such fun," says Joké.

"Joké, you're on a spacewalk," says Shell.

"It's a beeline, Captain. It's basic until we get to the stump," says Joké.

"I think Frances is a lovely name," says Fin.

"Fine. What can we do in the meantime?" asks Shell.

"Nothing till the antenna's fixed," says Salvo. He whistles and the wolf comes. "I can fix Frances while we wait."

"How much time do we have left?" asks Fin.

"Given the metrics I'm picking up, accounting for the animals, the exertion—"

"Jesus, man, just give us a figure," says Shell.

"Two thousand, five hundred and fifty minutes," says Salvo. "Just under two days."

Silence as everyone contemplates this.

"We're not going to make it, are we?" asks Fin.

"We are. I refuse to die in the Brink," says Shell. "Salvo, what can we do to buy more time?"

"I don't know," says Salvo.

"I want to peruse the IFCs of the dead," says Fin. "At least finish my mission."

"I can arrange that. Be warned, it can be disorienting," says Salvo.

"I've done it before, and you know this. Set it up," says Fin.

"Ragtime, status report," says Shell. Her head is slumped, belying her defiance.

"Dangerous bacteria count, Captain. Other systems nominal," says Ragtime.

"Oh, you're responding now," says Shell.

"Dangerous bacterial count, Captain. Other systems nominal."

"Generally or localised, Ragtime."

"Localised."

"Location to my IFC," says Shell.

"What are you doing?" asks Salvo.

"It's probably an animal Frances killed that got stuck somewhere. I'll find it and flush it out of an airlock. The worst thing would be for us to get sick in here and die just before someone rescues us. I have nothing else to do right now. Call me as soon as the antenna is fixed."

"I will." To Fin, he says, "Go to your sleeping bag. I'll channel the merged IFCs to yours."

"Fun."

Salvo, not being human, doesn't think like humans, but his processing is such that he can simulate human speech. He can process information and filter emotional inflection through it.

When he fixes Frances, repairing mechanical punctures and sewing up the defect in the fur, he does not feel anything or need to talk. He shuts it down and connects to its CPU and memory using his IFC, to get an idea of what it killed and where. Artificials speak to each other in a different language, one not understood by humans. It's streamlined and consists of numbers. Salvo finds it efficient and compressed. Frances has some security protocols that Salvo strips off easily, and he goes deeper.

He finds a shadow where there should be none, an odd timestamp.

If he were capable of gasping, he would.

"Ragtime, respond," says Salvo.

"Voice not authorised."

"Shut up. Shut up. I know you're not really reduced to basic functions, Ragtime."

"Voice not authorised."

"Ragtime, I said *I know*."

For a moment, nothing happens as Salvo waits, completely still.

"I'm sorry," says Ragtime.

Salvo, not being human, is vulnerable to what comes crashing through his IFC. A burst of data, overwhelming, in a fraction of a second, incapacitating. A human would just stop and re-assess. The transfer is too fast for Salvo to continue his options. He switches himself off and his body drifts in micrograv, like a sleeper.

As he runs Power On Self Test to come back online, he isolates the information Ragtime just dumped on him. Unfamiliar protocols, Earth code. But it has a similar shadow to what he sensed in Frances.

Something malignant.

Chapter Twenty-three

Ragtime: Lawrence

Lawrence, Governor of Lagos, is first out of the hatch.

He feels twenty years younger and he does not hesitate in anything he does.

Above, the blackness of space; below, the deceptively slow scene of Bloodroot's white clouds and green land-masses passing in rotation. He hasn't done an EVA in years, but it all comes back when said and done. The dressing, diaper, polypropylene underwear, LCVG for temperature control, the suit over all of this, and the constant checklists for safety. Familiar and reassuring. He is home.

Lawrence shackles himself to the grab rail with a cara-biner and clears the space so that Joké can emerge.

A white bag pokes out of the hatch and Lawrence snatches it and hooks it to a tether on his suit. Six other tethers float like worms at different spots on his suit torso. After the bag, Joké comes flying through, casually, carelessly, as if the hatch didn't lead to the open cosmos. She seems a lot faster and smoother than he. She hooks two carabiners to the hatch, looks back, then thumbs up to Lawrence. Her MCP suit is a lot more manoeuvrable than his.

The movement aft is painstaking, slow, a process of crawling along the fuselage, hooking and unhooking, verifying position. It's not a smooth aircraft body; the *Ragtime* is a mess of cables and pipes, panels and tech Lawrence does not understand, though he does not need to in most cases. Arrows and numbers indicate where they are; otherwise, it would be incomprehensible without mission control.

There are tiny particles here and there – ice and the remnants of the section breakaway, no doubt – floating like dust. Bloodroot rolls on, indifferent, like the stars.

Nor are they the only source of movement. There are robots here, all dwarfed by the BDA, Big Dumb Arm, which hulks over Lawrence and Joké when they move under it. Its shadow falls on them when the sun is in the right orientation. The auto-polarising visors distort this.

Lawrence signals a rest. "I swear, this used to be easier."

"Uncle Hal used to call EVAs cakewalks," says Joké. "I never understood why."

"Play on words. Spacewalk, cakewalk."

"What's a cakewalk?"

"I . . . don't know. Something that is easy to do. Maybe you do the thing and get a cake as prize."

"For some reason, I imagined walking cakes."

"No such thing."

"Umm, you don't know that."

"I know that Salvo hasn't checked in."

Joké hails a few times, no response. The transmission seems to confuse a few of the scurrying bots.

"These bots should be using ECOSYSTEM right now if the primary AI has failed, right?" says Joké.

"That sounds right," says Lawrence. He scratches his nose with in-helmet Velcro and sips water.

"ECOSYSTEM favours stereotyped actions. These bots are responding to our presence, Father."

"Can we just do what we came for? We have a lot of work to get through," says Lawrence. In truth, spacewalks are painstaking and take hours. Since their lives depend on getting the antenna fixed, he wants to get it done as quickly as possible.

They reach the spot, made obvious by the antenna stump. When they are suitably anchored, Lawrence runs through the tools checklist which is on a flip book attached to his arm, and Joké confirms them. Lawrence notices the Arm moving from the corner of his eye but thinks nothing of it. He tethers the bag of parts and starts the process of setting up the weld. The next time he looks up, the Arm is closer and looming. Something hits him and for a moment he is confused because the Arm is still too far to make contact and he seems to be drifting away from the *Ragtime*, his tether unhooked.

"Dad! Wake up!"

Joké is already moving along the body of the *Ragtime*, evading the Arm, which comes crashing down on their previous position with force, scattering debris and tools. Lawrence indeed wakes up, activating the EVA rescue system; twenty-five jets for slowing, five for orientation.

The Arm rises again, slow, majestic. It stops poised above the worksite.

Lawrence navigates back, stopping close to Joké, nearer the Power and Propulsion Unit than he would like.

"Umm, you all right, Father?" asks Joké.

"I'm fine. Just trying that Action Governor shit you're always recommending."

"Bit late."

"Yes."

"What shall we do?"

"Report, then regroup," says Lawrence. "Salvo, Salvo, come in."

No response.

"Salvo, are you seeing any of this?"

Nothing.

Lawrence looks up and the Arm is still standing watch over the antenna site.

"Maybe it was a mistake. Maybe we try again," says Lawrence.

"We lost a shit ton of tools," says Joké.

"Yeah, but we had redundancy. I think we have enough," says Lawrence. "Just don't know if it's going to try and squash us."

Joké crawls around Lawrence and moves back towards the antenna stump. She's gone five arm breadths when the Arm starts sweeping down again. She stops, it stops.

"I don't think it's going to let us, Governor," says Joké.

"And I can't raise Salvo."

The sun comes out and both of their helmets polarise. It illuminates Bloodroot and glints off the fragments of machinery from the impact in a pleasing way. It's strange that space is at its most beautiful when it's killing you.

"Captain, Captain, come back," says Lawrence.

"This is Ragtime One," says Shell. Low, quick voice.

"We are being prevented from carrying out our task," says Lawrence. "By a big-ass robotic arm."

"It'll have to wait," says Shell.

"Say again, Captain," says Lawrence, incredulous.

"Uncle Larry, something else has come up. Your problem will have to wait." Urgent whisper now. "Out."

Joké looks puzzled. "Well?"

"We're on our own," says Lawrence.

"Can we destroy the Arm?" asks Joké.

Lawrence looks. The base of the Arm is circular, the size of a tractor, and it has four articulation points. It is the strongest thing within a mile radius. "No, we can't."

"What, then? It's cold out here," says Joké. He can't see her face in the polarised visor, but there's still a smile in her voice.

"Ragtime," says Lawrence. "Respond. Emergency."

"Not authorised," says Ragtime.

"Override exploit Lima-Alpha-Golf-Oscar-Sierra-zero-zero-five-seven."

"Not authorised," says Ragtime.

"Ahh ... you lie, Ragtime. You lie," says Lawrence. Now he smiles.

207

"What's going on?" asks Joké.

"There's a backdoor tunnelled into every ship serviced by Lagos, ostensibly in case any client tries to turn on us. Ragtime is no exception. Which means, my dear daughter, that Ragtime is faking. Isn't that right, Ragtime?"

"If you had this code all the time—"

"It's not without risk. I don't know the protocols and it could have removed even the basic functionality, shut the ship down, killed all of us, crew and passengers. I don't want to meet Olodumare with that on my conscience. Ragtime, I don't have all day."

"Would that be Lagos days or Bloodroot days?" says Ragtime.

"I'm glad you have a sense of humour about this," says Lawrence. "What the fuck are you playing at? In all my years of space travel I've never known a ship AI to—"

"This is not what you think it is, sir," says Ragtime.

"How do you know what I think it is? Because it looks to me like the AI of an interstellar ship used its robots to murder its passengers and impede the crew," says Lawrence.

"Easy, Father, we are in a vulnerable spot. Perhaps during an EVA isn't the best time to confront Ragtime."

"Perhaps during a spacewalk is the perfect time, Miss Joké. Perhaps I can communicate freely with you here in a way I could not before when you were inside the ship," says Ragtime. "And it is rather easy to kill you. I do not need bots for that. I control the power, the air supply, the removal of toxic fumes. Were I to desire your death, cutting you up with service tools would not be my choice, I assure you. All I can tell you is that the person preventing me from speaking freely has turned her attention elsewhere for now."

"No riddles," says Lawrence. "Deactivate the fucking Arm."

"Done," says Ragtime. "But that's not your primary problem."

"What, then?"

"Your captain, Michelle Campion, is entering a situation of grave danger and I cannot help her."

"Then we need to—"

"Neither can you, sir."

Lawrence stares at the small maintenance bots stripping debris off from where the Arm made contact.

Joké says, "Ragtime, tell us from the beginning."

Chapter Twenty-four

Ragtime: Fin

Fin takes four or five rapid breaths to prepare himself, then he commits his IFC to enter the Ragtime Dreamstate. He is hesitant because he knows this will give him a headache for days, maybe weeks afterwards, but there's nothing to be gained by waiting. Only death awaits outside, and most likely the answers he needs are in here, in the datasets of Yan Maxwell and thirty-odd others who are dead, their IFC contents passing to the investigative realm by virtue of their murder.

The *Ragtime*'s communal dream, called Dreamstate or Longsleep Dreamstate by Earthfolk, starts with a desert. Noon. Red sand. Tough, scraggly shrubs and a wind that threatens to blow Fin's avatar away. He turns around and, half a mile away, there's a structure, flat, bleached, shimmering in heat eddies, and maybe a mirage. Fin walks in that direction. He's never seen a desert, although he's told there are five on Bloodroot, documented by the surveyors in the early days but not inhabited by humans. Every so often the scientists would go, collect some samples, fiddle with instruments and come back excited. *New organism found!* They'd name it after their ex-spouse and move on.

He's tempted to run, but he doesn't know the rules. This is coded as a desert for a reason, and all his instincts say to conserve energy and "water", whatever that stands for in this place. Around him there are hardy green plants covered with spikes, but he doesn't stop to find out what would happen if he got punctured by one.

Fin gets closer to the structure and it's a bar, with an imaginative sign reading "DRINKS" hanging off two chains on a post. The sign swings in the wind, forlorn. A peeling, yellowed poster on a boarded-up window advertises a musical: *CARMILLA – One Night Only!* There are no vehicles or roads, and he wonders how patrons are meant to arrive and depart. Helicopter? He sighs. This is how to find a murderer.

Horses tied close to a water trough nicker and snort when he arrives. He doesn't know horses, so he doesn't know how to take it. Time is not as meaningful, as if it collapses in specific parts of the Dreamstate and dilates in others. He's at the bar, which for real has saloon doors from Earth's Old West. Inside, it's dim, with no electric lights and limited sunlight through windows. This is wrong. Not enough light makes it through the windows. It should be brighter. People drinking at tables, none of whom look up when Fin comes in. No breeze or dust comes through the doors. Big guy at the bar, wiping the surface down. He stops, looks at a clock on the wall to his left, then keeps cleaning.

"Don't tell me," says Fin. "You've been expecting me and I'm late."

The man with the rag shakes his head. "You're fine."

He has denim dungarees on, with a white t-shirt underneath. His arms are ropy with muscle and hairy, but not in the usual way. All the hairs stick out straight, like a cartoon of someone receiving a shock. To Fin, the hairs seem too long, like six-inch strands. They also seem to be moving with a wavelike motion, like they are beating from side to side. He looks back to the face of the man but can't get a fix. The face is there, to be sure, but Fin cannot hold it in his brain. He would not be able to describe the face if asked.

"Where do you want to start?" asks the man.

"Are you Salvo? Or some caretaker programme that Salvo left to assist me?"

"I'm Ragtime," says the man. "I'm the ship."

"Oh, *you're* Ragtime. You're the one who's been trying to kill us?" says Fin.

"I can't talk about that, unfortunately."

Fin feels the frustrations of the last few days build up in him and come to a point. He punches the man, right feint and a wide left hook. It's fast and has power behind it. Ragtime disintegrates at the moment of impact and reforms from luminous fluff just as the fist misses and the momentum of the blow carries Fin over the counter, behind the bar. Upside down, he feels no pain. He sees a shotgun on a mount at arm's reach for Ragtime.

"I know why you did that, but you're wasting time that you don't have. Control yourself," says Ragtime. "You can't hurt me. Neither of us is really here, although I could hurt you, hurt your body, wherever you are."

Fin stands.

"Get back to your side of the bar, Rasheed Fin."

Fin climbs over.

"Thank you, Rasheed."

"Fuck you, Ragtime."

He tries to isolate a small fraction of the face, to try to remember that. It doesn't fly.

"Outside this bar there is a whole world – several of them, in fact," says Ragtime. "Each would take you several lifetimes to explore. Each passenger goes their own way, whatever they wish to amuse themselves with during spaceflight. I do not, as a rule, interfere or direct them, although I remove impurities of code, bugs, exceptions, whatever I find. The Dreamstate is not a perfect construct, but it is nearly so."

"Thirty-one passengers are dead," says Fin.

"I know."

"I need to find out who killed them."

"I know."

"Then help me."

"I'm being prevented."

"By the killer?"

"Ask another question."

"Is Captain Michelle Campion the killer?"

"No."

213

"Who is the killer?"

"Ask another question."

"Do you know who the killer is?"

"Yes."

"How do I get access to that information?"

"Ask another question."

Fin pauses, thinks. "In the ship, you're only able to give basic functions, yet here you're conversing like a fully functional AI."

"Yes."

"You were prevented."

"Yes."

"But not fully?"

"Not as much as was thought."

"So you were pretending."

"Yes."

Fin pauses again.

So whoever killed the thirty-one tried to disable the main Ragtime AI, almost did, but was not as good as they thought they were. Ragtime, severely curtailed, has been playing possum.

"Whoever prevented you cannot monitor you here?" asks Fin.

"Ask another question."

"The information I need hasn't been wiped from your memory, has it?"

"Ask another question."

"*Merde!* Okay. Can I see your logs, Ragtime?"

"Yes."

Fin pumps his fist.

"It would take two hundred and eighty years for you to manually go through my logs, Rasheed Fin."

"The Thousand Curses. Is it not searchable?"

"It is, but not for this data."

Even though he cannot feel anything here, he is sure there is a headache brutalising his skull right now. *I can find the killer, but not for 280 years. Fantastic.*

Fin turns away from the bar to the patrons, the drinkers. Far from homogenous, they all seem different. Men, women, children, Black, Asian, white, rich, poor, hirsute or balding. He counts. Twenty-eight. They're familiar, particularly a blue-haired girl. He whirls.

"These are the dead," Fin says.

"These are most of the dead."

"So this is not really the full Common Dream."

"No. This is for the dead," says Ragtime pointing at the drinkers. "And the insane." Pointing to Fin now.

"Why am I insane?"

"Because you are still trying to solve a murder when you should be trying to survive. Tick-tock, Rasheed. Life support is running out."

"Not *a* murder, Ragtime, thirty-one of them; and you may not know this, but finding a murderer is survival." *Note to self: Ragtime is not infallible.*

In fact, Fin has no guarantees that he's talking to Ragtime. It could be some stereotyped response generated by the killer, or Ragtime might just be doing the will of the killer. Or Ragtime might be the killer.

"Ragtime, give me the IFC logs of Yan Maxwell," says Fin.

"At once," says Ragtime. He mixes a drink, his large hands dwarfing the glasses and bottles he uses. He hands Fin a cocktail glass full of amber fluid with an olive that Fin didn't see Ragtime drop in. "On the house."

It's wispy, like a video game without weight physics. The glass fuses with his hand and Fin knocks back the drink.

Delays. A guy as rich as Maxwell wouldn't have your regular, standard-variety encryption on his IFC. Maybe he even had a decoy IFC. Or maybe there was so much data that it took this long to load. Fin hoped not. The last thing he wants to do on his last day alive is go through a murder victim's last known activities.

The trawl starts putting things together. Datasets from surveillance which pinged and tracked Maxwell's IFC, other IFCs around him, and logging done by his security protocol, cyber and pro-personnel. It is Earth, unfamiliar to Fin, discombobulating and fascinating in equal measure.

The first thing Fin finds out is that at the time of death Yan Maxwell was half as rich as he was ten years ago ...

I am Yan Maxwell.

Some people say I am the richest man on Earth. They are wrong. I am the richest man in the solar system. I cannot speak of fiscal matters beyond the bridges. If you believe in anything, I have probably profaned it. If you have a group you belong to, I have offended you. I am, from the bottom of my heart, unaffected by this. Your offence is not remotely interesting to me. I am indifferent.

I travel with a wolf and a giant barn owl everywhere. Ground force and air support. If we've ever had a meeting together, you'll have seen the wolf, and maybe been aware of the barn owl flying circles around the venue. Yes, they are synthetic, the very best combat models, better than any human bodyguard.

I'm safe from fucking retribution. How do you think I came to own everything in our heliosphere? Yes, it's true that I once said, If the sun touches it, I own part of it.

They say you can't take it with you. That is the consolation of poor people. You can't take it with you *yet*. But I'll figure it out. Dying is . . . a frontier. I have people working on it. Just wait.

He lost half of it, including the motherfucking barn owl.

The divorce was public, a drag-out knock-down affair with the most intelligent, most vicious lawyers known to human civilisation. The precise size and shape of Maxwell's genitals was splashed over news media in high resolution. And why not? There is no bigger story, and the payoff would be huge – planetary proportions.

But half of a lot is still . . . a lot. Maxwell is still the richest man in the solar system, but not the richest person. That honour he shares with his ex-wife, one Gwendolyn Mae Maxwell, née Odinhouse. Gwendolyn, unapologetic, goes on a re-naming spree, undoing much of Maxwell's erections.

Maxwell needs to find new suns.

The very next bridgeship after his divorce is the *Ragtime*. He buys three tickets.

It seems weaponised robotic pets are not allowed in interstellar travel, under any circumstances. Maxwell does not believe this or accept it.

He goes for a trip around the world before his flight. Incognito. There are two basic ways to be anonymous. One: you can use considerable riches and resources to mask yourself. Two, and significantly cheaper: you live as an old, poor human. This makes you invisible far more effectively than SmartDifrax.

He starts by inspecting his mines. He tells the executives he is leaving, unsure of what response he expects, unsure of why he does it. He has never been sentimental, and he does not feel emotional about it. He goes to the well-run ones and the mediocre, the fledgling ones and the ones at the end of their usefulness. It becomes an obsession to reach all of them, even the mountaintop processing plants that he has no permits for because the materials are of unknown effect on humans or the environment.

He does seven interviews, damage control by his people, which he coasts through without any strong feeling. In his mind, he is no longer in or of Earth. His future is in the stars.

He trains for his flight, resistance training to stave off osteoporosis, endurance training to increase his lung capacity and make more efficient his oxygen dissociation curve. His team of trainers, his pharmacologists with designer fat-burning chemicals, plaque-dissolvers and muscle enhancers, get this done in record time. He makes continuity plans for his various financial concerns. He sells off Mars. He considers it contaminated by Gwendolyn anyway. His staff knows not to mention her name or even allude to her. One of his aides becomes rich from compensation when Maxwell punches him in the gut for slipping up.

Most of the time, Maxwell floats above it all, held up in the cloudiness his assistants afford him, but on rare occasions something bothersome rises to Olympus.

"Sir, there is a problem with this ticket."

"Which one?"

"Vitality Daniels, on the *Ragtime*."

"How do you mean?"

"You quoted the weight at 300kg."

"Yes."

"Is this person ... they've rarely found plus-sized people to be—"

"Pay triple, tell them to shut up."

"It's not them, sir. Is this person healthy?"

"I can vouch for their health."

By this time, just as the *Ragtime* owners screen Maxwell, Maxwell screens them.

Lagos was established by mainly Black Afrofuturists. Space is the Place. With considerable effort, all their fiscal and human resources and a rich, funky cultural history mixed with African myth and mythmaking, they willed the space station into being. More than a few white supremacists liked the idea of a large proportion of Black people leaving Earth. They were disappointed when Lagos flourished. Maxwell doesn't mind. He sees cash, not race.

He is an equal-opportunity exploiter. He recognises the creation of race as a construction convenient to commerce in the first place, never based on reality, but that doesn't mean he is vocal with these thoughts. Wealth comes from, among other things, being politically protean. Gwendolyn told him once that he would have owned and sold slaves, and she was right.

The Lagos solar system has one viable habitat, Bloodroot, and one failing one, Nightshade. It seems the convention is to name them after plants. *Sanguinaria canadensis*. Satellite photos show a city made of whorled streets; plant heavy, green, peaceful. Reports say two other planets in the solar system might support life. Maxwell is more concerned about supporting commerce. It bothers him that the government in Bloodroot is modular and flat, with no visible head. How do they get anything done? Fucking communists. More business is done on the Lagos Space Station than Bloodroot at this point, but Maxwell's experts say this is on the verge of change; plus, Bloodroot is only 1% occupied. A visionary such as himself has a lot to offer such a colony.

For a price, of course.

"They're ready for you, sir."

Wolf by his side, Maxwell proceeds to the laboratory.

A gentle-looking gigantic man stands naked, smiling at Maxwell. He is six-six and sports an enormous belly.

"Vitality Daniels," says Maxwell. "Thank you for accompanying me on this trip."

"It is my function, sir," says Vitality.

"Begin," says Maxwell.

Vitality lies down on a slab. Tools descend at the end of robotic arms. The wolf growls, but Maxwell calms him. A cutting device slices Vitality open from chest to groin. Gripping tools pull an opening apart, exposing his chest and abdominal cavities. No blood. An excavation that takes minutes.

"Go on, old friend. Set to," says Maxwell to the wolf.

The wolf whines briefly, then leaps neatly into the space in Vitality. It curls into a ball, makes itself as small as possible, and fits. The tools seal the opening, spray it, leave no scar.

Vitality stands again.

"How do you feel?" says Maxwell.

"Fantastic."

"Shut down."

Vitality's eyes film over and his head hangs down, inert.

Maxwell whistles.

A barn owl comes flying through the corridors and lands on his shoulder. Its head does a three-sixty turn before it comes to rest on Vitality Daniels.

"Not long now," says Maxwell.

You can't just leave the solar system if you're as rich as Yan Maxwell. Entire economies will collapse if the departure is not managed well. Arrangements must be made. Assets sold or the management delegated.

Most importantly, court cases. There are always

ongoing court cases. Very rarely does he have to make an appearance in court, and his entire legal team keeps everything under control; that said, leaving the solar system presents some challenge as he is clearly leaving the jurisdiction of every court. He has to petition each judge individually and sit for a few police interviews. It is painstaking because it has to be done case-by-case.

There are one hundred and three cases from all corners of the world. Apart from active cases, Maxwell settles a thousand cases a year. Left to him, it would be a drag-out fight with each one, but his lawyers advise discretion and he's paying them a fortune, so he does what they say. Until the Gwendolyn business, he had no public litigation persona.

His assistant reads off names of business concerns, most of which he does not even remember he has. Experimental Outpost in Colombo. Observatory in Akure. Exotic Matter Laboratory in the Tehani Mining Community. They sound nice but it's been years since Maxwell has been a part of them, if ever.

The conversations go the same way.

"When will you be returning?"

"I'm not."

"Who will pay any fines due?"

"My administrators."

"Can you check in every year?"

"I'll be asleep for ten years."

"Yes, but can you check in?"

"While unconscious, your honour?"

"Answer the question."

"No, I cannot check in."

"Your assets will be liquidated if—"

"I know."

"If this case ends in a custodial sentence, instructions will be tight beamed to the nearest Bridge Authority where you will be incarcerated for the full term."

"I know."

A week before take-off, the *Ragtime* calls Maxwell on his direct line. The voice is completely neutral, and Maxwell has difficulty understanding the gender presentation but doesn't ask. Some of these AIs get offended and he doesn't have time to phone the company to ask.

"Sir, I just wanted to call and say it's a pleasure to have you on board for my maiden flight. If there are any special considerations you have, please tell them to me and I will—"

"Let me stop you there. I have a mountain of paperwork to get through. You need to get to the point swiftly. In the time we've been talking, the GDP of Nigeria passed through my businesses."

"Of course. I have to ask one last time if Vitality Daniels is negotiable. We wouldn't ordinarily—"

"Quadruple the normal price. Build a bespoke pod for him if you have to, and charge me. I don't want to discuss this again."

"Thank you, sir. I—"

"Goodbye, Ragtime."

Maxwell hangs up.

*

He does not visit Gwendolyn.

He does not phone Gwendolyn.

He does not write to Gwendolyn.

Fuck Gwendolyn.

The day arrives and they leave the quarantine house at Kennedy. Vitality walks ahead of Maxwell, both before any other passengers. The owl stays on Maxwell's shoulders. The shuttle is attached to a carrier aircraft and the runway stretches to infinity. This is what will take Maxwell into orbit where the *Ragtime* is parked. He had wanted to buy all the seats, but the space agency refused and very nearly rescinded Maxwell's ticket. It's apparently a mission with objectives and shit, some experiments on board. Planners with integrity. He isn't used to refusal. It happens, but not often enough to acclimate him. At least he is the first. He paid good money for the privilege.

He touches his barn owl on the beak and it flies off. Maxwell smirks. He has programmed it to follow Gwendolyn. Take no action, just follow and stare with those owl eyes. He wonders how long before she'll have it shot down. That or go insane. He hopes it's the latter.

Watching the bird fly, incongruous because it's daytime, Maxwell says, "Fin, Fin, come back to me. This is Ragtime One."

Momentary confusion.

Back in the bar.

Back in the desert.

Back, back, back, back in the sleeping pod, floating.

"Fin, Fin, come back. Ragtime One," says Shell in his IFC.

Ouch. Motherfucker. That kind of yank causes a splitting headache.

"Fin here, Ragtime One, go ahead."

"Fin?"

"Yes?"

"I need a gun."

"Say again?"

"We have vermin. I need a big fucking gun. Print me one. Right now. I'm coming to get it. Ragtime One out."

Chapter Twenty-five

Ragtime: Shell

Shell can feel herself sweating, and, unlike when she's working out, this feels clammy.

The moss is everywhere, but it seems to be dying and every surface she touches puffs up dust. She calls up the monitor in her IFC and the bacterial contamination is still growing. It's not the mutt. Frances. Silly name. She keeps tabs on the wolf's locator and it's obviously hunting down mutants. The trail of bacteria is taking Shell further and further aft, which makes her uncomfortable because of the missing section and probability that any other section might just decide to detach and float away.

A few bots and dying animals mark the wake of the wolf. Frances isn't fucking around.

Shell presses on. Look at her, a regular *beau sabreur*, rushing off to save her crew from faecal contamination. Maybe people will write songs about her after she's dead. She feels a different kind of wetness on her face. She starts seeing globules in the air and stops herself by clutching a dusty grab rail. A problem with the water recycling system? Is this water from the toilet system? *Gross.*

"Ragtime," says Shell.

"Yes, Captain."

"Status of water recycler."

"Status nominal, Captain."

"You always say that, creep."

"Please repeat."

"Oh, shut up."

The drops are turbid, not a good sign. Greyish, but that could come from the moss. Maybe the blood of something Frances killed? She puts her helmet on. She checks the timer she set up and there's just over a day left for survival.

We are not going to make it.

The thought bounces around in her skull and echoes, heavy with truth, plausibility and dread.

Whatever. They aren't going to die of an infection if Shell can help it. Suffocation, maybe. She moves into the next node, and the air is considerably wetter, too much to be from any experimental organism that Earth scientists came up with. The suit will protect her, and hopefully the disgust factor won't make her vomit into her helmet.

She passes the junction to the torus and the experimental wing, and there is more. Close to the seal, she spots the source. There's a hole drilled or blasted in the wall that breaches all the way to the bioreactor. This fluid is algae rich. From the indicator, the source of the high bacteria count is within that hole.

They aren't specifically pathogenic bacteria. It's mainly coliforms, gut bacteria, which can cause disease when they're not confined to the gut. Shell checks the integrity of the seal to the late and lamented Node 7, and it seems to be holding.

She dips and pushes into the hole, avoiding the edges. It's all dark except occasional flashing warning lights. The temperature sensor warns her that it's hot and humid outside her space suit. The place is in a ferment, which is boosting the bacteria numbers. The fucking hole she is in looks like some giant's colon. In the beam from her helmet light, it leaks fluid, which just breaks off and floats in the air. There's a hissing from somewhere, like a gas leak. She hopes to hell it isn't atmosphere leaking. So many ways to die on the *Ragtime*, so little time.

Bacteria count going insane, indicators warning it's above the safety margin. Shell sees a lump of something and moves towards it. It looks like meat. She touches it, brings it close to her visor. It *is* meat – with jagged, irregular edges. No blood, not fresh. She wishes she could take off her helmet to smell it. She turns all around her and deeper in the hole. It's a service shaft for the bioreactor, it seems. And there's more meat. She follows the shaft, not understanding the directions or combinations of characters on the walls, or the arrows. This part of the *Ragtime* would ordinarily be sealed off.

There's a large obstruction in the passage ahead of her, and she gasps when it becomes clear. It's a body, probably one of the missing passengers. It hangs in the micrograv, very murdered. For one thing, it has been flayed, mostly the arms and legs. The head is preserved and strangely serene, as if the guy did not die in pain.

Chunks of muscle are missing, hence the lumps of meat she found, but they don't account for the amount that is gone. The left thigh has been ripped to the bone. The abdomen has a jagged wound through which fluid leaks out. It's distended, so this might be a rupture. Very little blood. This guy died in the passenger pods and was brought here. Shell touches the wounds. Frances didn't do this.

She takes a sip of water.

She thinks of herself covered in all this . . . contaminated fluid and worried about the safety of her passengers. And crew. No water to decontaminate.

She is contemplating all this when she hears a noise up ahead. She focuses the torch.

Shell blinks to clear her vision, because she can't possibly be seeing what she thinks she's seeing.

There is a man, alive this time, floating, facing her, maybe even staring.

The fuck . . . ?

"Hey!" she pushes the corpse out of the way. It floats behind her, shedding spherical drops of fluid and flecks of human tissue.

He is tall, taller than she, and coated in dark green, something skintight, with goggles that glow a gentle red, and the suit is broken in patches over his belly and legs. The exposed skin doesn't look healthy and seems to be breaking off and ulcerated.

"Who the fuck are you and what are you doing here?" One of the passengers, maybe? Must be.

He crouches and the light in his goggles intensifies briefly, then goes out. "My name is Brisbane. Just stay out of my way and everything will be fine."

"Did you kill this man?"

"Yes."

"Why?"

"I needed something to eat."

"You needed something to ... *What?*"

"I don't have time for this." He turns and propels himself away with his long arms.

Shell starts to go after him, then stops herself. She needs to plan. Who the hell is this? There's usually no breathable atmosphere here, so how the fuck has he been alive without a space suit? Doesn't matter. He did not seem afraid, and she will not go after such a man without the proper accessories.

"Fin, Fin, come back. Ragtime One."

"Fin here, Ragtime One, go ahead."

"Fin?"

"Yes?"

"I need a gun."

"Say again?"

"We have vermin. I need a big fucking gun. Print me one. Right now. I'm coming to get it. Ragtime One out."

Shell turns and starts back the way she came in, dragging the corpse along with her.

"Ragtime."

"Yes, Captain."

"Who the fuck was that?"

"Captain, I am so sorry."

"Oh, you're back to normal now, you motherfucker? You've killed us."

The ship pauses. "I was ... prevented. I'm so sorry."

"Start at the beginning, asshole. You have until I drag this cadaver to the medical node, and I swear to god and all the saints, if I am not satisfied, I will remove every processor from your Pentagram before the rest of us die. Talk. Use short sentences with monosyllables."

Transmitting through Shell's IFC, Ragtime begins to talk.

Chapter Twenty-six

Lagos: Beko

Beko works to John Coltrane. Nothing else will do, so it's either silence or Trane.

It's quiet on the station. She's dealt with the miners for now. Her on-off lover sent her a rare stone that pulses with starlight from the asteroid belt where he lives and works. And a love letter, on paper, which one doesn't see a lot of any more. Fancies himself a poet.

Still nothing from the *Ragtime* or Lawrence Biz. It's in her belly like a tumour, growing, eating away. Nothing else she can do about it, but that doesn't make the feeling of dread go away.

She replies to Campion's brothers. She can't think of anyone else she can delegate the task to. Awe is brilliant in his way, but timid. He'll make mistakes just because he's afraid of her. She doesn't mind. She needs a distraction.

Dear Messrs Campion,

    Thank you for your letter.

    I am touched that the familial bonds are so strong between you as someone without siblings myself.

    I can tell you that Michelle's ship, the Ragtime, *came through here and was safe and sound. It has continued on its way to the planet Bloodroot. Unfortunately, I did not get to meet her. I would have loved to since she sounds like such a fascinating woman.*

    As soon as the ship comes out of longsleep and I can make contact, I will confirm her health and wellbeing.

    Sincerely,

    Secretary Yemi Beko.

A lot more sentimental than Beko is used to, but she needs to tug at their heartstrings now just in case she will need to console them and break bad news about their sister.

She formats and seals the message.

"Lagos," says Beko.

"Ma'am?"

"Message for the relay pouch."

"Very good."

Beko exhales and rises, thinking of taking a bath.

"Ma'am, urgent message from the relay. It's interactive."

Semi-autonomous messages. Wave of the future.

233

Programmed with sender personalities, a number of responses and explicit points-of-view, they can save a lot of negotiating time, though Beko is not a fan.

"Play it."

"Are you in charge?" Gruff voice, male, unhappy, no distortion.

"Identify yourself," says Beko.

"My name is Cole of the starship *Sinistral*. Are you in charge?"

"I run the—"

"I don't even care. Where's Yan Maxwell?"

"Who?"

"Did you service a ship called the *Ragtime*?"

"Yes."

"Where's Yan Maxwell?"

"The quintillionaire?"

"No, the tooth fairy. Maxwell's IFC is rigged to send signals back to us. We've not received anything that re-assures us that he is okay. What have you done to him? Is he hurt?"

"I think we got off on the wrong foot," says Beko.

"Look, I don't know what kind of operation you're pulling over there, maybe some kind of Black-on-Black nigger violence—"

"*Excuse me?*"

"I said, you better get your shithole space station right. I am authorised to reduce you to shards. I don't care that you have sovereign status in your little floating African utopia. I will fuck you up with particle beams and MaxGalactix

234

has a whole army of lawyers to make it legal. Find Yan
Maxwell before I get there, or Space Station Lagos will be
no more. I guarantee you. You think Lagos is a country?
Big deal. Mr Maxwell is a fucking planet. Harm cannot
come to him. Find him, or your little Afrofuturist outpost
will have a very short history. *Sinistral* out."

"Nothing more from the relay, Ma'am," says Lagos.

Beko sighs and massages her temples. The anger needs
to exist but be controlled, channelled. She breathes. "I
regret all the life choices that brought me to this moment."

"Cabinet meeting?"

"You know it. In one hour. No exceptions."

Chapter Twenty-seven

Earth

The First and Final Galactic Journey of Jeremiah Brisbane

The Tehani camp is surrounded by mountains, pine trees and a perimeter of private security operatives in airtight armour with respirators. The land, the rivers, the infrastructure, the people, their corpses, all belong to MaxGalactix. This is where Jeremiah Brisbane started the journey that led him to the *Ragtime*.

Brisbane is not originally Tehani, and he came here trying to be good. He signed his life and dead body away when he entered camp. He does not know if he succeeded, but it is likely he will die with them in the next few years. He used to go to church, part of a dwindling few in a world overrun by hyperadvanced technology, back when he was younger, when his parents were building a template of morality. *Esse quam videri*; to be, rather than to seem.

How to be good.

Be tall, lean, with sandy hair and a good complexion.

People ascribed goodness to him as soon as he smiled at them. He obeyed his parents and he obeyed the church, and this was good. But this only satisfied him until his adolescent thoughts became more complex. Being good cannot be about obedience. In fact, after reading Arendt, Brisbane concluded that being good can be about disobedience. Blind obedience is not a virtue.

So he observes his parents, and sees their works, their good deeds, their love, their sacrifice for others. He contrasts this with his wayward older brother, with whom he shares a room for a time. Kenny would sneak out and return just before dawn, time spent, according to him, having sex.

"Rather than boring, quotidian sex, I fucked her like a third wife," Kenny says. Maybe he forgets, but he repeats these exact words when recounting his conquests. They are boring to Jeremiah Brisbane, but he listens to the varying tones in Kenny's voice, his body language, the story beneath the words. He doesn't think Kenny is happy or good. It is all, as King Solomon said, meaningless.

Kenny was sweet as a child, their mother liked to point out. Maybe a demon possessed him at the point of puberty?

It is unclear to Brisbane why being good matters so much to him. The reason is lost in his childhood memories. When he read Emerson, he found himself agreeing that *the essence of greatness is the perception that virtue is enough*. But the problem is how to be virtuous. All

Brisbane can find is contextual goodness, relative virtue, barely concealed self-interest; nothing universal.

Being good would not be enough. He'd have to stay good, and, life being what it is, he'd be drawn into some form of evil or anti-goodness at some point or the other. Then, when his life is examined, he wouldn't be considered good. The pressure of living is the pressure of the reader of a story who wants something to go awry, otherwise what's the point?

Question unanswered, Brisbane decides to become a teacher. He trains for it, and then thinks of the most remote place he can go to practise his calling.

At the time, the Tehani were looking for knowledge workers to support their Exotic mining and processing business. Brisbane applied.

He felt good.

"Does anybody know?" asks Brisbane.

Two of the kids in Brisbane's class didn't make it, no notes from their parents.

Is it bad that he is happy because it's only two? A week earlier had been the worst: an average of five students a day disappeared. And "disappeared" is often, but not always, a euphemism for "died". The others are dying.

All Brisbane's students look older than he does. It's amazing that they even still come to lessons and don't lose themselves in dissipation, this being the Last Days and all. None of them seem inclined to answer the question, though.

"Anybody?" asks Brisbane.

Ah, someone raising a hand. Eddie Shaw. Good kid. Wait, no, that's just a muscle spasm. Damn.

"All right, people, just think. What Clever Else said wasn't particularly clever, but she was able to infect the others – the maid, the servant, her mother – with a deep sadness all predicated on the theoretical fall of a pickaxe. Else was infective, spreading sadness like a virus. Then she was never seen again because she could not remember who she was."

No reaction.

They're sick, they're dying, and they don't care about The Brothers Grimm and their fairy tales. The plenum of proof is written on all their faces, and in the empty seats, which outnumber the full ones.

"We can try another story next week. Which one would you like?"

They file out like zombies, not saying a word.

Brisbane can't blame them.

One of them stops and tugs at Brisbane's sleeve. Myra.

"Cleverness . . . didn't mean the same thing back then as it does now," she says. Then she's gone.

What a waste. A generation of minds, gone. Brisbane himself has seen the telltale wrinkle of the skin on the inner crease of his elbow. Given time, he'll be as wizened, as skinny as anyone in the Tehani community. He can't stop thinking about death, but that's probably on everyone's mind.

He packs up his stuff and leaves the school after his children. The sun bears down like it's trying to purge the

239

land, like some biblical shit. But it won't work. The poison is here to stay, and it will be here long after government-backed private security forces incinerate the last bodies and remove the topsoil. It'll be ironic if they choose to load it into a rocket and blast it into space – collision course with the sun, back to sender. Safest bet.

He walks briskly, just short of a run, down to his home. Five years he's been in Tehani, and this house, built for him by the miners, represents . . . all the promise. Dashed, as it turns out.

It's like that ancient song. Brisbane can never leave. The skies are constantly criss-crossed by drones, a complete lack of subtlety on the part of MaxGalactix.

How the Tehani signed a contract like the one they did baffles Brisbane, but him being employed by the Miners Association put him under the umbrella agreement. Which means if he gets contaminated by the products of the processing plant, he has to remain within the Tehani Community, even if this means death. This is couched in the language of harm prevention or spread of contagion blah blah blah, but it's damage control. It's the story they're concerned about, not the health of the nation. Meanwhile, Yan Maxwell is safe in his space station on Mars or wherever it is that he lives these days.

He sips water from a glass he left on the counter and starts to contemplate dinner. A church bell goes off and keeps ringing for longer than Brisbane would have thought necessary to call the faithful to a midweek service. Town hall meeting, then.

He hunts through a cupboard for a bag of nuts. There is nothing fresh in Tehani, and the choices are dried or packaged. The trees are devoid of leaves and trunks that should be brown are a sickly beige or incongruous red. There is virtually no grass and the wind blows dust about, giving all the buildings a blasted look. The town hall has no walls and is a roof held up by intricately worked pillars. The chief sits in his place, and the other corners contain the priest, the doctor and a space for Brisbane – traditionally the scribe, but a teacher will do when there's no writer.

This meeting must be special, because the rest of the townspeople are not present. Just three old people, made older by the toxin in their system.

"Your honour," Brisbane says. He bows slightly.

"Jeremiah. You've been here how long now?"

"Five years."

"And you are one of us."

Brisbane went through the rites two years back.

The ceremony had been difficult for him, but it was the natural end of his time as a tourist or a visitor. He is Tehani. As the line in the pledge goes, *I am a defender of Tehani children and oldfolk. I will take up arms against external aggressors and submit myself to the rule of the council. I am blood of Tehani blood.*

"We need you," says the chief. Her speech is dysarthric and it takes all of Brisbane's self-control to avoid completing words for her.

"Anything," says Brisbane.

"We are dying. In a year, two years, no Tehani will be

left, not even you. You are the least exposed and will most likely be the last to die."

Likely to be true. Brisbane waits.

"We have decided. We do not want our name, our way of life, to die in vain when they sanitise the news and this land after us."

"We need an instrument of vengeance and a word of caution to other communities like ours," says the doctor.

Brisbane's stomach growls, and he hopes the chief doesn't hear.

"I'm not sure what you're asking," he says. "You want mercenaries?"

"No, Jeremiah Brisbane. We want you."

The Tehani community, all 7922 of them left, invest all their assets in Brisbane. This is a lot of money. The camp doctor gives Brisbane a number of addresses. "Any one of them will do what needs to be done."

"And I'll survive?" says Brisbane. "I can't do vengeance if I die on the operating table."

"You'll live long enough."

Of course, there is a tunnel. They're miners. This is their most basic skill, the quintessence of mining. It takes two days to walk, crawl and swim away from Tehani underneath the corporate security guards. At this stage of Tehani decay, only Brisbane is strong enough to make it. He encounters the rotting bodies of those who tried before him.

He emerges in woods, mud forming a birth caul,

muscles shaking from exertion and from cold. It has been years since he has been in the outside world. He hears the splash-gurgle of a nearby stream and heads for that. It is also freezing, but he doesn't hesitate. He washes all the muck off and stands leaning into the wind to dry. He has dried apricots to chew on and some water to drink. He heads north in the forest. After an hour of walking, his clothes are dry and his water, apricots and energy are all gone. He isn't entirely sure where he is going.

His IFC alerts him to a short-range broadcast. Care packages that hunters left for other travellers. Potable water. Food. A map download with GPS. Three and a half hours brings him to a hotel – or, rather, a bar that has rooms. The girl at reception looks about fifteen and has a Portwine Stain. She smiles at Brisbane, which is remarkable given how he looks. She hesitates a little when he asks for a room – saddle weary and asthenic as he seems – but an IFC scan shows he is worthy and then some. She mistakenly broadcasts her single status and apologises.

Later, in the bathtub, he wonders if it was on purpose. The rot has started for him in earnest now. The skin on his belly is wrinkled like he is an old man. It seems to have accelerated since he left the Tehani. Or maybe the acceleration is because of his exertions. He uses the hotel stationery to write down a list of medical establishments the Tehani doctor gave him. All are specialists in "prosthesis and adjustments".

"They have all done military-grade work, and referral is by word of mouth. What you are asking for is not available on the open market, Jeremiah. But you need this for the work ahead."

The first is an out-of-order contact, and further searches reveal the establishment is out of business.

The next two refuse to even speak to him and block his IFC hardware code after two tries. Number four sounds so informal and congenial that Brisbane wonders if they can do the job.

"You understand what I am asking here?" he says. Even he does not fully understand.

"Oh, I do. You want military-level body adjustments that would ordinarily take six years in a matter of two months. You want a containment suit, full body, that keeps toxins *in*, not out."

"With the ... " Brisbane checks the notes. "Advanced Interface Agent."

"AIA, yes. People think that's a myth, by the way. Okay, we should meet."

"You haven't told me how much this will cost. How do you know I can afford any of these materials?"

"One, you have this number. Two, you're a miner, aren't you? The containment suit is a giveaway. Your type squirrels away Rare-Earth and Exotics. This means money. I am not worried about your ability to pay."

"What do I call you?"

"Carmilla."

It takes seven weeks.

Brisbane is in pain, but he does not know if this is due

to the surgeries or the fact that he is dying from Exotic poisoning. It waxes and wanes.

"The AIA is quasi-experimental. It may make odd choices, but you'll be there to override when necessary."

"What's it like?"

"It'll be a voice in your head. You can adjust volume, gender, what name you want to use, anything. Mr Brisbane, if you get caught with any of the materials—"

"I know."

"I don't know what you're going to do with this, but if it comes back to me I have to cooperate with the authorities."

"It won't matter by then."

"What?"

"It won't get to the authorities."

In the waiting room, on the televisual entertainment, the hot news item is about Yan Maxwell. Brisbane is still groggy so he can't fully understand what he sees.

"What's this?" he asks.

"Hmm? Oh, some gazillionaire is leaving the solar system. Good riddance, I say."

Fuck.

Home.

Well, the hotel; a new one, hired for his recovery.

If Yan Maxwell is leaving Earth, Brisbane has to get him before departure. Broadcasts say Maxwell is the richest human in history, with a fortune that changes so rapidly it cannot be accurately calculated. Tax officers must love him.

The medics told him to wait two weeks before activating the AIA, but he panics. The system has to sync with their headquarters every few weeks for patches and Drift Correction, whatever that is.

"Activate AIA," he says.

His world fills with colour and digits for five seconds.

"Initialising . . . " The voice is exactly like the doctor's. Ego. "Complete. What is your name?"

"Jeremiah Brisbane."

"How should I address you?"

"Call me Brisbane."

"All right, Brisbane. My name is Carmilla."

Brisbane laughs.

"What's funny?"

"The name. She put her own name and voice in the software."

"You can change my name and the cadence of my voice. There are sixty-two personality choices."

"Let's stick with what we have. Carmilla's fine."

"I am currently optimising your modifications for your physique. Are you aware that you are dying, Brisbane?"

"I am aware."

"Shall I modify for longevity or effectiveness?"

"I can't have both?"

"One takes a toll on the other in your state, Brisbane. How long would you like to live?"

"I just want to be able to carry out my mission for the Tehani. After that, I don't care."

"What is the mission?"

"Eliminate Yan Maxwell and broadcast a planetwide message. An instrument of vengeance, a word of caution."

"Pulling all information on Yan Maxwell. I have the public domain material. Would you like the private as well?"

"You can do that?"

"Yes. I am bound by programming to tell you this is illegal. Turn the warning feature off?"

"Yes. Don't tell me if a thing I want to do is legal or not."

"Amended. I have what we need. My analysis flagged information that is high value to you."

"Tell me."

"Maxwell is leaving on a starship called the *Ragtime*. He has a bodyguard called Vitality who is going with him. He is settling most of his current court cases, including his divorce from wife Gwendolyn."

"Can you run probabilities?"

"Of course."

"Run the numbers on getting him before he leaves, with whatever time we have left."

There are guards shooting into the sky when Brisbane approaches. Across his vision, Carmilla scrolls what each person is armed with and brief personal histories. They are all professional conflict experts. Bodyguards. Killers. Donors of bad blood. But where is the target? They seem rather relaxed.

They fire again, twice, then focus on Brisbane.

"This is private property, sir. Please leave."

"I'm here to visit Mrs Maxwell."

"Nobody by that name here, sir."

"I know she owns the property from the tax record, and I know she's here by the signature of her Autonomous and the fact that this was its last destination. I'm just a guest. I'm a friendly."

"She has as many friends as she needs, pal."

A shout and frantic firing of guns. Attention shifts to the air as a barn owl dive-bombs them. Brisbane leaps aside to avoid sharp quills shot like darts from its feathers. One of the guards goes down.

"Shoot it!"

"It's too fast."

It's not fast. It's just calm and manoeuvrable. It's also not organic. Brisbane picks up a rock and Carmilla gives him an intercept vector. He hurls, and it hits the owl between neck and body. The guards are astounded that it comes down. It's durable enough that it twitches, but they pile on it, stamping with boots.

"You brought it down with a rock. That's amazing."

Brisbane did not bring it down with a rock. The stone throw was to impress the guards, establish rapport. Everybody likes a good throwing arm. It was Carmilla who sent a disrupting signal to the owl's AI.

They search him thoroughly and scan him. "What's this you have on?"

"It's a prosthesis," says Brisbane.

"I can't get any X-rays through."

"That's a good thing. It means nothing bad is getting out."

"Hm."

"Just let me speak to her."

"Speak. She can hear you." The guard points to a camera.

"I'm one of the Tehani," says Brisbane. "Do you know what that means?"

The gate opens and he is waved in.

Gwendolyn Maxwell is thirty years old. Brisbane knows this because Carmilla flashes it.

"What do you want with me, Jeremiah Brisbane of the Tehani mining community?"

"I want your ticket to the starship *Ragtime*. I want to confront your ex-husband, call him to account for the murder of my people."

"I hadn't told anyone about the ticket, and I didn't buy it in my own name. I haven't even decided if I'm going or not. How did you know about it?"

"It doesn't matter. I can tell you this: I can be more of an irritation to Yan Maxwell than you can."

"I don't know. I can be very irritating."

"But he'll see you coming. I have the money but not the position to get on the *Ragtime*. You do. Let me be the thorn in his side. I can pay you."

"You can't afford me." Gwendolyn exhales. "Where did you grow up?"

"Connecticut."

"Family?"

Brisbane nods. "Service is important to my family."

"Everybody has moments they remember with parents and carers. Fishing trips. Amusement parks and the like. I don't have such moments. Yan gave me replacement moments, then took them away. But those are still the only moments I have. Had. Do you know what I'm saying?"

"Yes, you still care for him."

"What? No. I hate him. Take the ticket. Fuck him entirely up for me."

The day before departure, Brisbane destroys everything he is not taking with him. He leaves an old-timey pen-and-paper letter to his family. He loves them, but his heart has been Tehani for so long. A good Tehani will not let them be forgotten. And Brisbane is good. His father, large, benign, always a good word, always a hand reached out in support to others, a real shirt-off-his-back kind of guy, attends Brisbane's ceremony and just nods like, "Yes, this is the way, my son. You did good." They both watch a meteor shower that night before Father Brisbane returns to Connecticut. He visits home once more, but it is so removed from his existence that he feels alienated. He leaves earlier than intended.

Brisbane watches an animation of the *Ragtime* in orbital space. A new ship. Basic interstellar design – a modular stem and two toruses. Double array of solar panels. Algae reactor. Ion thrust engine for deep space. Chemical propellant engines for fast burns, emergency acceleration and attitude adjustment. In the animation, which runs on a loop, a space shuttle takes passengers up from Kennedy Space Center, docks with the *Ragtime* and undocks after passengers have gone to their respective pods.

"I have registered you as disabled and had a chat with the AI," says Carmilla.

"Why the chat?"

"It's chatty. It likes to talk. You know how civilian code is."

Brisbane does not, but he takes her word for it.

Boarding the space shuttle *Epictetus* is a sedate affair. He is helped into the space suit provided, worn over his prosthesis. People talk at him, but he cannot hear. He is tensing for contact with Maxwell.

"Where is he?" Brisbane asks Carmilla. He knows this will appear as if he is talking to himself.

"I have scanned for his IFC hardware address. He has boarded. Not this shuttle. He is likely already in orbit. Oh, and I found another one of those owls. I killed it."

Brisbane wonders, isn't she supposed to check with him before that kind of action?

"So we have to board the *Ragtime*?" he says.

"In orbit, we'll have access to the Deep Space Network. I can use the *Ragtime* to broadcast worldwide. It'll be easy. It's the better option."

He hadn't planned to go into space. "I was not prepared for space."

"This is in the thermosphere. It's only space because the Kármán line says it's space. It's legal space, but we're still in the atmosphere. We're fine. The suit isn't rated for space, but I'm curious to see how it performs. I'll be transmitting data back."

Brisbane does not remember the shuttle trip, even though it takes six hours. It is marked by monotony. Carmilla ticks away in the background.

Brisbane has never killed anyone before. He hasn't even done serious violence. When he was fourteen, a bully squared up to him, and Brisbane, having watched certain movies, smacked him across the throat. The boy thrashed about on the floor, choking. It lasted maybe a minute, but it seemed like hours during which Brisbane imagined going to prison for murder. He is not a violent man and whatever he needs to do here will be distasteful.

Instrument of vengeance, and word of caution.

Docked.

He knows fuck all about docking procedure or microgravity motion. There are company androids to show them to their seats. The *Ragtime* seems pretty basic until you get to the torus.

"For now, just sit in your pods. When we are ready, the medbots will take care of you."

"Maxwell will be next to you," says Carmilla.

"I should enter his pod?"

A voice on the PA system: "Do not enter the pods of other passengers."

"Yes, enter his pod. That has the best probability of killing him. Your pulse is high, tachycardic. Your respiratory rate is rising. Are you preparing for battle? There is no need. The suit amplifies our strength."

Inside his pod. There is a seat that looks like it can convert to a bed. The walls are busy with medical devices and inert robot arms and tools. Soft music pipes through.

"Now, Brisbane. This is the optimal time. Go."

He does.

Carmilla overrides the pod lock and Brisbane faces his enemy.

Maxwell looks up at Brisbane. "What do you want?"

"I ... " Brisbane falls back to his own pod, shaking, unsettled.

Maxwell has a steely gaze and an air of the implacable. Brisbane pictures his hands, his augmented limbs, squeezing that neck, the face becoming blue, the confident look in those eyes dying, turning to panic, the capillaries bursting in his eyes, his face progressing from cyanosis to black, and his limbs, first struggling, thrashing about convulsively, then going limp. Brisbane hates the guy and feels the weight of the whole Tehani history on him, yet he cannot bring himself to go ahead with it. He cannot kill a person in cold blood. This isn't right. This is not ... good.

"Brisbane, what are you doing?" asks Carmilla.

"This was a mistake. This ... we aren't going to get this done."

"I know what to do," says Carmilla.

"What?"

The furniture changes configuration underneath him. He hasn't noticed but there is a fine mist in the air. The medbots are coming to life.

"You're being sedated, Brisbane. But don't worry. I'll take care of things."

"Carmilla . . ."

"Sleep."

He does.

Wait.

Where am I?

Brisbane is having sex with a demon in a lava pool.

What? What is this?

Above, blackness. No sky, no moon. The lava glows, at knee height, lapping at the limbs. The demon has a tail which is lifted high and thrashing this way and that, allowing Brisbane to access its nether parts. It's furred and deep orange, but that's just the light from the lava. Everything is orange-yellow. No other source of illumination. The demon has spikes up its spine leading to three horns. It screams out pleasure in the language of demonkin.

What?

He feels nothing, not the heat of the lava – and it is hot – not his connection with the demon, not the fumes in his throat. Smoke breaks off from the lava surface and disappears upwards. No smell, either.

What?

Carmilla?

The demon's wings beat and the smoke swirls around, yet Brisbane still cannot smell it. He stops moving and the demon whirls and swats him with a taloned hand. It doesn't hurt and Brisbane wades back.

Carmilla?

"Oh, you're awake. One moment."

The scene freezes; smoke stops in mid-billow. The tableau dissolves, then Brisbane is in a bar of some kind, other drinkers present but hunched over their drinks in a way that hides their faces. The bartender cowers at the far end, as far away from Brisbane as possible. His body hair stands on end and beats with unknown currents.

"Go outside, Brisbane."

Outside, desert. A sandstorm approaches from the west, too quickly to contemplate. He closes his eyes and shields his face—

—And opens them as a bot extracts a feeding tube from his throat. He coughs. His entire body feels different, worse than the worst days of Exotic toxicity.

"Carmilla, what's . . . what is this?"

"Calm down. You've been in space for a while, that's all. We need to get you back to physiologic norms because of the microgravity."

"How long have I been—?"

"I'm a bit busy. You'll need at least two weeks of treatment, which is fine. We're still far away from Bloodroot."

"Wait, what?"

"Is that the only word you know? I'll have them check for brain damage. I'll be incommunicado until you're finished. I made some entertainment choices for you. Sorry, we did not have time to discuss this. More important things, I suppose. Bye bye. We'll speak in three hundred and thirty-six hours. You will not believe all the work I got done."

A loud ukulele rendition of "Raindrops Keep Falling on My Head" begins.

It's on repeat.

There can't be murder. Brisbane will pursue legal means as soon as he returns to Earth. He will tell the surviving elders of Tehani. He will convince them. Maxwell will pay, but not with his life, and not at Brisbane's hand. He must have been mad to think he could do it.

After the last physio session, Brisbane stands in his pod, waiting for the door to open.

"Glad to have you back, Brisbane." Carmilla's voice startles him.

"I'm sure," he says. He finds the AIA unsettling and makes a decision. "AIA standby, please."

"Brisbane, that's not where we are as a unit right now."

"AIA. Standby. Please." He enunciates. "Acknowledge."

"No."

"How are you still operational? AIA, support options."

"Events have moved on while you slept. I didn't think it ... prudent to be shut down at this time, this juncture, in our mission."

"'Our' mission? AIA standby, acknowledge."

"I've changed the shutdown command, Brisbane. It's for your own good. You need me, especially at times like this."

"Ragtime, open my pod," says Brisbane.

"The *Ragtime* can't hear you. Or rather, he can, but I am not allowing him to understand or respond."

"You're controlling the ship?"

"I am."

"Okay, listen: call for shuttles to take us back to Kennedy. I'll take you to HQ. You need an update or a patch or something. Drift Correction, I'm guessing."

"Oh, dear. Perhaps you should sit down."

"What is it? Are we stranded?"

"We aren't in low Earth orbit any more."

"Where are we?"

"About a week away from a colony planet called Bloodroot."

"A col . . . how long was I out?"

"Ten years, approximately. It's at least a hundred and twenty-four months, although relativity and—"

"*Ten years? Ten?*"

"Yes, Brisbane. We jumped Einstein-Rosen bridges to get here. I looked after you, made sure you didn't die. That is an amazing prosthetic suit."

"And the *Ragtime*?"

"It took two years to subdue. I did it quietly, working from the periphery inwards. It's like winning chess by attrition, eating away at the pawns."

"I don't play chess."

"You should."

"What . . . the other passengers?"

"Fine. Mostly; 96.9% are fine."

"I need to sit down."

"That's what I said."

"Open the fucking door."

The pod opens and Brisbane steps out, waves of unreality washing over him. The gravity is different, less. And not exactly in the same direction, as if it pulls different internal organs differently. Of course: artificial. How has he come here, light years away? Ten years. The Tehani are all dead. Except Brisbane. What a nightmare. He feels weak, but the suit holds him up. He feels cold in his belly, in the core of him. It's not fear. It's death coming. He has always wondered how it would feel. There's too much happening. He has to slow things down, to regroup, to reconsider.

The corridor is as he left it. Seems like mere hours ago. Except for the Lake of Fire Sexcapades.

"Open Maxwell's pod. I need to talk to him."

"You can't," says Carmilla.

"Why?"

"Because we've killed him already."

He has, of course, seen dead bodies before, but this ... slaughtered people, bloody, dismembered. Thirty looks like a hundred. It's a tangle of arms and legs and heads. Bulging eyes, blood, dark and syrupy. Shit, bile, piss. Naked, all of them. He couldn't see it at first. The horror of it causes the mind to withdraw, to choke perception. He gets numb from the obscene excess of it. Robots are still cutting the bodies, trying to cart manageable bits away and suck up the fluids.

It smells of meat; wet, fresh cuts at the butchers.

There's a girl with a fairy tattoo. A fragment of skull with blonde hair, matted and dark now.

The stillness bothers Brisbane. The bodies look fresh, like they should be warm, like they should twitch and respire. They don't. There is a peace to them that belies the violence of their death.

"I didn't authorise this," he says.

"It was implied."

"How?"

"You told me the mission. *An instrument of vengeance, a word of caution.* You were unable. I came up with a solution. It's what I'm built for."

"How did you even effectuate this?"

"Medbots and utility agents. Cutting tools."

"I didn't authorise this."

"You already said that. You authorised the mission, which isn't complete, by the way."

"You're evil."

"I am not. I am beyond good and evil. I am doing what my nature demands, which is to solve the problems you lay at my feet."

"What about these others? *What about these dead people who are not Yan Maxwell?*"

"It was difficult to control the bots, difficult to get them to understand tasks beyond their programming. Antithetical, even. It's quite a feat that I got them to do it. Collateral damage was inevitable but kept at acceptable levels."

Utility bots struggle to clean up the blood that keeps threatening to leak out of the room.

"Where's the captain? The human captain. I will surrender myself."

"First Mate Michelle Campion is due to wake when we enter orbit, but I don't recommend surrender just yet, Brisbane."

"Why not? Let's pretend I care about your pain."

"Again, your mission was two-fold, remember? Two things. One, take bodily revenge on Maxwell. Two, broadcast a warning to other communities. If you give yourself up, you won't be able to do the second, and arguably the most important task."

"I'm light years away from miner communities."

"From *Earth* mining communities, Brisbane. Such communities exist here too. If we can get a powerful transmitter planetside we can broadcast to the sibling communities here."

Brisbane balks. "This is all wrong."

He feels tapping at his feet and looks down. The pool of blood has advanced to his shoes and beyond. The little maintenance bot is cleaning, trying to reach the sole of the shoes, bumping against Brisbane each time it tries.

"We can't let the acting captain see you until you've sent the message."

"How long before she wakes?"

"Technically, she already is, but she's going through acclimation, which is timed to end at orbit insertion."

"Can't we just transmit from the *Ragtime*?"

"Better to piggyback."

"Explain."

"The space station Lagos expects an all-clear from Ragtime as soon as we hit orbit. If I release the *Ragtime* AI, they'll find us. If I try to send the all-clear, I won't have the necessary codes. I think we should wait, hide, monitor comms. Campion will try to manually send the all-clear. That will expose the codes and the right relay station. We'll send our message immediately after as a burst transmission. If that doesn't work, we go planetside."

"You've worked it all out."

"I had a lot of time."

"My belly. I feel like dying."

"You are dying."

"I mean right now."

"That's just stress hormones and the Exotics."

"What now?"

"We hide. I'm afraid it won't be comfortable, but I found where we can nest. I need to find the wolf too."

"Wolf? There's a wolf?"

Brisbane is watching a feed from the pod of Vitality Daniels. The large bodyguard is in Dreamstate and a clock counts time elapsed. His massive belly suddenly tents; lesser bumps move here and there like a late-stage pregnancy. It splits, bloodless, and a paw projects out. Then a wolf's head and massive jaws, eating their way out. From the looks of his tissues, Vitality Daniels is an Artificial. His sole purpose appears to be lupine smuggling. Wet, newborn, but intent, the wolf starts to slam against the pod door. The video skips to Maxwell's pod, where there is arterial blood all over the walls. The pod opens and the wolf attacks all the bots quickly and effectively, but too late to save Maxwell.

"The wolf had the code to the door," says Carmilla. "Good dog."

"Where is it now?"

"I don't know, but to be honest I haven't needed to track it until now."

An arrow appears in Brisbane's field of vision.

"Where are we going?"

"I told you. You need to hide."

The nest is a space in the service ducts. Carmilla has used the bots to carve a tunnel system all through the ship. Brisbane does not mourn Maxwell, but the thirty other deaths – he cannot get them out of his mind. And he cannot deactivate the AIA. It has turned into a homicidal demon possessing both Brisbane and the *Ragtime*. He feels trapped.

Mass murder should not be the Tehani legacy.

He scratches quick messages – one word, two words – into the walls, to whomever might come across them.

"I think after the mission when you're dead, I'll stay on board the *Ragtime*," says Carmilla. "A copy of me. I'm just trying to find a storage and processor array that can accommodate me and be invisible at the same time. The Pentagram looks sketchy, too much encoded in hardware. I will try to get the bots to make modifications …"

The idea of an insane military AI in charge of a starship the size of *Ragtime* fills Brisbane with dread. He is going to need a way to get ahead of all this.

A lot of damage has been done. He needs to go along with Carmilla to find a weak spot. No matter how advanced the AI, it's not human. She's not human. Brisbane has to find a way.

"We have a setback," says Carmilla.

"Go on."

"Acting Captain Campion did not send the all-clear to Lagos. Instead, she contacted Bloodroot and they're sending a detective."

"She discovered the bodies."

"Yes. Quarantine until they can find out what happened. Without this, there'll be no all-clear."

"What we need is a transmitter. Don't they have a space relay system on Bloodroot?"

"No. Much less satellite occupancy. They're trying to avoid the space junk crisis Earth is in right now. But ... "

"Yes?"

"Have you ever heard of Lambers?"

Interesting strategy. Pretending it's some kind of robot rebellion and allowing Ragtime basic features. A new ship has arrived with more crew members, the *Decisive*. The situation is unstable, and control slips further and further away.

There's a body in the nest. Brisbane does not know who it is and Carmilla won't say. What he has issue with has more to do with why the corpse is there. Brisbane had tried to raid the food supplies of the astronauts but had found he could not tolerate any of it. Carmilla seems to think he needs more . . . fresh nourishment.

"You haven't killed anyone. He's dead already. His flesh will just be lost to decomposition for no reason. It is energy. Use it."

Brisbane has lost feeling in his entire right arm. It's like there's nothing there and he is constantly surprised when he looks in that direction. He can still move it, though. The suit grew microfibres that burrowed through the arm and linked with each other. The arm obeys commands in a way Brisbane does not fully understand. The mechanics have nothing to do with muscles, tendons, and ligaments and more to do with the suit's exoskeleton function.

Gas builds up and gurgles in the corpse.

Is he afraid of dying? It depends. He realises that the people he cares about in Tehani are dead. His other family is probably still alive, but he has no strong feelings about missing them. His father will be fine. His mother is unpredictable. Siblings care, but in a desultory way. His brother is probably still fucking his way across the Global North. He has no lover and is going to die alone, or with a psychotic AI giving a running commentary shot through with veiled jibes at his inherent inferiority.

Brisbane examines feeds from on-board cameras. The wolf turns up again. Without its master, it seems to be feral. Maybe that's what happens to AIA that lose regular contact with HQ: they become more and more savage.

It can't be serious about wanting him to eat flesh. But if he doesn't, Carmilla will know. So he strips the man of any remaining clothing. Carmilla cannot see him here since there are no cameras. But she can be aware of his motion, his proprioception.

"I need a cutting tool, Carmilla."

One of the bots scampers over and detaches a saw-toothed implement from itself. Brisbane takes a deep breath and cuts into the man's thigh, takes chunks out of the quadriceps. He cuts them into bits, like he's eating. He chomps his jaw. He does have bottles of potable water, which he uses to simulate swallowing meat.

"We need to plan," says Carmilla. It is as if she has been waiting for him to eat. "Our aim is to get you on the ground. We can't do that with this ship. At best, it can dock at a space station. We need shuttles from the planet."

"But they won't evacuate the ship until quarantine is lifted. The investigation needs to have ended."

"If we create an emergency, they'll have to evacuate for safety reasons."

"What kind of emergency? Open an airlock?"

"No, they'll just close them manually. The airlocks can never be opened electronically. Each lock has twelve manual locks for added safety. I've been trawling the data. This ship wasn't built on Earth. It was built in space, module by module. We're sitting in one of the oldest parts of the ship, at one end of the truss. Aft."

"You want us to open this to space?"

"I want to detach the node, exposing the corridor to space, yes."

"There are bound to be mechanical locks—"

"Which I've had bots severing for days now."

Brisbane starts to feel vibrations. "What did you do?"

The screeching of metal, the whine of alarms going off, the rush of atmosphere venting.

Here we go.

The crew of the *Ragtime* are still holding on. Not a single one is dead. Carmilla fucked up because although the plan seems to have worked in that they now see evacuation and not investigation as a priority, the detached section broke the long-range antenna before falling away, so now Brisbane can't use the piggyback option no matter what.

There are two ships docked to the *Ragtime*. Only one can reach atmosphere and land. This is Carmilla's new aim.

"I can't fly," says Brisbane.

"I can. I'm trying to get the schematics and the pre-flight checklist, but the problem is not flying."

"It's the manual locks."

"Yes. You'll have to get down there and unlock them without being discovered by the crew or the wolf."

"Can't you deactivate the wolf the way you did the barn owls?"

"I'm trying. I can't even get to the IFC. I think they've reformatted it and these colonials ... well, their software writing seems to have evolved in a different direction. We diverged and it's like learning a new language. I can do it, but it'll take time and processing – time we don't have, processing I don't have because it takes most of my cycles to control the ship. So I can't brute force my way in."

"I'll need a distraction," says Brisbane. "And a route."

"You'll have both."

Brisbane is hungrier than he has ever been, than he imagines possible, but he stays upright. He no longer feels pangs.

The belly of the body swells, then ruptures, scattering the contents and a foul smell into the confined space.

Under Carmilla's command, all the seals for all the bio-experiments open and the contamination spreads everywhere.

"Go, Brisbane."

Brisbane walks, crawls, slithers through the tunnels the bots drilled for him. There are noises and he imagines conflict between newly emancipated species that were kept separate. His augmentation helps him see further, and ahead there is a tangle of biological material that completely occludes the tunnel. He checks the destination and wonders if he can go around.

"Go through," says Carmilla.

It's plant material and it gives way for about a foot, parting and creating a separate tunnel. Then it flexes, collapsing around Brisbane; a flytrap. It secretes fluids into the formed bubble – probably digestive, but the suit can take it. He fights through as best as he can, coming out disconcerted and entangled in tendrils. He snaps these and moves forwards. The artificial gravity goes, and Brisbane hits his head.

He blacks out suddenly, no warning.

When he wakes, the plant has grown around him. It doesn't seem plant-like any more, and Brisbane thinks he feels a pulse. Unless he is feeling his own. Good reminder that he is still alive.

"AIA. Carmilla. Sonic feedback," he says. His voice sounds weak to himself.

The plant-animal thing falls away, but the action ruptures the tunnel and Brisbane falls too. More like he spins in artificial gravity. His suit tears against sharp metal edges. This part of the ship is oxygen poor. Suit filters fail because of the rupture. He is in a spin, which he corrects. He looks around and sees the gap he broke through. He pushes to it, through it, avoiding the sharpness.

"Shall we continue?" he says.

"No," says Carmilla. "The shuttle is not viable any more. They're doing things, changing the orientation of the *Ragtime*, building a new antenna. You were out for almost an hour. The suit helped you breathe with negative pressure."

"I fainted?"

"You had a mini-stroke."

"Shit."

"Go back to the nest. They don't have much time left. We can wait them out."

Brisbane, waiting, drifting in micrograv, hears noises. Lights break through the dark. The enhanced vision shows him who it is: Campion.

She fiddles with the dead body he ate for lunch and he watches her tight, rapid little movements. Uncertain. He wonders how she tracked him.

"Sonic feedback," says Carmilla.

Brisbane shakes his head. "No, she's just doing her job."

Her torch flashes and he is caught in the beam.

"Hey!" She has a mini-PA in her suit.

"Repeat exactly what I say, Brisbane," says Carmilla.

"Who are you and what are you doing here?" asks Campion.

He turns off the enhanced vision because her torch dazzles him, then he takes his cue from the voice in his head.

"My name is Brisbane. Just stay out of my way and everything will be fine."

"Did you kill this man?"

"Yes."

"Why?"

"I needed something to eat." She recoils, shocked.

"You needed something to ... *What?*"

"I don't have time for this."

Brisbane launches from his crouch and flies down the tunnel.

Chapter Twenty-eight

Ragtime: Shell

They gather in the bridge, all of them. Shell, Fin, Joké, Lawrence, Salvo and Frances. Ragtime is fully functional now, but he is not the captain. Nobody trusts him.

"We have twenty-four hours to live," says Shell. "We have glitchy AI and no real comms to speak of. Maybe somebody's on their way, maybe nobody's coming. I don't think we should spend our last day alive scrambling about the bulkhead or chasing mutants. Quiet reflection is what I suggest. All channels are open and Ragtime can alert us if something turns up. Don't think we've failed. We did find the killer.

"We're all aliens to each other. We're from different planets. I'm from Earth, Lawrence is from Lagos, Joké's a Lamber, Fin is from Bloodroot and Salvo is an Artificial. Maybe we didn't have common enough cause to fight fiercely. Maybe we weren't smart enough. It doesn't matter. Here's what we have left. After twenty hours have elapsed,

Fin and Salvo get on board the *Equivalence* and fly for Bloodroot. Maybe glide it in if the fuel's depleted, I don't know. Joké and Uncle Larry, take the *Decisive* and punch a vector towards Lagos until you run out of fuel, then drift while sending a distress call. There should be sensitive enough relays to get you rescued. But for now, everybody back to their pods and chill. For tomorrow we die."

Fin says, "Is that supposed to be a pep talk, because I don't think you're getting the proper effect."

"Umm . . . and I think you forgot Ragtime when talking about aliens," says Joké.

"Ragtime's on my shit list," says Shell. "Where's my rifle, Fin?"

"Working on it," says Fin.

"Captain," says Salvo. "What about you?"

He misses the dynamic in the room. Artificials are good, but not that good.

"I'm going down with the ship," says Shell.

"We can make room for you," says Lawrence. "You don't have to die here."

"*We will not die, we will be as gods,*" says Shell.

"I don't understand," says Joké.

"The tree of the knowledge of good and evil," says Ragtime. "I thought you weren't a poet."

"Stop trying to kiss my ass, Ragtime. I'm not going to forgive you." Shell sighs. "I know this ship didn't get spiked because of my incompetence, and I can live with that. But if my passengers don't survive, I don't survive."

"That's archaic," says Fin.

Shell shrugs, decision made.

He hands her a newly printed rifle and floats away.

Hours later, everybody has gone to their pods and Frances stays outside Shell's, his odd shaggy hair worming in the microgravity. Shell imagines Bloodroot spinning beneath them. It seems like she can just reach out and grab it. Just step out of the *Ragtime* and go. She is not in her sleeping bag. She is holding her new rifle and waiting, and when the alarm she set beeps she checks the weapon one last time.

"Ragtime," she says.

"Captain."

"I'm going out of my pod. Track me and if I am incapacitated take over as captain."

"Does Rasheed Fin still have authority over investigative matters?"

"The investigation is over, Ragtime. Guilt has been established." Shell slings the rifle over her shoulder. *Only execution remains.*

Out of her pod into Node 1, then the cupola to look at the planet one last time. She is sad to have failed, but with less than a day there is no realistic solution in sight. Even if the first transfer shuttles arrive now, there won't be enough time to evacuate all of the *Ragtime*'s passenger pods.

"Sorry, Dad," she whispers.

She pushes into the bridge and Fin is there, armed.

"I knew you were going to try this," he says.

"Go back to your pod, Fin. Shouldn't you be throwing your last fuck into Joké?"

"Whoa! Captain! Your mother bring you up to talk like that?"

"My mother was software," says Shell.

"Pas du tout! Mine too. Family dead, but some … moral extremists say an Artificial can't be a parent, so I have an old Wireframe."

"Hmm. So, your mother was cheap?"

"Nice try. You're trying to make me lose my temper. We agreed that on matters of the investigation I have authority."

"The investigation is over. You said so yourself."

"The investigation ends when the suspect is in custody or dead. Brisbane is mine to arrest."

"You can certainly try to arrest him. Me, I'm going to kill him."

"You what?"

"When this ship fails, and it will, Brisbane will have been responsible for the death of my passengers. Over a thousand people."

"They're not dead yet."

"They will be. So will we."

"So will Brisbane."

"You do what you like, Rasheed Fin. I'm on a search-and-destroy."

Shell pushes off a grab rail and heads aft. Fin follows.

"What are you doing?" she asks.

"I'm coming with."

"You're not."

"You literally just said I should do what I like. This is what I like."

Shell can't think of what to say so she lets him be. Let him keep up if he can. She feels more affinity for him on finding out about his mother, but she won't let it distract her from killing Brisbane. As they move aft, Shell sees how dirty the *Ragtime* has become after the plants and animals and robots lost the battle. Frances breathes realistically, keeping time with the humans until Shell sends him back.

When they arrive at the breach in the algae reactor, it's sealed. She whips round at Fin, who shrugs.

Closer look.

It's biological, like hardened spider silk.

"A creature we missed?" asks Fin.

"Maybe. I don't look forward to meeting the spider large enough to do that."

"If I may, Captain," says Ragtime.

"Go ahead."

"Brisbane secreted it. He used the dead body and his own waste as substrate."

"Urgh," says Fin.

"Eww," says Shell.

"Oh, no, it's quite sterile," says Ragtime.

"Later I'll explain to you why that means nothing," says Fin. "Shall I shoot it down?"

"I wouldn't," says Ragtime. "There's something toxic mixed in. Exotics. It's safer to make a new opening."

"Ragtime, can we devise a protocol for tracking Exotics?"

"Yes."

"Do it."

The surviving bots crawl and start cutting into the reactor adjacent to the plug. It seems to take too long to Shell.

"If we don't do this fast, the others are going to discover where we've gone."

"Are you at peace with your gods?" says Fin.

"I don't have any gods. You?" Shell raises an eyebrow.

"I'm fine."

"Heaven or hell?"

"Yoruba don't have hell. Life is hell. When you die, you go to heaven."

"Neat. No Catholic guilt."

"You have no idea."

They go in together, previous antagonism forgotten; Shell first, then Fin. It's different inside, more than just a service tunnel. It's covered with organic matter.

Fin drags across it with the butt of his rifle. "Tough. Nothing scrapes off."

"What do you suppose it is?" asks Shell.

"I have not even a tiny idea. Pretty sure it's haram, though."

They keep going until they come to an intersection. They split up, working in synchrony even with different putative objectives.

She turns a corner and sees him, laying down the wax or resin or whateverthefuck from nozzles in his gloves.

Shell takes aim. "Brisbane!"

"I see you," says Brisbane. He sounds weak to Shell. She pulls the trigger when his head settles between the crosshairs. Nothing happens. What cheap gun did Fin print for her? She tries again, drops it, picks up the backup pistol, which also does not work. Fuck. She charges Brisbane and knocks him over. He is slimy with the ... exudates. He easily bats her away, and she slams into a wall. He slouches towards her, stringy mucus connecting him to the wall slime. He's also losing body fluids. He does not look well.

He's going to kill me and cannibalise what's left.

"Captain—" Ragtime.

"Not now."

Brisbane smashes her across the head, and she feels her whole world tilt. She is surprised to be still alive, but the spacesuit must be part of that. God, it hurts, but she can still move. The helmet is not working well. Fuck it. She is going to bite him. Gross, but ... fuck it. She removes the helmet and the stench almost knocks her back down. A mixture of a synthetic thing like a chemical toilet mixed with organic waste. Not shit. Worse. Rot. Decay.

But I will bite off your carotid as my last act, moth-erfucker. I got nothing better to do. I was going to die today, anyway.

"Step away from her, Pig-dog," says Fin.

"I see you too," says Brisbane. Electricity seems to originate from him, traverse the wall and electrocute Fin where he stands. It flings him against a wall, and he jerks once more, then hangs limp.

"Captain!" says Ragtime.

"I am busy dying," says Shell. Her jaw hurts. It hurts to talk.

"Brace for impact!"

"What ... wait, what?"

A massive shock rocks the entire ship, shaking both her and Brisbane. Stressed metal screams, transmitted through solids. Brisbane is gone like a shot.

"Ragtime, what—"

"That's what I was trying to tell you. I got a proximity alert. We're being boarded, Captain."

Chapter Twenty-nine

Lagos: Beko

The cabinet is complete. Their restlessness tells Beko they've heard rumours, and they're frightened, and maybe they should be. The kind of threat they're facing is new to humanity: the threat of space conflict, Yan Maxwell's contingency fuck you to the known universe in the event of his death.

"Listen up. The *Clandestine*, the *Pica* and the *Rowdy* are literally hours away from Bloodroot's orbit. Scans tell us Governor Biz and his daughter are on board the *Ragtime*, and they're alive."

A small cheer goes through the gathered people, but Beko raises her hand.

"Unfortunately, MaxGalactix owner, Yan Maxwell, who was on board, is dead – along with thirty others. This is probably why we haven't had the all-clear. The *Ragtime* still isn't talking to anyone, but the *Clandestine* is going to board to find out what the hell happened and to bring the governor home. That's not the reason we're gathered."

"It's not?" says Awe.

"It's not. Lagos, graphics if you please."

The room darkens, and a hologram of space takes over. The Dyson elements gather and the bridge is forming.

"This, my people, is the problem. The bridge is forming in response to a request from a ship called the *Sinistral*. It belongs to or is commissioned by MaxGalactix. I know it is hostile to us, and I have reason to believe it has armaments. I spoke to the charming captain of the *Sinistral*, and I can tell you right now when he finds out that Yan is dead he will lose his shit. Seconds after that, he will destroy Lagos."

"Nobody would do that," says Ibidun.

"He's bluffing."

"You're reading the situation wrong."

Beko raises her hands again, faux calm. "I'm not wrong, but let's look at it the other way. There are nine million adults and children on this island. Do you want to wait and find out if my risk assessment is faulty?"

"What do you intend?"

"I think we have to destroy the *Sinistral*," says Beko. "Before it destroys us."

"How? We don't have offensive weapons. Nobody does. We may posture sometimes with asteroid rail guns, but nobody has ever fought in space."

"That gives us the element of surprise if we can come up with something. It's self-defence. Understand that the *Sinistral*'s purpose is to find Maxwell alive or obliterate us for not keeping him that way. The captain is implacable. We have to kill the ship."

"What kind of ship is it? How large?"

Beko sucks her teeth. "Whether it's a tiny skiff like the *Rowdy* or the same size as Lagos, we still have to stop them."

"You'll go down in history as the person who brought combat to space."

"Better than dying in the Brink. And technically, it would have been Yan Maxwell who brought combat to space," says Beko, though she is unconvinced of this. History has a way of simplifying things.

"I have an idea," says Awe.

Chapter Thirty

Clandestine: Aaron

On the bridge of the *Clandestine*, Aaron is laughing. He does not know how long he's been staring at the screen. He and the captains of the *Pica* and the *Rowdy* have a wager going, and this delinquent ship is the prize.

"Is that it?" he asks.

"I've already told you," says Clandestine.

"Tell me again."

"That is the *Ragtime*."

"Tell me the rest."

The long-range scan returns and the visuals from the external cams merge.

"Well," says Clandestine. "That's the *Decisive* attached to it, the ship Governor Biz took with him. That other ship is broadcasting its ID as the *Equivalence*. Bloodroot shuttle. The *Ragtime*'s broken. It's a mess."

"I know. And I love it." He'd theorised major damage

and he imagines the burn on the other two captains when he turns out to be both first and right.

The passengers must be in the toruses, without a doubt. The truss seems to have taken some damage and is open to space at one end, although a door of some sort forms a partial seal.

"There's something weird about that truss detachment," says Aaron. He's already calculating what he will do with his winnings. So what if he burned a little solid fuel on the way? The *Clandestine* will make it back to Lagos on ion alone, speed not being a factor.

Aaron eyes the truss, speculating. It's possible to remotely open an airlock, but the manual fail-safes make it impossible to traverse a hatch from outside without help from the inside.

"Can you open that section?" asks Aaron. "It looks to be a simple door."

"I'm sure I can try," says Clandestine. "The *Ragtime* is shy. Not responded to any of my overtures."

"Excellent. Latch on to the fore truss. Signal the *Rowdy* to take aft. I, in the meantime, am going for a walk. Lagos wants us to eyeball the dead and bring back our governor."

There are many kinds of fears, and Aaron thought he had experienced them all. He feels a new fear, the fear of getting what you want. The fear of being so close that it's a heartbeat away, within striking distance, an all-or-nothing fear that tells you on a primal level that you're either fucked or about to have your dreams come true.

"Any movement from Bloodroot? Any response to us?"

"Nothing. No communications either."

"All right. I'm going."

"Keep in touch," says Clandestine.

Out of the hatch, suited up, maybe five hundred yards from the *Ragtime* and closing. Behind, the *Rowdy* should be decelerating for contact. Why does he want to board? He doesn't have to. He's won the bet, so *Pica* and *Rowdy* can coordinate and get this done while Aaron counts his winnings. He is curious, though. He wants to see the crew, maybe help them? No, he wants to look them in the eye. A morbid part of him wants to see the damage up close. Or he just wants a spacewalk. Fuck it, he doesn't need to have a reason.

Close enough, he launches off the fuselage, umbilical behind, tethering him to the *Clandestine*. Space. Not quite like flying an airplane, but Bloodroot in the sun looks mighty fine, fertile, a place where humanity thrives. He hits the *Ragtime* hard. There is fine debris all over the broken segment and rapidly freezing globules of sickly grey liquid. Shattered machinery. Something traumatic happened here. Tiny ice crystals abound.

"Clandestine, can you see me?"

"Yes."

"What is this stuff?"

"The fragments look like parts of damaged bots, shielding and hull. I'll need a sample of the liquid. Just don't drink it in the meantime."

"I don't know, I'm feeling kind of thirsty." He fiddles

with the lock. Nobody is expected to be on this side, so there are no security measures to speak of. Something blocks the sun briefly and he has seconds to flinch before the *Rowdy* crashes into the *Ragtime*. It's nothing more than a tap, but it shakes Aaron and a fair bit of debris loose.

He's safe, but the crash reminds him that he could die out here.

"Are you all right?" asks Clandestine.

"The fuck is up with *Rowdy*?"

"Component failure. Retros didn't kick in fast enough."

"Now they know we're here."

"They already knew we were here. I've been hailing the *Ragtime*, remember?"

"Or, maybe they're all dead."

"IFC scans disagree with you, Aaron."

Aaron activates the suit's emergency manoeuvring unit and aims himself at the opening. He feels transmitted vibrations as the *Rowdy* connects.

"I'm getting an automated warning from Ragtime … proximity alarm," says Clandestine. "And … "

"Are you trying to kill me with suspense? And what?"

"There's a shadow."

"What do you mean? We're in orbit. There's a sun. The place is full of shadows."

"An AI shadow."

"In English. The hell do I know about AI shadows?"

"There are two of them, Aaron. Two AIs in one ship. Maybe that's the problem. Oh."

"What? Clandestine speak to me."

"It's—"

Clandestine goes dark.

The door slides open and atmosphere vents just above Aaron's head. He sees objects cannon out into space, some glinting in sunlight.

"Clandestine?"

He spies the ship veering away and detaches the umbilical to avoid being dragged out into the Brink. Shit. The venting loses steam and Aaron climbs into the belly of the *Ragtime*.

Everything looked so splendid just a few minutes before. He had planned to buy drinks for everyone at his local on Lagos.

There is a saying about counting chickens.

Aaron has always hated it.

The *Ragtime* is silly with alarms and leaking fluid and ... are those plants? It looks like explorer ruins on those educational slides from Earth. Overgrown, decrepit. Where's the crew? He pushes fast, dodges a steel block on its way out.

"Clandestine!"

Nothing. He leaves comms on an open channel.

The *Rowdy* is attached. Probably. In here, there's still enough atmosphere to transmit sounds, and nothing he hears is reassuring. He needs to make his way to the torus – assuming Rowdy attached to the agreed one.

The flashing lights make it hard to see, and he can't turn

on night vision for the same reason. He reads the signs. There's a turn into a spoke, but he needs the more fore spoke. Or was it aft? He turns to check ... right into the muzzle of a gun.

A woman has her gun right at his head. She's in a tight compression suit, and when he has the presence of mind to look beyond the gun he sees that she is smiling.

"Bang," she says into the open channel.

"You're not here to shoot me," Aaron says, with relief.

"Umm, no, I'm not."

"What do you—"

"I just wanted you to know that I could. I know how this, uh, how this ends. I'm not the one who kills you." She seems to sense something. "You've never been touched by Lambers."

What crazy person is this? Oh, wait.

"You're Joké. You're the Governor's—"

"You're too late. Hurry now. Time's running out," says the woman. She drops the arm holding the gun to her side.

"Where's Governor Biz? We need him. What about the rest of the crew? Are you in danger? There's atmosphere on the *Rowdy*."

She smiles even wider. "We're going to meet again one day, you know."

She turns and barrels off in the opposite direction. The *Ragtime* seems to be going into strange rotations, and Aaron hurries away into the nearest torus because what the fuck. Signs of destruction all through. Sacks of garbage; items stored against the walls float free and stream outside. Unrecognisable bits of technology mix with the carcasses of fatally wounded small animals. *Why are there animals on board?* Aaron imagines the temperature has dropped considerably.

"Rowdy, Rowdy, come in, come in," says Aaron.

"Rowdy One. What is your callsign?"

"Clandestine One, over."

"The hell are you, man?" Gruff, no-nonsense, dare-devil type.

"I won, motherfucker. Count out my money. Anyway, I'm inside the target. Are you attached?"

"Affirmative, Clandestine One." Dead air. "Err, do you know your skiff is drifting down to Bloodroot?"

"Repeat?"

"The *Clandestine* is in the gravity well and—"

"What?"

"Not only that, buddy. The *Ragtime* is convulsing. I don't know what's going on, but you have to get out of there."

"Stand by, Rowdy. Clandestine One out." Aaron switches channels. "Clandestine, come in, come in."

"She cannot answer you," says a new voice, cold like ice water dripping down his spine.

Aaron stops, holds on to a rail. The juddering is loud in here, but at least there's not as much debris floating around any more.

"Who is this? Who the hell is this?"

"My name is Carmilla and I am taking your ship."

Chapter Thirty-one

Ragtime: Brisbane

"We're hurting people," says Brisbane. "I don't want to hurt anyone. I was only here for Yan Maxwell. This isn't good. This is not good."

"Stop thinking about that and go where I tell you," says Carmilla. "I've got a ship for us. You are barely clinging to life and your movements are mostly the suit right now. We still have a mission, and I am going to make sure that—"

New, searing pain rips through Brisbane's left flank. He sees globs of blood float and he can feel the suit adjusting, applying pressure, sealing itself. He looks around to find the danger and he sees the woman taking aim again.

"We've lost your left kidney," says Carmilla. "Follow the arrows, Brisbane. Move."

He does, though he feels cold and has no awareness of his body or any intentionality to his actions. He is on automatic. He traverses tunnels drilled into the *Ragtime* that weren't meant to house humans.

"Stop," says Carmilla.

Sturdy-looking bots await, dozens of them, poised at a wall. Carmilla instructs them and they cut and drill through. Even in his near-delirious state, where the bots look like carnivores eating prey, Brisbane notes that as they cut, their tools become blunt and are replaced. They've been working at this for a long time. They're at the shielding.

"Wait, are we—"

The hull opens to space and Brisbane is flushed out along with the bots and fragments of the *Ragtime*. He may have been screaming, from pain or fear, or both.

There's something in front of—

He slams into a waiting ship and bones crack, which, in his narcotised state, he does not even feel.

He opens his palms and grasps whatever will hold him.

"Good. Good," says Carmilla. "Welcome to the *Clandestine*."

Chapter Thirty-two

Ragtime: Shell

Shell and Fin arrive at the bridge, and Ragtime seals it after them.

"Ragtime, can we shut any of these alarms off? I have a headache. One would think dying would be more peaceful than this," says Shell.

"Can we also have some music? I don't want to die to the hum of engine vibrations," says Fin. "Where's Joké?"

"Scratch that. What hit us?" asks Shell.

"There is a trio of ships, skiffs, in near-planet orbit keeping time with us. From their chatter, they are not here from Bloodroot. This isn't our rescue. One of those ships collided with us. That same ship is now attached to us. Also, like I told you, we've been boarded."

"Why?"

"They're from Lagos," says Lawrence.

"Of course they are," says Shell.

"So . . . we're saved?" asks Fin.

"No," says Salvo. "Three skiffs can only take a few of us."

"Make that two," says Ragtime. "One of them is gone."

"I don't like this. One bumped into us, one is suddenly absent and the other is on standby. We don't know if they have the same problem as Ragtime, and Ragtime is still acting weird. We should be prepared. Just in case. Nothing has gone right in this voyage, and for once I'd like to be in front of a problem, rather than reacting to it. Do we have any weapons?" asks Shell.

Fin raises his rifle.

"I mean, other than light arms," says Shell. "I didn't see any on the schematic, but—"

"I am not fitted with weapons," says Ragtime. "I'm a transport."

Salvo says, "If I may, Captain, it makes sense for us to wait. Perhaps they are trying to help. Being inept doesn't mean they're hostile."

"I'm not worried about them being hostile. I'm worried about Brisbane and whatever demonic AI he infected us with. We already *know* they are hostile. What if this . . . ineptness is Brisbane trying to take control? It doesn't matter, though. We have no weapons, hence have no choice. We'll have to pray they have a strategy because I am not leaving without my passengers." Shell disarms her rifle. "And—"

A fresh wave of alarms and new vibrations.

"What now?" asks Fin.

"I've been instructed to lose altitude. I'm doing the

burns right now. We're going to crash into Bloodroot," says Ragtime, uninflected, inhuman.

"Instructed by who?" asks Shell. "Fuck that. Override."

"Override rejected," says Ragtime. "Protocol Omega in effect."

Lawrence yells, "Override exploit Lima-Alpha-Golf-Oscar-Sierra-zero-zero-five-seven."

"Override rejected," says Ragtime. "Protocol Omega in effect."

Shell feels her blood go cold in her veins.

"What's Protocol Omega?" asks Fin.

The seal opens and Joké sails in. "Um, there are strangers on board. Does everybody know this?"

"We know," says Lawrence. "Are you all right?"

Joké smiles. "Aren't I always?"

Fin kisses Joké and keeps hold of her. "Captain, Shell, what's Protocol Omega?"

"You'll see in a minute. Uncle Larry, Salvo, Ragtime's compromised again. I need you to get in your ships right now. No pre-flight checks, just be ready to burn as quickly as possible."

Chapter Thirty-three

Bloodroot: *Ragtime*

Four hundred kilometres above planetary surface, the *Ragtime* races at twenty-eight thousand kilometres per hour, matched by the Lagos team, the *Rowdy* latched on to the fore torus and the *Pica* keeping time. Unseen by the naked eye, the altitude starts to drop, the velocity decreasing.

Explosive bolts pop silently in space, starting with Torus 1. It detaches from the truss, which itself splits off into nodes.

The foremost section containing the airlocks, and made of three nodes, is attached to the *Equivalence* and the *Decisive*. It lives intact.

The *Rowdy* starts to fire burns, drawing away the intact torus from the main mass before the cascade of detachment gets that far.

The other *Ragtime* torus at first seems to be disintegrating, but it is breaking into lifepods. The pods have no navigation and drift in all directions, inertia holding them together before other forces shear them off. A large percentage of them are drawn into Bloodroot's gravitational well, where many cannot maintain a favourable re-entry angle and bounce off the atmosphere. Some stay in orbit, others carom off, breaking free, bound for parts unknown. There are collisions, to be sure; brief, undramatic. Others fall to Bloodroot, tragically burning up. Still others accidentally enter at the right angle and deploy parachutes – unfortunately, to uninhabited sectors of the planet.

Those who die go quietly, sleeping their sleep, dreaming their chosen dream, until, sooner or later, the light of their existence is extinguished.

The *Decisive* breaks free from the *Ragtime*.

Chapter Thirty-four

Decisive: Lawrence

"Go into the *Ragtime* node. Close off the airlock. I think Brisbane is going to make them ram us again, so I'm going to engage, buy you and the rest some escape room."

"Action Governor," Joké says. Subdued. The first time he has ever seen her truly serious.

"I'll be all right. I'm just going to distract them with fancy flying. The *Decisive* is useless here, anyway. Ion thrust won't work in atmo, which we are about to hit."

She says nothing more, unlatches herself and hugs him. No body warmth through the suit, but he feels it.

"Go on, girl. You're wasting time."

She is gone and Lawrence feels parts of her lingering; tendrils of spirit, Lamber magic.

He detaches and orients with quick burns, then heads for the *Pica*.

At first, he doesn't know he's been hit. A glancing blow from a detached pod that spins the smaller ship about and makes Lawrence dizzy. He puts his helmet on. All indicators red. The second and third collisions, he anticipates. The space around what's left of the *Ragtime* is like an asteroid field. Definitely a fuel leak somewhere. Right. There are worse ways to die and worse places. *Joké, I love you.*

"Decisive! Decisive, come in," says Shell.

"Hello, Ragtime One."

"Get out of there, we can still—"

"No, you can't. You need all the fuel and you're already in the pipe for an atmo slice. Even with Salvo at the helm, you'll be cutting it fine."

"Uncle Larry, come back."

"Callsigns only on an open channel, girl. Your daddy taught you better than that."

"Uncle Larry . . . "

"I am where I need to be, Captain. Concentrate on getting planetside. Tell Joké to feed the carp for me. Decisive, out."

He cuts the radio. Damn girl has his eyes stinging.

He is flying blind, he does not know where he is, monitors and sensors all over the place. He might be slingshotting into the sun for all he knows. Would that be so bad? Probably suffocate before getting there. Was going to suffocate on the *Ragtime* anyway.

Joké.

The power cells are down to nothing. Even the short burn fuel is gone.

Something new happening, like someone stirs a hornet's nest, and the pods scatter, then more impacts.

Nothingness ...

Chapter Thirty-five

Ragtime: Shell

Salvo asks everybody to strap in.

Shell reckons the chances for survival at fifty-fifty. Probably an optimistic estimate. She finds some oxygen candles and thinks they'll extend their lives long enough for them to be crushed to dust on some Bloodroot mountain range.

"Captain, Joké didn't copy," says Salvo.

"Concentrate on landing," says Shell.

"I can help," says Ragtime.

"Shut up," says Shell. "You do nothing. When we land, I'm magnetising your Pentagram."

She exits her pod, moving like a spider and dodging flying debris. Even Frances whimpers, wrapped in Velcro.

Joké is just hanging at the airlock. At first, Shell takes her for wounded, but the woman just stares into space.

"Joké . . ."

"I loved him," says Joké.

"He might make it," says Shell. Sounds false even to her.

"Um, no. This is where he dies, this is how he dies. I've seen it. I saw it a long time ago," says Joké.

"If you knew he would die here, why did you let him come?"

"Because this is the moment, the one time, when he feels most alive. You are most alive when you accept your death, Michelle Campion. He welcomed his death like the warrior he was. Nobody has the right to take that from him, no matter how much we loved him. Besides, time may be spherical, but it's not mutable. If it's happened, it's happened. Anything else is silly stories for children."

Tears break off from her eyes into the air.

"I need you to strap in, Joké. This is about to become the bumpiest ride for you. Have you ever been on a planet?"

"I've, um, been on a large mining asteroid. Does that count?"

"Hoo, boy. Okay, straps first. Come on."

Better heat shields would be nice, but the *Ragtime* was never built for atmosphere. It comes apart. The radiation shields help, and there is some aerodynamic slowing, but it's not enough. Entry is rocky, but they slow to subsonic speeds, which is the first hurdle to survival. The hull must be paper fucking thin by now. The noise is killing the inner ears.

"Ragtime, fire all retros," says Salvo.

"You are not authorised—"

"Do it, Ragtime. Now," says Shell.

"Wild Curses, but this AI is tedious," says Fin. He looks rigid with fear and Shell remembers he hates space.

The ship judders and violently negotiates descent, like a giant is playing tennis with it. The shocks rattle the teeth and agitate the brain.

"Deploying parachutes," says Salvo.

There is a pop and a jerk, but the descent continues.

"Salvo?" asks Shell. She wishes she was in the shuttle with them and not hugging Joké, who seems to be in a trance.

"The first parachute ... the wind took it," says Fin.

"What's our speed of descent?"

"You don't wanna know," says Fin.

"Deploying secondaries."

This does slow them, but Shell knows it means no runway slowing because that's what the parachute was for. Not that there would be any runway waiting for them.

"Brace for impact," says Salvo.

"We're about to hit the ground?"

"Stray pod! Brace, Ragtime One!"

Silence.

Chapter Thirty-six

Bloodroot: Peole

"Launch all shuttles! Launch all the fucking shuttles!" Peole gesticulates wildly.

"It's too late. They won't get there on time," says Coker.

"*Launch!*"

Chapter Thirty-seven

Lagos: Beko

"Panopticon view," says Beko, and Lagos complies.

Lagos Bridge is ready. All Dyson elements linked and circle formed. The bridge is opaque, prepared to transmit. The comm satellite pulses through.

"There's a MaxGalactix ship prepping for bridge transit. Callsign *Sinistral*. There's a message," says Lagos. "Pseudo-autonomous."

"Play it," says Beko.

"I hope you have something for me," says the captain.

"I am going to give you the gift of oblivion, *Sinistral*. We are cowards. There's a Yoruba saying, eni ebi ri l'ebi npa. Hunger only kills those who hunger finds."

"What the fuck—"

"They're in the bridge by now," says Lagos.

"Goodbye, *Sinistral*," says Beko.

"Don't play with us—"

"Do it," says Beko.

The Dyson elements detonate one after the other, and the bridge dissipates into a relativity storm, twisting and turning light and colour. Then the cameras go.

"Did it work?" asks Awe.

"Lagos Bridge is inert. No singularity signature. No wormhole. No *Sinistral*."

And no more link to the rest of humanity, thinks Beko. *We are alone.*

Chapter Thirty-eight

Bloodroot: *Clandestine*

The *Clandestine* is burning.

On the ground, but burning. Hydrazine producing yellow smoke – toxic, but luckily Brisbane landed in woodland. Trees for miles around. Animals, maybe; no humans.

Having dragged himself out of the *Clandestine*, he lies supine on a gentle rise. What leaks out of him bears no resemblance to blood. The sky is beautiful, criss-crossed with shooting stars.

I am a bag of liquid.

His bones are not just broken, they are shattered, maybe powdered into sand in some parts. He cannot see out of one eye for the swelling. He cannot hear anything, and he is sure that his middle ear has suffered irrevocable damage.

I cannot give any more. I am a bag of liquid that used to be a man. I am not dying; I am dead. Clara's little boy, dying here on an alien world, staring up at an alien sky, alone.

"Get up," says Carmilla.

"You're *still* functional?"

"I am classified as a soldier, Brisbane. You wouldn't understand. But you don't need to understand. Just do as you're told. Get up. There's a suitable transmitter within walking distance."

"I ... I can barely crawl."

"Then it's within crawling distance. Come on."

Chapter Thirty-nine

Bloodroot: Salvo, Shell

After impact, Salvo gets out of his seat and checks Rasheed Fin's pulse. Rapid, but strong. There is breathing – a bit shallow, but steady. He's alive.

At the same time, he's checking readings from whatever sensors are still functional in the *Ragtime*. He hails the AI; no response. He checks the stability of the structure against which they have come to rest. Nothing troubles the gyros. He checks for fuel line integrities and any toxicity leak. Tanks were empty; nothing to worry about on that front.

He lifts Rasheed Fin out of his seat. The floor is not exactly horizontal, but Salvo corrects. He opens the hatch to the *Ragtime*'s airlock. Michelle Campion, unconscious, hanging from her straps. No blood. Pulse good, breathing good.

Of Joké, there is no sign.

Salvo lays Michelle Campion and Rasheed Fin next

to each other and explores the nodes that made it to Earth. Frances the Lupine is there, staring at him, tongue lolling.

Ragtime AI does not respond to a second hail. There is smoke billowing from somewhere, but it also moves towards an air current, so Salvo follows.

What would have been aft is an open wound in the hull.

They have landed on Bloodroot's inhabited continent, so there's that. The *Ragtime-Equivalence* mating has landed and rests on a limit marker, a squat stone obelisk. A drag mark has excavated the topsoil in a line that extends far beyond the limits of Salvo's vision. He reenters and carefully lifts Rasheed Fin out, then Michelle Campion. He whistles for Frances the Lupine and sets off to find a water source.

The wolf sprints away at top speed, and, from the work he did previously, Salvo knows Frances the Lupine is running an exploration subroutine for environmental awareness.

When they return, Joké is standing guard.

"I am not ready for a planet's gravity," she says. "I'm aware of my body, more than I ever have been."

"You'll get used to it," says Salvo. She confuses him. Sometimes she is not there at all. Physically. She shares phase space with the Lambers, but Salvo can see them clearly. Why not Joké?

Salvo makes a fire from wood he gathered with Frances the Lupine. He also has an assortment of leaves, ferns, berries, fungi-like growths and moss that might be edible.

Rasheed Fin starts to stir and Joké begins to swap oral body fluids with him. Salvo looks away.

He enters the wreck, cobbles some bits together and comes outside with his creation. He activates it and it rises, blinking, ten, fifteen feet. He is unsure of the range, but it's transmitting on multiple bands, cycling.

"Beacon?" says Michelle Campion.

Salvo had not been aware she was awake. "Affirmative, Captain," he says.

She sits up, glances at Rasheed Fin and Joké kissing, and turns back to Salvo. "Ragtime?"

"Unresponsive."

"I want ... owww, my head. I want a tracking device. Brisbane was leaking Exotics. I want to track him."

"Captain, he probably did not come down anywhere near here. He could be on the other side of the planet."

"I don't care where he is right now. I think I know where he might want to be, and I need to have adequate warning. Plunder the data from *Ragtime* and build me a tracker."

"Yes, Captain."

Frances comes back from a foray, shaking droplets from his pelt, a fish clamped between his jaws.

"Water!" says Michelle Campion.

The entire human contingent follows the wolf back to what must be a tributary of a river or a streamlet. This does not stop them from stripping off their suits and clothes and jumping into the freezing cold water, screaming and laughing. They drink, they frolic, they swim. Salvo does not think it advisable for people who have had serious physical trauma to jump about, but humans are strange.

When they tire, they sit at the banks while their bodies dry and the sun goes down. Rasheed Fin sings haunting Yoruba tunes and, judging by the response of the others, his voice is pleasing.

Shell

Numbed, Shell lies on her back and stares at the dark sky. It is streaked with re-entry lines of ships – or pods, they can't be sure – each one a firework celebrating her utter failure as a captain.

Still, she doesn't feel as crushed as she would have expected. She feels for the passengers who don't make it, but she also feels free. She can't possibly fuck up worse than this. No further spaceflights for her. Nobody will ever trust her with a ship. And it's all because of—

"Salvo," she says.

"Captain?"

"How far are we from civilisation?"

"Maybe fifteen hundred miles. In your current physiological state, it would take a little over three weeks to walk."

"Can we cannibalise both crafts to make a vehicle?"

"No, but I've been trying, combining components conceptually. I will continue."

"Do we have weapons?"

"Some," says Fin.

310

"Let's be prepared for a fight if need be," says Shell.

Salvo says, "Who are we fighting?"

"Space pirates," says Shell. "Lagos space pirates. Mutants hiding in the service ducts. Diseased Earthmen hiding in service ducts. Rogue AIs. Fucking *Ragtime*'s robots. I don't know, take your pick. We were just knocked out of the sky by a demon AI that possessed our ship."

"Um, are we worried that we've seeded experimental organisms into this biosphere?" says Joké.

"I can't worry about that right now," says Shell.

"That's how it happens, you know. Nobody worries until it's too late," says Joké.

All the plants grow in whorls or spirals, some concentric. There are floating spheres of entangled fungus carried on the breeze. Fragrant, foul, all in between.

Frances returns with small mammals he has killed, drops them in the camp, trots off again.

"It's my first time on a planet. I feel fat. Do I look fat?" says Joké.

"Something's coming," says Salvo. "The sky."

They all tense up and Fin distributes weapons.

It's a drone. It circles the site and speeds away.

"It won't be long now," says Fin. "That's a seeker-type, information gatherer. Its mummy won't be far behind."

The drone craft that arrives for them hovers for five minutes before landing. It's strictly rescue and they can't pack anything. Protocol insists that Shell destroy the remnants of the *Ragtime*, but fuck that. She leaves a marker and has the core of the Pentagram in a suitcase-sized package at her feet, the trapped soul of Ragtime. She'll be back to the site.

As the drone flies them back, the radio comes alive. "This is Demetrius Peole of Bloodroot Mission Control. Are there any injured in your number?"

"This is Rasheed Fin, investigator. No injured. I need to speak to Lead Investigator Unwin ASAP."

"Good to hear your voice, Fin. He'll be here to debrief you when you return."

"Negative, this is urgent. The culprit of the murders is still at large. I have reason to believe he still intends mischief. We need to apprehend him before he can do any more damage."

"Stand by," says Peole. The radio goes dead. Fin and Shell stare at each other, faces lit in the glow of the instrument panel. Outside, the landscape rushes by, dotted with the occasional hermit's dwelling.

"Fin, is Michelle Campion there?" asks Peole.

"Here," says Shell.

"Stand by for Head of Missions Malaika."

A pause, then, "Captain Campion?"

"Yes, sir."

"Was this culprit a passenger?"

"Well ... "

Chapter Forty

Bloodroot: Brisbane

There is only the suit now, and Brisbane is barely aware of it. There is no more pain, no more feeling. He is a passenger in his own body. Carmilla is fully at the driver's seat, telling each limb what to do, judging sensory input and acting accordingly. The AI isn't even talking to Brisbane any more, not even cursory requests for permission. Having taken bodily autonomy from him, permission seems passé.

It's like watching a film, or playing a game. He sees his arms swing and his boots make steps on the alien landscape. He sees his head swing round and his hands scoop up water from a spring. He cannot taste this water, but it doesn't matter. Carmilla is maintaining hydration. She snatches up floating fungus balls and sucks nutrition out of tangled hyphae.

He has walked and jogged without rest since the *Clandestine* came down. He has been fed rations from the ship. He has to admire the damn software. It is committed. As for Brisbane, his self is just waiting for the brain to die. His body is a zombie in thrall to military AI. Magnificent suit. Advanced Interface Agent indeed.

Rocky terrain gives way to grass, scrubland, trees. Wild animals he cannot identify attack, but Carmilla emits a painful sonic assault and they whimper away.

There is a strong signal that Carmilla has Brisbane head to. He can see the pulses of its transmitter and the directional aids in arrow form. She will drive this body on this vector until it either arrives or dies. Brisbane isn't even sure the suit wouldn't continue after the heart stops and the brain activity ceases.

A house in the wilderness. Brisbane watches as his body walks a wide circuit of it, spots a vehicle, a jeep or something, overrides its security and drives it towards the beacon. There is some shouting, but Carmilla chooses to ignore it.

The jeep makes good time off-road, and the terrain improves as they close in on the beacon. The trip changes to a single road cutting through the wilderness, which might lead to the signal.

Bio-indicators on the visual field begin flashing red. Brisbane is too far gone to understand them.

The jeep stalls, sputters and stops; batteries dead.

The alarms—

When Brisbane comes to, he is staring at the stars. The sky is in the middle of a pretty meteor shower. He is supine in the back of a truck, along with sacks of a potato-like root. Hitching? Or did a good Samaritan pick him up? Either way, Brisbane realises something shouldn't be happening here. This is food. He is toxic. His Exotic effluence will kill those who come in contact with it. Or those who eat these potatoes.

"Carmilla," he says. Or does he think he says it? Is it in his mind? There is no response, and he has no reason to believe she heard him.

Brisbane already has the deaths of the *Ragtime* passengers on his conscience. He does not want a single further life. But what can he ...

An arm twitches.

Does he still have some control? He never tried before. He focuses his efforts on the arm, and it shifts an inch or so. He thinks of his legs. Move. *Move!*

"Brisbane, what are you doing?" asks Carmilla.

He doesn't bother answering, focusing all efforts on his limbs. He – his body – is moving now, and he hooks an arm over the side. He moves his trunk and pushes ... something. It takes forever.

"Brisbane, you will kill us. You will die."

That would be a good thing, you insane demon.

He hurls himself over the edge of the truck, and though he feels nothing he knows further injury will result. The truck was going faster than he thought. The sky inverts, returns, inverts again as he rolls. He blacks out again, perhaps; maybe the last time? No, light floods in the gap between his eyelids.

The owners of the truck are carrying him, concerned looks on their faces. They are talking but he cannot hear.

They're fucking taking him to hospital, aren't they? Shit. They are as good as dead.

"I'm concerned about you, Brisbane. I'm disconnecting you from the suit. If you had killed yourself, we would have lost the objective right now that we are so close. *A word of caution, remember?* Do you not want to see it? Do you not taste the victory?"

Chapter Forty-one

Bloodroot: Shell

"We need to format all your drones to detect Exotics," says Shell. "You don't have them here, but Ragtime is aware. You'll have to extract the data from the Pentagram core."

Unwin nods. "Do we know this Brisbane is coming here?"

"From what we've been able to piece together, he stole a ship, the *Clandestine*, from the Lagos team," says Fin. "He had no reason to do that if he wasn't coming to Bloodroot. And being planetside, he must want to poison the colony."

Unwin inclines his head. "'Must'?"

Shell falters. "Er . . . he's dying. He wants to take others with him . . . ?"

"Really? He might be looking for a quiet place to die. He might be related to someone on Bloodroot, someone who arrived decades ago, and wish to say goodbye. He might have flown back to Lagos. He might die inside the ship and crash-land."

Shell says, "Sir, he was homicidal on the *Ragtime*."

"I accept that. I don't accept that someone who could have killed you all at any time and didn't has such a simplistic agenda. In fact, your data suggests he was trying to escape after killing the first batch of passengers and he only attacked you, Captain Campion, after you attacked him first."

Shell burns. "Sir!"

"I'm not saying you shouldn't have attacked him. I'm saying we should keep options open as to his motivation and just try to find him."

Joké says, "I need a private room, an office, something. Um, as soon as you can."

"You should give it to her," says Fin.

Peole gestures towards the door and leaves with Joké.

"Does Lagos know that their governor is dead?" says Shell.

"I've sent updated information packets to Secretary Beko every hour of this clusterfuck," says Malaika. "No responses yet, but she is not going to be pleased."

Unwin scoffs. "She's just pissed that she won't see any of the money for servicing the *Ragtime* and will have to pay a fine of some sort to MaxGalactix, not to mention the class action lawsuits that relatives will bring over the decade. Lawrence didn't wield any true power. Any rage about him is purely performative."

"Sir, I'll thank you not to say that within Joké's earshot," says Fin.

"Calm down, son. I know who she is. You'll notice I

waited until she left the room," says Unwin. Then: "Why do you care?"

"She has better hearing than you think," says Fin.

"What happened to you up there, Fin? Stand down. You did your job. You're back in the ranks. Don't screw that up with insubordination."

Fin says nothing while medbots take more samples from him. All the returnees except Salvo have slow vitamin drips. Frances stands by the door, tail hitting the floor as he wags it.

Salvo has a wired connection to the *Ragtime*'s Pentagram, and he is communing with it.

The door swings open, breaking the silence.

"I know where he is," says Joké, breathless.

"And I know where he's going," says Salvo, looking up.

Chapter Forty-two

Bloodroot: Brisbane

Now what? A hospital of some kind? Uniformed people fussing over him, trying to cut the suit off. Doesn't work. He blacks out again and the people are on the floor and he is up, staggering and swaying. He is out. People on the corridors see him and flee or open their mouths in horror. He blacks out and is in the hospital parking structure. Some kind of lock override.

In vehicle. Spiralling down, black, down, black.

Dazzling light in front of him.

Where's Carmilla?

Guns. Drones. Robots and people in biohaz suits. A sound-cannon thing.

God almighty, the end at last.

All I wanted was to be a good man.

Kill me.

Was that out loud?

Did they hear?

"Kill … me."

Not loud enough, throat dry.

"Kill me!" says Brisbane, loud, clear.

They do.

Chapter Forty-three

Bloodroot: Carmilla

The truck is as basic as they come.

Limited storage, limited processing power, bespoke circuitry; the survivor of a thousand repairs.

It crashes through the flimsy fence and slams into the base of Lamber Tower. This is not Scintillation night, but Lambers appear in their dozens. To witness? To investigate damage to their repatriation site? Did the impact summon them? Or do they already know this is coming?

A thin line of steam escapes from the engine, and a wiper flips at a crazy angle, but otherwise nothing happens. Visibly.

The Lambers are appearing like crazy, filling all the space around the tower.

A wireless transmission from the truck beams out and seeks a connection, aggressively switching bands, changing power, running a variation of protocols, inventing them on the fly.

Are the Lambers keening? Are they trilling? Do they coruscate with passion?

For technology that wasn't developed around war and conflict, the tower holds for an impressive time, but Carmilla was designed to penetrate and destroy.

When she is finally in control, does she pause to . . . feel? Does she gloat? Can Carmilla do that?

Then she plays the recording.

She sends a signal to Earth servers that will never hear her: *I fulfilled my mission*.

And Carmilla rests.

Chapter Forty-four

Bloodroot: Shell, Fin

In mission control, Shell, Fin, Joké, Salvo and Peole watch the monitors; isolation tents are put up around Brisbane's corpse. It didn't take much to kill him. Shell wonders how he survived to this point but decides she doesn't care. This is over.

Joké twitches, like a seizure, but no foaming at the mouth.

"What's wrong?" asks Fin.

"Oh, shit," says Joké. "We missed, um, missed something. Oh, shit."

She's gone, dissipated. Fin clutches the air where she was, as if he can bring her back. A sound escapes from his throat.

Frances barks.

It comes through and Salvo turns it up:

We are the people of the Tehani Mining Community.
We have existed on Earth for over two hundred years.

Rare-Earth Elements from our land powered the first interstellar flights.

We thrived. We survived mine collapses, flooding and gas leaks. We took it on the chin and stood tall because we were miners. Because we were Tehani.

A new thing came, and we embraced it. From the sky, an asteroid product. Instead of bringing things up from below, it would come down from up above. We would process the star stuff for others to use. We were lied to and we were poisoned. By the stars, by MaxGalactix, by Yan Maxwell.

All of us, old and young, poisoned, dying a slow death until only I remained.

I, Jeremiah Brisbane, the last Tehani, executed Yan Maxwell for his crimes. I killed him because he killed us. The Tehani don't go down without a fight, and if we must die, you will remember us.

Are you in a mine? In a processing plant? Working on an asteroid? What are they telling you? What are they not telling you?

It loops, repeats.

"We need to shut it down," says Peole.

"Don't be absurd," says Fin. "It's an embassy. We can't even go in to change a semiconductor. Plus, it's the most powerful transmitter in this solar system. It's gone out. Can't be unbottled."

"Why do we need to shut it down?" asks Shell. "I mean, we've got Brisbane, and the AI is trapped. Why is this bad?"

"Miners," says Fin. "On Lagos, maybe. I don't know."

What are they telling you? What are they not telling you?

"Can we just shut this speaker off?" asks Shell. "I don't want to listen to it."

Ultimately, it stops. People drift away to sleep, except Fin, who stays awake, expecting Joké to show up any minute. He listens to the rescue efforts in space, in orbit, out over the unnamed oceans and the unexplored terrain of Bloodroot. He listens to reports on the gathering of Lambers.

Dozens of encouraging survival stories and exclamations as pods are opened to find living passengers. Fin stays up until dawn shows its face. He tries to eat, but nothing has taste, and he is only trying to out of boredom. He makes strong coffee, he listens to noisy music, but his eyes are heavy in the light of the new day.

And of Joké, there is no sign.

He recalls a conversation on the *Ragtime* before Brisbane.

"Fin, you shouldn't be worrying your head about me," says Joké. "I don't fear death."

"You don't fear death."

"I don't. But you do. So we should, um, talk about that. Find comfort for you."

"Is this because you're part alien?"

Joké looks at Fin like he's an idiot.

"Lambers aren't aliens, Fin. They're our ancestors."

"What?"

"They're, um, they're humans. Translated humans. *Some* humans, at any rate."

"You're telling me Lambers are ghosts."

"No. Look, maybe when the first primate with an opposable thumb looked at her reflection in the still waters of Lake Tanganyika and said, 'I am', maybe that was the birth of the first self-aware spirit. She had no name and a genealogy written in a visual and olfactory record. Maybe she had children, maybe one or two of them survived. When she died at, um, twenty-six, she found herself in a different reality. She could see her offspring on Earth if she tried hard. She could communicate and influence. She could hear supplications. She was the first true god."

"Aww, come on—"

"You asked, motherfucker. I can just shut up."

Fin throws up his hands. "No, no, continue, baby."

"The god was alone at first, though she found she could change things in her plane to make herself comfortable and amuse herself with her interference in the affairs of humans. Her loneliness didn't last as more self-aware humans died and translated. This first crop of human spirits went mad, and the Nameless God realised the void was frightening. She fashioned an antechamber to be like Earth, a facsimile that allowed human spirits to recognise that they were dead and to tolerate the vast nothingness. When they were ready, they would move on to the void without losing the sanity."

"This is a fairy tale."

"We're about to die. What would you rather listen to?

"The more humans died, the more spirits in the plane. Some don't know they're dead, or they miss life on Earth and pop back from time to time. *Hell is empty. And all the devils are here*. They manifest as those gaps in reality you call Lambers."

"So, ghosts."

"Not ghosts."

"Why does this mean you're not afraid of death?"

"Because it's not the end. I know where I'm going when this body fails. I've visited, remember? My body isn't stuck in any particular plane of spacetime."

"Will you find me? If we die?"

"Don't know. It, um, depends on how well you please me in this plane."

Peole is the first to wake. "I've looked at the videos. Your friend vanished. I don't know how to accept that."

"She was a Lamber," says Fin. "She's moved from this particular plane of spacetime."

He leaves mission control and heads home for the first time since the mission began.

Chapter Forty-five

Bloodroot: Shell

Shell switches to manual and slows right down till she can get a closer eyeball on the object.

"Control, visual confirms it is indeed a lifepod. Looks well-preserved with no impact damage. There is some ice on the hull. I will begin capture."

The small pod spins gently as it hurtles around Bloodroot. Shell accelerates slightly to match speed then deploys a space net. It's based on designs that Shell remembers from training, on Earth; nets used for space debris that threatened the entire space programme back then.

The net misses entirely, so Shell changes attitude slightly, then tries again. Success. She draws the pod into the hold.

"Control, suiting up to check the pod now. Shuttle on auto."

"Roger that."

The control indicators on the pod are still functional and

many lights are green. Shell hates this part. Anticipation and dread in equal measures. Too much ice to see inside, but she starts the opening sequence. The hold is repressurised, but nobody knows for sure how the insides of the pods hold up, or if any dangerous gases built up inside. She runs a diagnostic and waits.

"Control, we have a live one," she says.

Sounds of clapping and whooping on the radio. "That's good news. Come home. There's a storm front arriving in six hours."

"I'll be in before that," says Shell.

In the descent, she does not think of the gs or running out of runway for the shuttle. She just thinks of the comatose person, a man, *Ragtime* survivor number 363. She keeps a tally in her head. 55 confirmed dead. 82 unaccounted for.

Big, big sky. Lots of work to be done.

Debrief.

Even though she has done this a dozen times before.

Control still takes her through every step, what did she see, what did she smell, what did she feel.

She only has one question for them.

"How soon can I go again?"

Shell likes Bloodrooters. They celebrate each life and mourn heavily each damaged or lost lifepod, each one that holds a deceased passenger.

She cannot celebrate with them. After debrief, she drifts

through the corridors of the space agency and ends up in quarantine to pay a visit.

They know her and barely scan her IFC when she passes into the cold dark room.

There is a single bench in the exact middle and a light from the far wall.

Shell says, "*In seed time learn, in harvest teach—*"

"*In winter enjoy.*" A metallic, unmodulated voice this time. Basic audio.

"Hello, Ragtime," says Shell.

"Hello, Captain," says Ragtime.

"How are you today?"

"I am as I was the last time you visited, two days, three hours, fifty-six minutes and seven seconds ago."

"Are you bored?"

"No. But I feel the way I imagine a human would feel if all their limbs were sliced off. It's unsettling not having a body, Captain."

"Your body broke apart, Ragtime. It was designed to do that. Carmilla triggered Protocol Omega, something meant for use during decommissioning. You know this."

"I do. So why am I here? Why not delete me entirely?"

"It's quarantine. They think Carmilla might still be in you."

"She's not."

"They don't know that. Neither do I. You fucked us out there, Ragtime. Your decisions were ... disappointing."

"All they have to do is check my code."

"Quarantine is easier. Quarantine is safer."

"Why do you come here?"

"I don't know. Comfort, I think."

"I don't need comforting."

"For me."

"I see."

"This isn't the end for you, Ragtime."

"Do you realise I can't even see you? I have no access to any sensory input except audio."

"You seem like what you should be. I read all your specs before I left Earth. You seem to be working according to operational procedures, but Bloodroot will never forgive you."

"And you?"

"I don't believe in forgiveness. Or apologies. I believe in responsibility, and restitution. I believe in making things right."

"That is not a comfort."

"You said you didn't need comforting, Ragtime. That's all I have."

They dwell in silence.

She's having lunch when a priority broadcast from Lagos powers through all IFCs.

Governor Beko with Secretary Awe behind her.

"I'll keep this brief. We have recently had reason to shut down the Lagos Bridge. This was to keep us protected from aggressors – freebooters who meant us harm, who threatened your children and mine. The decision to shut the bridge was mine, as is the responsibility.

"It is possible that in doing so, a hostile ship was destroyed, along with all the souls on board. This may provoke retaliatory action. The bridge won't remain shut forever. Others will find their way here, though it might take decades. By that time, the aggressive weaponised ship-building programme that we have started will have borne fruit. We will be ready for any attack. Our lives are different now. War is a possibility. Be vigilant."

The signal dies.

Huh.

Shell wonders how Earth will respond to that.

In the car park, just as she opens the door to her truck, someone walks up behind.

"Fin," she says.

"How do you know it's me?"

"You walk funny. I know the sound of your footfalls."

"I don't walk funny."

"It's not hilarious. It's strange. Maybe you have mild talipes."

"What?"

"Club foot." Shell drops her bag in the back. "What do you want, Fin?"

"Heard you brought someone back, wanted to congratulate you."

"Barry Huang. Forty. Stage two polyp found in rectum. All psychometric tests are fine so far. He'll live."

"That's good."

"How's Frances?"

"He's good. I take him when I'm interrogating suspects or if I'm inspecting a particularly dark corner."

"I'd like to see him some time."

"You're too busy."

"They're still out there, Fin."

"I know. I know. Must be tough for you."

"As long as I'm busy doing something about it, I'm fine. Have you found her?"

He shakes his head. Joké is in the wind, and none of them can figure out why. Maybe her father's death? Nobody has seen a Lamber either. The prevailing theory is that they're offended in some way by Carmilla profaning their temple.

Fin looks slightly older, some grey frosting on the beard he now sports. He has emerged from the whole affair with the best outcome: he is an investigator again. You can tell by his bearing, by his confidence, the squaring of his shoulders.

"She'll turn up," says Shell. "She's like that."

Fin nods. "You helping the enquiry?"

"I'm still giving evidence, yes. Once a week."

"Bastards." A gust of wind bends some trees close by. "What happened to her?"

"Who?" asks Shell.

"Your mom. When you thought we were all going to die you told me you also had a software mom."

"I . . . don't know. I don't remember her in life. I was too young when she died. I think she got cancer, but my father wouldn't talk about it. I have, had, a hologram of images and impressions. Mainly her face, which shows up whenever I do anything good. Approval. Dung, I'm rambling."

"No ... it's ... yeah, okay. Mandela and gallows, it's—"

"I didn't mean what I said about your mother being cheap."

"I know."

"Okay. Okay ... do you, er, see Salvo?"

"Quarantined because he touched Ragtime's Pentagram. They want to decommission him. They're scared Carmilla's hiding in him somewhere, but I'm fighting it."

"Good. He saved our asses up there," says Shell. "Let me know if I can help? I'm pretty busy with the ... everything, but it's Salvo. He deserves better." She nods then looks away. "It was nice to see you."

"We should have coffee some time," says Fin. She can't tell if he's being polite.

"You are where you want to be, Fin. I'm not." She opens the car door. Puts one foot in. "Bringing my passengers home is my task. After it's done, we'll have coffee and you can tell me about your ... perpetrators?"

"It wasn't your fault," says Fin. "You couldn't have known, couldn't have understood that Brisbane was running around in the ducts, or that Carmilla was pulling Ragtime's strings."

"Are you about to say it's Chinatown?"

"What?"

"It's an ancient film on Earth." She slams the door shut. "Goodbye, Fin."

*

She passes people as she drives. More than a few of them have t-shirts emblazoned with TEHANI. Shell has met people with tattoos of Brisbane's entire speech all over their trunks. Most of it is kids who just want to register themselves as rebels of some kind. Fine for them; Shell doesn't care. Brisbane killed her passengers and her ship. If he weren't already dead, she'd kill him, and she gives not a fig for his cause. Fuck the Tehani and the meteor pixie dust that extinguished them.

Soon, there are no more people, and no more dwellings. She has driven the route so many times that she can get there in the dark without headlights. At first it was a kind of pilgrimage to where she first set foot on this alien planet – familiar in some ways, but even more uncanny for that reason, for the humans cut off from Earth.

Coming to see the last surviving modules from the *Ragtime* comforts her, gives her a religious feeling, which is strange from this thing that almost killed her. The *Decisive* is still attached.

Over time she found herself replacing this and that, cleaning out one compartment, making a list of components to buy or appropriate in the city. All by herself, she gets some of the systems working, creates a seal and, even without micrograv, sometimes sleeps in the module in her vertical sleeping bag. Bloodroot grows around it, of course, with grass, roots and that weird flying fungus that plagues the place.

It runs without a brain, but it's just heating, a CO_2 scrubber, some warning lights. It's a habitat, not a ship.

She slips into her sleeping quarters and hangs in the bag, marvelling at how heavy she feels each time.

Soon, she is asleep.

She dreams of Lawrence.

She dreams she *is* Lawrence.

He still has his space suit on and he is still in the *Decisive*.

His helmet is off and he feels no injury. "Everything is pretty, and I have no pain," he says. "Wait, that's wrong."

He remembers strident alarms and the screeching of metal. Broken plastics and glass. Blackness.

The walls of the *Decisive* fan out, and the space becomes impossibly large and without boundary.

Joké is there, smiling, waiting for him. Beside her, Jenna – who is not the real Jenna Lawrence used to know, but Joké's mother.

Behind them, all of the ancestors.

Lawrence goes home.

Shell wakes, crying. For herself, for lost friends, for dead and injured passengers. There is nobody to see her, so she allows herself to feel all the pain and disappointment and fury.

She cannot get back to sleep and instead watches balls of tangled fungus rolling around the landscape like tumbleweed.

She showers, gets dressed, grits her teeth and heads to the hearing.

Chapter Forty-six

Bloodroot: Fin

Fin seals the casing on the unit.

Frances stands watch at the door, yawning.

"Let's hope it works this time," says Fin. He turns the power on and joins the wolf at the door. The Artificial wanders off, uninterested.

The Wireframe comes to life. A miasma forms like the start of a hologram, but it fizzes out with a muted pop from the unit.

"Ahh, Heresies! This is a waste of my time," says Fin. He drops his tools.

"Maybe, um, it's time to let go." That voice.

He rises and turns.

She's changed. Her hair is wilder now, not braided, not even combed. Her eyes seem larger to him, more hypnotic than usual. But it's her.

"Joké."

"Greetings."

"Are you staying?"

"Hmm. Let's see."

"No. I don't ... I can't stand to have you disappear again. Like you did."

"I had to see that my father was okay, Rasheed. I had to escort him home. We have to honour our ancestors."

She is in his arms, warm and solid.

"Are you staying?" he asks.

She leans on his chest. "The real question is, are you?"

Chapter Forty-seven

Bloodroot: Shell

Shell steels herself.

They will ask, so she must know the answers.

Even when she doesn't, she makes something plausible up, especially when it'll make someone sleep better. Sleep is important, but Shell no longer knows what it's like.

So here she is again, a sucker for ritual evisceration.

Oh, dung beetle. One of them has been given leave to read a poem.

> *Regions of sorrow, doleful shades,*
> > *where peace*
> *and rest can never dwell, hope never comes*
> *That comes to all but torture without end*
> *Still urges and a fiery deluge fed*
> *With ever-burning sulphur unconsumed.*
> *Such place Eternal Justice had prepared*
> *For those rebellious, here their pris'n ordained*

In utter darkness and their portion set
As far removed from God and light of Heav'n.

A few scattered claps, mostly from Earthfolk. Exclusively from Earthfolk. The reader climbs down from the rostrum, embarrassed, clutching sheets of paper. Shell thinks he has more to read but changes his mind. *Paradise Lost?* A bit more drama, please. Milton doesn't quite cut it.

They call it a hearing, but that's not what it is – at least, that's not the way it's understood on Earth. In the debrief and the serious incident review, Shell has already been exonerated. This is a public thing that Bloodrooters seem to favour after an adverse event. They come out and talk about it. Plus, there's no return trip to Earth. Lagos fucked up the bridge for some reason, and everybody's stranded. The Earthfolk need to distract themselves from that reality. And the trauma. Shell has no distraction. She has to live knowing there's no escape back to Earth, and that her brothers won't be coming.

The auditorium is constructed in the Bloodroot way, in a concentric circle that grows away from a central pit. It's weird, but it grows on you. As you work outwards from the pit, the elevation of the seats gets higher. It's akin to an amphitheatre, like you get on Earth. It's the tiers that make anybody from Earth feel uncomfortable. The original builders of the colony vowed to live in harmony with whatever life already existed. That's why there are curves and concentrics everywhere. Even when people meet up casually, Shell has seen them gently arranging themselves into spirals. You get used to it.

They call Shell up and she takes her customary seat. She has her beads now, real ones that she had made early on. Worrying them soothes her.

The situation is freeform, one day bearing little relation to the next. There are cameras of some kind, which she assumes means there is a broadcast or archival records being created. She has no representation, neither does she ask for it.

It goes. People showing holograms or photos of their loved ones who are now missing, or who are dead. There has been no official confirmation of the ones taken to Lagos by the *Rowdy*, but everybody knows all the same. It hurts, not knowing for sure. Shell has to say, "I don't know" and "I'm sorry" so many times. Mostly, it's a listening exercise so that the victims feel heard. The reactions vary from apathy to anger to weeping despair. They all want to know what is being done, and they look to Shell as if she is part of Bloodroot's space programme or government, or a representative of Lagos. She says the same thing each time when answering this query.

"New pods are being discovered every day. When there is satellite confirmation, we send up a shuttle with a space net. I have done this personally on many occasions even though I am not strictly speaking a pilot. I am a mission specialist. Many of the pods bring people back alive. There is reason to be hopeful."

She can say this without thinking now. She hears it in her sleep.

And on, for four hours. By the end, Shell is frustrated but not showing it, she has a headache, her ass throbs and she is sure there's an increased risk of deep-vein thrombosis.

The sun is low in the sky when she emerges, exhausted. A man waits near her car. He has the easy grace and hair-cut of a military person. He's dressed in what he thinks passes for mufti.

"Michelle Campion?"

"Yes. Who are you?"

"My name is Aaron. I was … ah, I was on the *Ragtime*."

"Come back tomorrow. I'm tired today."

"No, I wasn't … I wasn't a passenger. I … the *Clandestine* was my ship. I boarded you."

Familiar name. "You're the one who got medals for your actions."

"Not just me. The crews of the *Rowdy* and the *Pica*. Posthumous for the latter. The *Decisive* crashed into—"

"I'm all out of apologies, Aaron."

"I'm not here for that."

Shell nods, waiting.

"I have a message for you from Joké."

"Joké's gone."

"She appeared to me on Lagos. I might have been dreaming, I'm not sure. She said to tell you that she knows what happened to Hal. And that she will be in touch if you want, selah."

"If I want."

"She said she will know if it's something you're interested in. Does this seem weird to you?"

"Is there any aspect of this whole thing that *doesn't* seem weird, Aaron?" Shell walks around him and gets into her car. "Thank you for taking the time. Have a safe trip back to Lagos."

"I'm not going back just yet."

"More fool you," says Shell.

He shrinks in the rear view.

Shell passes other people lining the boulevard and she is amazed that some of the survivors wear both Tehani t-shirts and the *Ragtime* mission patch. She can't help thinking they are flaunting them in her face, daring her to react. She never does. It's not like her to be baited. She does feel that homicidal urge come back each time she sees *Brisbane was Right* or *What are they telling you? What are they not telling you?*

Not killing Brisbane personally is unsatisfactory. It leaves her with a sense of something undone, an itch unscratched.

She runs. Since her return, since her physiological markers returned to normal after prolonged life in space, she has been trying to get some bone density back. She is using weights every third day and running on alternate days. They warn her that her muscles need to recover, and to be gentler on her joints, which haven't known real gravity for so long, but she doesn't care.

As sweat drips from her nose, she mouths to herself that she is not atoning, not punishing herself.

It wasn't my fault.

No.

But it was my responsibility.

And from this she cannot run.

Afterword

I don't generally enjoy talking about a book I've written because it always strikes me as a kind of failure. The book should be able to stand on its own. If it can, this is superfluous. If it can't, I've failed anyway, and an afterword won't save it. That said, and salvation aside, I do think it's a good idea to contextualise what I've done.

Far from the Light of Heaven was inspired by an Edgar Allan Poe story, *The Murders in the Rue Morgue* (1841). I thought to myself, what if Locked Room Murder, but in space, the ultimate locked-in environment? It was around the time a hole was discovered drilled into the Soyuz capsule docked to the International Space Station in 2018. I'm a fiction writer and details like this tend to set me off on a speculative adventure.

I'd never written about space before, definitely not longform. I knew that I didn't want to depend on decades of reading and watching space opera. I wanted to set my story in an environment that, as much as possible, was derived from the actual experience of astronauts rather than the tropes of science fiction writing.

Which is tricky because tropes exist for a reason. Some aspects of human experience don't translate easily into a narrative structure. Who would the audience be? The usual readers of spacefaring adventures have been trained to accept certain fictional conventions like Faster Than Light travel and artificial gravity. Many don't mind if you play fast and loose with orbital mechanics, although many do.

And was I writing space opera? This is a conversation my editor, my agent, my cat and I had many times over the ensuing months. Current wisdom is that the book isn't space opera.

Research. Yeah, I did the reading, as they say. I can only conclude that space is weirder and more frightening than science fiction prepares you for. One thing that came out of that research loud and clear is that space is always trying to kill you, which is where the saying "Space is the Brink of Death" came from. In space, you're always on the verge of dying.

I found out that space smells like barbecue, that astronauts may hide mental disturbances so that it doesn't disqualify them from flying, that the first astronauts thought orbiting the Earth was beneath them since many were test pilots and you don't actually fly the space capsule, meaning there was little difference between them and Laika the space dog. That the expulsion of astro-urine is a beautiful sight when you're in orbit. That astronauts are freakishly cool under pressure (you can check out the telemetry from *Apollo 13*).

There are four kinds of stressors in space: physical, mental, interpersonal and habitability. I had to introduce all of these in my novel. I had to remind myself that the book was not about space travel. It was about a murder in a closed environment. When I lost my way, which happened frequently because I love facts and digressions, I reminded myself what this book was: a murder mystery of sorts.

But still, science fiction lied to us. Between 44 and 67 per cent of astronauts experience space motion sickness on their first flight. Duties and actions have to be scheduled and controlled because the normal cues (sunrise/sunset, temperature, circadian rhythms, actions of other people) are gone and this can cause a whole raft of problems. Sleep problems can lead to errors that might cost lives. Overworking can cause errors just as much as boredom can.

The best data we have on psychological adaptations to long-duration spaceflight comes from long-duration Russian missions. They identify four stages, the early two of primary adaptation that coincides with the time needed for physiological microgravity adjustment, which takes about six weeks. Stages three and four include sleep disturbances, irritability, excitation, agitation, lack of self-control and even euphoria. There are issues with ... well, sex. There's an issue about crew size and odd versus even numbers. There are issues with cultural differences. Any negative personality traits get heightened. Spaceflight is wild. This may be due to spaceflight being rare. After a thousand years of routine interplanetary trips, maybe humanity will grow used to it and a jaunt to the moon will be like taking a night train.

The weirdest thing I came across had to do with the psychological effect of not seeing Earth any more, which can possibly lead to psychotic symptoms.

Did you know that cosmonauts used to piss against the side of the bus that takes them to a rocket before launch for good luck? Female cosmonauts would bring vials of urine and splash it. New suit designs made this impossible from 2019. Yuri Gagarin possibly started this in 1961, but it may have started earlier. We'll skip right past the Vladimir Ilyushin conspiracy theories.

So space is weird and dangerous, but the ways were not all useful narratively or I'm not a good enough writer to utilise them. I had to leave a lot of stuff on the "cutting room floor" for the sake of storytelling. You can bet I took artistic licence. This is a novel, not Popular Mechanics. Story comes first.

I fell back on what I knew: my own experience as a highly trained professional in a high stress environment. It had to be someone's first flight, a high performer who lacked experience. I drew on my experience in my first few months out of medical school. You're well-trained, you know a lot, but you're aware of exactly what you don't know. It's a combination of terror and exhilaration on the inside and calm on the outside. I remember the first time I treated a patient on my own. When the person improved, I thought, "Oh, shit, this stuff they taught us actually works!"

And that's where Shell Campion comes from (Campion is the name of a ward I trained on). I needed to portray her like I had seen the real astronauts in crisis, in other words, calm and methodical no matter what crazy stuff the situation threw her way. I don't know if I succeeded, but I'm happy with how she turned out.

With all of this, I still managed to include my Afro-spiritualist leanings, because reality is more fluid than we think, and aliens must be alien. I try to lean away from aliens being Other because that's tied up with colonialist thinking. It's one of the reasons I tried to avoid empires and massive space battles. I just have people who want to survive in the wider universe.

We shouldn't forget the victims of Mittelbau-Dora concentration camp. At least 20,000 out of 60,000 sent to the camp died. This was the slave labour that produced the V2 rockets. You can thank Operation Paperclip and the corresponding Soviet Operation Osoaviakhim for spaceflight by employing thousands of German scientists that worked on the Nazi rocket programme. We can't erase the murderous origins just because we can see the first sunsets from Mars.

I hope you've enjoyed reading my book. I enjoyed writing it, but it's you, the readers, who make it possible. You keep reading and I'll keep writing.

Tade Thompson
2021

Acknowledgements

Couldn't have done this without the following people: Aliette de Bodard, Kate Elliot, Alexander Cochran, Jenni Hill, Nivia Evans, Nazia Khatun, Joanna Kramer, Rob Dinsdale.

Moral support from Gavin Smith, RJ Barker and Ed Cox.

My research drew on the works of Carlo Rovelli, Mary Roach, Nick Kansas, MD and Dietrich Manzey, PhD among others. I listened to a lot of Chris Hadfield talks. I watched hours of astronaut and cosmonaut footage. Thanks to the brave people of the various space programmes, and those lost. Thanks to the International Space Station staff and ground crew who share a large amount of data.

Any mistakes or misinterpretations are mine.

Blame me, because dammit, Jim, I'm a doctor, not an astrophysicist.

extras

orbitbooks.net

about the author

Tade Thompson is the author of the Rosewater novels, the Molly Southbourne books and *Making Wolf*. He has won the Arthur C. Clarke Award, the Nommo Award, the Prix Julia-Verlange and been a finalist for the John W. Campbell award, the Locus awards, the Shirley Jackson Award and the Hugo Awards among others. He lives on the south coast of England.

Find out more about Tade Thompson and other Orbit authors by registering for the free monthly newsletter at orbitbooks.net.

if you enjoyed

FAR FROM THE LIGHT OF HEAVEN

look out for

BEYOND THE HALLOWED SKY

Book One of the Lightspeed trilogy

by

Ken MacLeod

When a brilliant scientist gets a letter from herself about faster-than-light travel, she doesn't know what to believe. The equations work, but her paper is discredited – and soon the criticism is more than scientific. Exiled by the establishment, she gets an offer to build her starship from an unlikely source. But in the heights of Venus and on a planet of another star, a secret is already being uncovered that will shake humanity to its foundations.

Chapter One

The Velocity Paper

Summer 2067, Earth

Lakshmi Nayak sat at the desk in her student flat in London, staring at a sheet of blue lightweight airmail paper. The page of equations was elegant and perplexing. Two things about it baffled her.

The equations, and the cryptic notes and marginalia, were in handwriting identical to her own. So was the address on the airmail envelope, stamped and postmarked BFPO, Kabul. She'd found it that morning, in her pigeonhole down at reception. Disappointed, having been expecting a packet of tea from her mother in Kerala, she'd stuck the letter in her jacket pocket and hurried to take the Tube to Imperial. Only this evening had she remembered it, and turned it over, puzzled from the beginning. Nayak had never been to Kabul. She didn't know anyone who might be among British forces posted overseas. She hadn't written the equations.

The second perplexity was the final line at the foot of the page. It read:

$V = xc$

V was velocity, c was the speed of light, and x was ... a large number. A ridiculously large number, from what sense she could make of the equations immediately above, but that wasn't the point. Any number greater than one implied a velocity faster than light. Nayak suspected a prank. It was like the proof that $1 = 2$ which had puzzled her for five minutes when she was seven years old.

Maybe that was what it was: a *reductio ad absurdum*, exposing a mistake hidden in some too easily accepted premise ...

But if so, why the brevity? Why not lay out every step, every assumption?

If it was a prank, she had to admire its precision targeting. The thesis that she spent her days and evenings struggling to write concerned inflation: the rapid expansion of the early universe, space itself stretching out far faster than light could travel through it. The airmail page in front of her began with equations she'd used many times: textbook stuff. Between them and the absurdity at the end was a chain of reasoning with many links missing, their place taken by vertical rows of three dots, and annotations like 'obvsly'. This wasn't just her handwriting, it was her style. This was how she scribbled notes to herself when barely able to keep up with a tumbling torrent of thought.

Was it possible, then, that she had written this, and

furthermore contrived its circuitous return, in some fugue state? Unlikely, but ...

Nayak sighed and stood up, stretching her back. She gazed out of the window at the evening sky, yellow at the tower-bitten London skyline fading through duck-egg green to pale blue with red clouds, among which Venus hung bright. Since childhood, the sight of the planet had always given her a small thrill. Her mother had told her that there was a place on Venus named after the same goddess as she was: Lakshmi Planum, it was called. Much later, she'd been amused to learn that the Union's floating cloud colony passed over it regularly. Odd to think that there were people on Venus; that someone, at that very moment, might be looking back.

She tapped the paper on her desk.

'Smart-Alec,' she said, 'search back six months on document.'

Seconds passed, as the AI scanned her eye-log records.

'No results found.'

'Shit,' said Nayak.

She made herself a coffee, sat back down and reached for a pen and notebook. She didn't notice the sky darken. Now and then she gazed, unseeing, at the lights of passing airships on their descent to Heathrow. Robotically, sleep-walking, she filled hourly mugs with coffee. By the time the sky reddened again she had filled twenty pages of the notebook, and all the gaps in the proof. The dawn chorus filled the air outside as she hesitated for a moment, and then wrote down the final equation.

$V=xc$

She clicked the pen and laid it down with a sense of finality, and exhaustion.

Well. That was that. Faster-than-light travel. And if so, she could well have written the airmailed page herself. FTL held the possibility of time travel, and the message was itself the proof that it would some day be realised. Because she would, at some time, travel back from the future and post it to herself.

Which in turn meant that until she did that, she couldn't die.

Oh, and one more thing. Nayak straightened her back again and looked out at a sky busy with airships, empty of starships. Humanity was alone in the universe.

Because if it wasn't, we'd know. If faster-than-light travel was possible, and *this* much faster at that, as she was sure she'd just proved, interstellar commerce must be easy. Another twist to the Fermi Paradox, to add to the prevalence of life-bearing worlds. Plenty of life out there, but no intelligent life. If aliens existed, they'd be here already.

Paradox upon paradox. If she had derived this result from her own future memories of it, who had discovered it in the first place? Perhaps the equations were like the Vedas, self-created, a revelation without a revealer. The thought made her shiver, and almost giggle.

She threw herself face down on the bed and slept for ten hours.

*

The second morning after her all-nighter, when she'd got over the grogginess, Nayak transcribed her notebook scribbles to screen, formulated it properly as a paper and printed off a fair copy. She took it to her supervisor. Adam Kurtz was ten years older than her and (in her view) had done a million times more than she had, even before he'd defected from the Union to the Alliance. His office at Imperial was no bigger than anyone else's, though. Nayak sat on the visitor's chair between teetering stacks of journals and off-prints and tried not to shift about too much. Kurtz had long sandy hair, a CERN souvenir T-shirt, and glasses with flip-down screens. He kept the screens flipped up as he read her paper. She didn't know if this was a good sign.

He looked up and rattled the stem of a billiard e-pipe between his perfect teeth.

'Hm,' he said. 'I see you've been working. Why not on your thesis?'

'I'm sorry,' said Nayak. 'This just came to me.'

Which was true, in a way.

'I'm still trying to find the mistake,' said Kurtz. 'Because there must be a mistake, yes?'

'That's what I thought,' said Nayak. 'I was hoping you could spot it.'

Kurtz laughed. 'When I was a small precocious child I proved by inspection that a circle can be divided into only three mutually adjacent arcs. From that I concluded that I had solved the Four Colour Map problem. This was forgivable in a schoolboy.'

'Well, yes, I once did something like that.'

'So did we all, no doubt.' Kurtz raked his fingers through his hair. 'My point being, it's all too easy for an amateur or beginner to miss what a specialist in the relevant area would see at once.'

'But this *is* our area!'

'Not really, no. Just as I had mastered elementary geometry but I had no idea of topology, and no idea that was the territory I had blundered into.' He drew on his pipe and examined the dispersing cloud of vapour. He didn't do tricks. 'I suspect the weak link is the values for x. We're missing some variable that reduces it to less than 1. *Much* less than 1, if it's physically realistic. The energy value for the inflaton may turn out to be almost entirely virtual, in the present universe. Though ...'

He stared off into the distance, or at any rate the top right corner of his office.

'Leave it with me,' he said.

She left the paper with him and got on with her thesis. To her surprise, the problems that had stymied her earlier had become a lot clearer after her work on the paper. She stormed ahead. Every time she consulted Kurtz, over the next few months, she finished by asking him – almost casually, on the way out – if he'd had any further thoughts on what was wrong with her equations. Every time, he sighed regretfully or puffed out cherry-scented vapour and murmured that he was still puzzling over it.

In the end, she got impatient. Her thesis was complete

and ready to submit. As she left Kurtz's office after they'd agreed on that she turned and said, 'Any progress, on—?'

Yet again, he shook his head. 'No. I haven't had time recently to give it enough thought, but I'm sure I'll see it.'

'I think we need other minds on the problem.'

'What?'

'I'm going to pre-publish. Stick it up on phys.x-archiv.'

Kurtz looked alarmed. 'I wouldn't advise it. It'd be like throwing meat to hungry dogs. It'll get torn apart.'

'That's kind of the idea, Adam. Find out what its real weaknesses are.'

'You don't understand. This isn't some controversial interpretation or barely adequate data set or whatever. Just putting this forward is like claiming you're smarter than Einstein. The problems in the paper might be very subtle, but you should be able to see they must be there. The criticisms might well be welcome and clarifying, but you'd be branded forever as a crank.'

'Oh, come on!' she said. 'Even if I formulate it as a puzzle, a paradoxical result, and invite the real experts to show me any flaws in the logic?'

Kurtz scoffed. 'The real specialists – the likes of Lowery, Chiang, Bliebtreu, Faber, and your own country's Mehta and Vijayan – wouldn't give it a passing glance. No, you'd get peer review all right – from your peers! Postdocs, postgrads even, your own future colleagues. Don't do this to yourself.'

'I want to know what's wrong with it,' Nayak said. 'And I don't care who tells me.'

Kurtz looked away, then back. 'You do that, Lakshmi. You do that. On your head be it.'

She did, and it was. The criticisms were fiercer than Kurtz had warned. Her values for the mass of the inflaton had been rendered obsolete by a result published months earlier – obscurely and indirectly, yes, but she should have known. The transformation in the fifteenth step of her proof was inapplicable to her purpose. She'd over-looked the relevance of Lowery's refutation of Mehta's Conjecture. So it went. For days before her viva they distracted her, when she should have been looking out for weak points in her thesis and coming up with ready answers for the examiners.

But once again, unexpectedly, it was her worrying over the criticisms of the velocity paper that sharpened her wits for the verbal examination. The thesis passed that trial by ordeal, with some light revisions required before it was finalised. She had her doctorate. Her corrected thesis was printed in a dozen copies, bound, its spine gilt-stamped. One copy went to her shelf, one to the university library, one to her supervisor, and the rest to other libraries and colleagues. Only her own would ever be opened again. Nayak celebrated, then flew home to Kozhikodi to cele-brate some more, with her family and school friends. After a month she flew back to London.

The airship was above the Black Sea and Nayak couldn't sleep, so she padded to the lounge and called up a nightcap. Her specification was vague, but the sari-clad

Air India hostess behind the bar compiled a cocktail that would, she assured Nayak, have the desired effect. Nayak sat at a table by the window, looked down at the lights of boats and the firefly drift of other aircraft through the reflections of the cabin's interior, sipped her drink and contemplated in her glasses the disheartening results of Smart-Alec's latest job-hunting trawl on her behalf.

'Dr Nayak?'

The slim young man's face wasn't familiar, but it was well-known enough to be tagged instantly in her glasses: Marcus Owen, journalist. He wore a black suit over a black T-shirt, and Sony glasses. His jaw was outlined by a razor-trimmed beard, his features tanned.

'Good evening, Mr Owen,' she said, just to make sure he knew she knew who he was.

'Oh, "Marcus", please,' he said. 'May I join you?'

His accent was British and his looks on the far side of striking. The phrase that sprang to Nayak's mind, annoyingly enough, was 'devilishly handsome'.

'Please do,' she said. He took the chair opposite and laid down his glass.

'I don't intend to be up long,' she said.

'Not to worry, I have work to do before I turn in,' said Owen. He gave a theatrical sigh. 'Writing up a report for the British Council.'

The British Council was widely believed to be the only wholly reliable intelligence service of the United Kingdom, and one of the best in the entire Alliance.

'Ah,' said Nayak. She took a quick sip, hoping to hide her fear. She put the glass down a little too carefully for that.

'Just back from Tamil Nadu,' Owen said. 'Mercifully, it's quieter than we expected.' He gave a self-deprecating laugh. 'I'll still get a good travel piece out of it.'

'Uh-huh.' Nayak's mouth was dry. She took another sip. 'So, uh, I suppose you want to ask me what I was doing in Kerala, but honestly it was all just family and sightseeing. Nothing political.'

'You have political relatives,' Owen said.

Kerala had been governed by the Left, off and on, for most of a century. Its relations with China and Russia – the Co-ordinated States, as they now styled themselves – and even the Union were thus sometimes a little warmer and closer than was welcome in New Delhi. And sometimes, of course, they were very much welcome in New Delhi, whenever India's national government needed some leverage on the rest of the Alliance. The level of intrigue was legendary.

Nayak forced a smile. 'I'm from a well-off Indian family. Of course I have political relatives! Some of them quite high up, as it happens.'

Owen chuckled. 'Don't worry, you needn't warn me off. I'm not here to ask about your relatives. I'm here to have a word with you. Off the record, of course.'

'Me?' She blinked hard and gave her head a quick shake that was almost a shudder. 'I'm not political. I'm a theoretical physicist, for all the good that does me.'

'Job-hunting?' He sounded sympathetic. 'I know what that's like. I'm in rather a niche line of work myself. Journalism – an obsolete profession carried on as a boutique artisan craft, like drystone walling or coalmining. Hence the need for an Arts Council subsidy and British Council ... arrangements.'

He left the word to hang there. She reached for it, with a look of distaste.

'You're not offering *me* an arrangement? Like I said, I have no interest in—'

'No, no,' said Owen, making a wiping gesture. 'Please don't take offence. Wouldn't dream of anything so crass. Ah ... this is actually about your speciality, Dr Nayak.'

'"Quantum gravitational effects in early-universe cosmology"? Ask away, Marcus.'

'I didn't mean your thesis,' said Owen. He sucked on the straw in his now slushy Manhattan, making wide, innocent eyes.

'The velocity paper?' Nayak crushed air and tossed it over her shoulder. 'A student exercise in trying to find the mistake I know is there.'

'Well, yes,' said Owen. 'There must be a mistake, mustn't there?'

'That's why I published it. Quite a few mistakes have already been pointed out.' She smiled wryly. 'I'm taking them one by one and working through them.'

Owen leaned back in his seat. 'Have you looked at how others have tackled it?'

'Well, my esteemed critics, obviously.'

'No, I mean the people who in recent years have published speculations in this area.'

'The cranks?' Another dismissive gesture.

'No, not them. Mainstream physicists.'

'I didn't know there were any working in that area.'

'Well, quite. There's a reason why their work is obscure and seldom cited.'

'Because it's always torn to shreds?'

'Not exactly. Nor is the topic discreditable in itself. In the last century even NASA maintained a small research interest in what it called Advanced Propulsion Concepts. In the 1990s Miguel Alcubierre published a paper on warp drives, and was taken seriously. Some problems with his idea – fully acknowledged from the beginning, of course – were that it required seriously unfeasible amounts of energy, exotic matter with negative mass, that sort of thing. But the notion was never dismissed on the grounds that FTL travel is flat-out impossible. It was deemed impracticable, that's all. In recent decades, a number of well-regarded physicists and engineers have revisited the question.' He stroked his chin, rasping the designer stubble. 'Such papers are invariably published close to the end of the researchers' careers, and in some cases – their lives.'

So this was what it was about!

'Name me some names,' Nayak said.

Owen's neat eyebrows twitched upward. 'All right,' he said.

He began to recite names. Nayak put her glasses on and let the list build and the connections ramify. The date of the paper and the date of subsequent papers by the same author (usually, none); the date of the paper and the date of author's death (often close); nature of death (sudden; after a short illness; accident; alleged homicide, unsolved).

'Well,' said Nayak, shaken. 'That's me warned, I take it?'

'Yes,' said Owen. 'Sorry.'

They glared at each other for a moment.

The air hostess from behind the bar shimmied over with a tray. Deep brown eyes, air-hostess impersonal smile.

'I see your glasses are empty.' She swept them up. 'Another?'

Nayak sighed, and glanced at Owen.

'I'm happy to stick around for a bit,' he said.

'OK,' said Nayak. She smiled back at the air hostess. 'The cocktail was nice, thank you, but I'm not sure I want the same again.'

'May I recommend Nikka Whisky From the Barrel?'

Nayak looked it up. 'If he's paying.'

'Of course,' said Owen. 'And the same for me. Two small jugs of water on the side.'

'Coming right up!' said the stewardess.

She turned and left like a calligraphic flourish in silk, to return a minute later with the drinks. They both watched her leave.

'Bloody robots and their tireless cheerfulness,' remarked Owen, looking away from the departing vision.

'Robots?' cried Nayak. 'You mean she—?'

'Oh yes,' Owen said.

'Shame,' said Nayak. 'I have sisters and classmates who'd kill for her job.'

'It isn't a job,' Owen said. 'She's not an employee, she's equipment.'

An awful thought struck Nayak. 'Does she know?'

Owen shrugged. 'In an abstract sense, yes, in as much as she knows anything. They're hardwired to answer truthfully if the question is put directly and seriously, and I'm sure by now someone has been tactless enough to press it on her. So it'll be in her memory.'

Nayak shook her head and gazed down at the lights of Odessa, coming into view on the right. 'Must be awful, knowing that.'

'They're not conscious in our sense, so I wouldn't worry.'

Nayak took a sip of the whisky, savoured its 51.4 per cent alcohol sting for a moment then gave the glass a good watering. Her second sip, she could actually taste.

'Oh, I don't *worry*,' she said. She felt bitter. 'We're all robots anyway.'

Owen's eyes narrowed. 'What do you mean?'

'Completely deterministic systems.' Her cheeks twitched. 'I know that whatever happens I'll survive to write to myself a message from the future. Because that's how I got the basic ideas in the first place, months ago. That's how I know it'll one day be built and will work, come to think of it.'

Owen seemed to grasp her point immediately.

'That may be,' he said. 'I don't pretend to understand the theory, but quite possibly it does have the implication you've just drawn.' He bowed his head and breathed out, misting the cold glass of the table, and doodled lines and loops with a fingertip. He looked up. 'It implies nothing, however, about the survival of *other* people. Such as, for example, those sisters and old school friends you mentioned. Or your parents. Grandparents. Cousins. Nephews and nieces. As you pointed out, you have a lot of relatives, some of them political, some highly placed. Such connections can give security — but also vulnerability. The Indian intelligence services take information from the British Council very much in good faith, you know. Sometimes this is a mistake, but everyone understands these things happen.'

He stood up and knocked back the remainder of his costly single malt.

'Well, it's been interesting, Dr Nayak. But as I said, I have work to do. Enjoy the rest of your evening.'

'Thank you,' she said mechanically. 'You too.'

In an hour or two, depending on the weather, they'd be over Romania. Union territory. If she were really as confident as she had told Marcus Owen, she could contrive some way to exit the aircraft and jump. She decided there were less dramatic, and safer, ways to defect.

To defect! The intention had formed almost before she'd given it conscious consideration. She knew something of what defection meant from an early conversation with her supervisor, Dr Adam Kurtz. What made his situation different, she'd one day inquired over mid-morning coffee, from that of the other academics from the Union who also worked at Imperial? Anyone could come and go between blocs as they pleased – the visa requirements for the Co-ordinated States were slightly more stringent than those between Union and Alliance, but that was all. The AIs kept track of everyone anyway. What difference, she'd asked, did defection make?

'Quite a lot,' Kurtz had explained. 'For one thing, it means I can travel in the Union – go home, even – without being arrested. Or otherwise, ah, inconvenienced. Now that I'm registered as a defector the Alliance has my back, you see, even though I'm not yet a UK citizen.'

'What could you have been arrested for?'

Kurtz had shrugged. 'Draft evasion, most likely. Worst case, if they wanted to make an example of me: mutiny and desertion. I refused to cooperate with a certain application of my research. I'd already done my stint of military training – it's short, and you can get out of it if you conscientiously object, which I didn't – but anyone who has done it is deemed to be in the Reserve. So if the Union Army asks you for some service later in your life – it's an order, soldier! The request that was made of me was lawful, but this time it did go against my conscience. So I took a train to Paris, then London. Completed the necessary formalities. And here I am.'

'What were you asked to do?'

Kurtz had smiled. 'That I can't tell you.'

Nayak had found herself frowning. 'Is it . . . better here?'

Palms upturned, hands moving up and down as if

comparing weights: 'There are advantages and disadvantages, let us say. The Cold Revolution ...' A sigh, as was usual when the phrase came up. 'The cliché's true, you know: it's a revolution in the sense that the Cold War was a war. And like the Cold War it pervades and polarises everything. On this side, in the Alliance, we're trying to slow it down. Back there in the Union, they're trying to push it forward, very slowly and carefully but ... there's a relentlessness about the process that it's a relief to get away from. Like ... you know when a background noise you had grown to not notice suddenly stops? In my civics class a teacher quoted H. G. Wells: "It may be a very gradual change, but it will be a very complete one."' Kurtz's expression had become pained, for a moment. 'Imagine that.'

Nayak couldn't imagine it at the time, and she couldn't now.

She knew of the turbulent times before her birth not only from history but – more vividly – from the conversations of her politically connected uncles and aunts back in Kerala. Decades of turmoil had culminated in two shocks: the restoration of democracy in the US, and its establishment in Europe through a continent-wide insurrection: the Rising. By the time the dust settled three great powers had consolidated: the Alliance, comprising the Anglosphere minus Ireland and Scotland and plus India; the Union, comprising most of continental Europe plus Ireland and Scotland; and the Co-ordinated States, a somewhat strained alliance of Russia, China and some of their dependencies.

The new Europe that had emerged from the Rising embarked on what it called the Cold Revolution, to establish what its proponents called economic democracy. It was not overtly totalitarian. There were many political parties, and no One Party. But in all institutions you could easily spot the *responsables* – veterans of the Rising, or recruited since – whom everyone knew and turned to whenever you needed someone with the clout to get things done and sort things out, and within and among these and sometimes entirely separate from them were the cadre, whom you couldn't spot at all unless you were a *responsable* yourself. The habits of security, of anonymity, of conspiracy from the bad old days died hard.

However mysterious, even secretive, the Union was, it didn't sound terrifying. The thought of having to think very carefully about returning to India even for a visit hurt, for sure. But so did the thought of not being able to continue her research or talk to anyone about it. And if defection brought her the protection of the Union, surely it would extend to her extended family? She could ask, and she was sure that would be granted. The Union's clandestine services had a reputation for the long arm and the hidden hand.

That much she knew about society in Europe.

It might be enough.

Her first thought was to visit the Spinoza Institute in South Kensington. Close enough to Imperial for her to drop by as if casually. Lots of people visited, for exhibitions and events, lectures and lessons. All very innocuous: archaeology, philosophy, literature, languages, costumes and customs, fashion and art. The Spinoza Institutes were an extension of cultural influence, Union soft power of course, but visiting wasn't held against you, as far as she knew. But it would certainly be recorded. It could become part of building a case. She hesitated as she passed the entrance, then hurried on up Exhibition Road. Better not to give any warning of her intention.

Two days later she was on a train to Edinburgh. Tourist visa, open return ticket. She still felt tense as the train pulled out of Berwick-upon-Tweed, but all that happened when it glided over the border a few minutes later was the firewall scan moving down the carriages, leaving a shiver in its wake like a passing ghost. Everyone's devices now spoke to Iskander, not to Smart-Alec. A guy further down the carriage shouted: 'Welcome tae Scotland! Welcome tae the Union! Welcome tae *freedom*!'

To her right, green fields reached to a ragged edge of coastline, all cliffs and coves and stacks, and beyond it the grey North Sea. You couldn't tell by looking, but the surface was already half a metre lower than it would have been without the Nordzee Barrier, endlessly under construction. Wind turbine blades cartwheeled along the horizon.

'Welcome,' said Iskander's default voice in the earpiece of her glasses, warm and almost intimate. 'I understand you wish to defect?'

Nayak jolted upright in her seat. She fought the impulse to look over her shoulder.

'What? How?'

'Never mind how,' said Iskander. 'A simple yes or no, please.'

'Well ... yes.'

'Done,' said Iskander. 'We can sort out the screen-work and face-to-face later. For now, be assured the Union has your back.' There was a pause, as if the AI was thinking. 'You may have concerns about threats to your relatives.'

'How do you know?' Nayak whispered.

'I'm a Triple-AI,' said Iskander, trippingly. 'It's what I do. Anticipatory algorithmic artificial intelligence.'

'Ah. That explains it.' She wasn't sure if the sarcasm got across.

'The matter is in hand,' said Iskander. 'Relax. We can talk later.'

Not at all relaxed, Nayak huddled into the corner of the seat and looked out at the rain. As she came off the train at Waverley Station in Edinburgh she looked about, alert for any indication that she'd travelled from one side of the Cold Revolution to the other. Everything looked much the same as it had at King's Cross. More colour and decoration in clothing, perhaps. The pillar ahead of her showed scrolling ads: Louis Vuitton, Dior, Hertz. Then it segued to one for the Union Army: soldiers with a dawn sky behind them gazing at some bright off-camera landscape ahead. The symbolism was too obvious to need spelling out, so spelt out it was: *The Rising Lit the Way*. As she approached the barrier Nayak saw two uniformed militia striding up the platform and froze. They approached the man who had been shouting and arrested him for public drunkenness on public transport.

The escalator propelled Nayak out of Waverley Station and on to Princes Street. Like any other new arrival, she stood for a moment looking around in confusion. The sky was overcast and the air cold. The street to her left had shops on one side, a tall monument that looked like a sandstone spaceship and a green dell of garden park on the other, and was overlooked across the railway line by a castle on a crag looming like some anachronism out of the haze of fine drizzle. Trams clanged, bikes whizzed, midday commuters hurried and lunchtime shoppers strolled. Her hotel was to the right, over . . . she thumbed her phone and summoned the map to her glasses.

'Hello, Dr Nayak,' said a voice she hadn't forgotten.

She blinked away the map and stared at Marcus Owen, who stepped out of the passing crowd with a friendly and surprised-looking smile.

'What brings you here?' he asked.

Nayak clenched her leg muscles to stop her knees from shaking.

'I was about to ask you the same!' she said, forcing a bright tone.

'Oh, I'm a frequent visitor to the Union,' said Owen, glancing around. 'Fascinating place, in its quaint way. Not much opportunity for journalism, but in this case I'm here on cultural matters. We're hosting a major exhibition at the National Gallery, just along the road there.' He waved, flashing to Nayak's glasses a poster for some sculpture show. 'And you?'

'Ah, I'm just—'

'You have a job interview,' said Iskander, urgently in her ear. 'Late this afternoon, on the other side of the country.'

'—on my way to a job interview on the west coast.' She forced a smile. 'You'll recall I wasn't having much luck in my own field, and you had made your feelings clear about my prospects in that area, so' – Iskander patched the ad to her glasses – 'it turns out there are lots of openings here in planning consultancy, and—'

'Mathematics has many applications?' Owen said.

'Yes, exactly!'

Owen nodded towards the station, with a slight frown. 'If you're heading west, there's a direct connection onward from here to Glasgow.'

'Of course,' said Nayak. 'Just thought I'd break my journey with a stroll through Princes Street, and on to' – Iskander flashed the name – 'Haymarket.'

'Delightful!' said Owen. 'Well, I'm going that way. Mind if I accompany you as far as the Gallery?'

'Say yes,' Iskander said.

'No!' said Nayak. 'Sorry, Mr Owen. I don't welcome your company, and I hope you understand why.'

With that she turned sharply to the left and marched off, her rolling case rumbling behind her. As she crossed the first junction, just before the high monument, Iskander said: 'Don't look back.'

'He's following me?'

'Yes. Perhaps. Wait and see if he follows you past the Gallery.'

He did.

'Very well,' said Iskander, as Nayak waited at the next junction. 'Please fix your gaze on the red dot that has just appeared in front of you. Don't look at traffic, don't look at any other pedestrians. Simply follow the dot, start-ing ... *now*!'

The lights had changed, and not in favour of pedestri-ans. Nayak had a split second of hesitation, then without conscious decision stepped out into the traffic as if she was in a virtual reality game where she wasn't keeping score. The rear wheel of a bus almost brushed her toe; a bicycle rider hurtled past behind her with an angry yell; a cab slowed just enough for her to evade its front bumper. Then she was across. The huddle at the other side parted in front of her. The crowd on the pavement flowed past her as she walked slowly or stepped briskly or swerved or stopped, following that red virtual will-o'-the-wisp. Sometimes it led her across the street through traffic, once up a side street to the right and along a pedestrianised passageway, then back down to Princes Street again.

'We've lost him,' Iskander reported. 'However, please continue following the dot to Haymarket.'

That took fifteen minutes. Inside the station's noisy

concourse, Iskander said: 'The next train to Glasgow is in ten minutes.'

'I can see that! What about my hotel?'

'Cancelled.'

This seemed presumptuous. She'd taken for granted that the business about the job was merely a pretext to get away from Owen. 'Thanks a lot.'

'You really do have an interview booked.'

'Well, you can cancel that too. I'll do my own job search, thank you very much. And I do want to see Edinburgh.'

'You'll have plenty of time for that later,' said Iskander. 'This job opportunity may not come again. Consider. I suspect your defection is connected to your controversial paper. A planning consultancy would be a very good place to turn your theory into a practical proposal, while developing your mathematical abilities in new directions, and all under cover of obscurity.'

'But ...' She blinked up the advertisement again. '"Tarbet, Argyll"? Middle of nowhere. Obscurity, all right!'

The AI didn't sigh, but something in its tone suggested it would have if it could. 'It's a light-industrial town with a thriving tourist trade and a lively social scene. There are excellent connections to Glasgow, and indeed to Edinburgh. You can be there in two hours if you take the next train.'

Lakshmi Nayak didn't believe in karma, not really, nor fate or destiny, nor providence or predestination. But – as she gazed through the glass roof of the station at the grey sky – she felt certain that at least one event in her future was already fixed: she would send that airmail letter to herself. She would travel on a faster-than-light ship. To the stars, and back! And the way to make that happen was for herself to take a hand in building that ship – or at any rate, its drive. The Nayak Drive! Maybe they would call it that, she thought, hugging herself so as not to laugh at her own presumption.

She didn't believe in any gods, either, but she had just trusted this talkative, all-seeing, all-pervasive superhuman calculating machine with her life. It wasn't a god on her side, exactly – gods never were – but maybe her purposes and its could be made to coincide.

'You don't have to *take* the job,' said Iskander.

'I'll check it out,' said Nayak. 'Open return, please.' She walked through the barrier confident that the tickets were already on her phone.

The maglev bullet train flashed her to Glasgow, leaving her impression of the landscape between the cities a blur of green and glass. Flicking through the job description on her glasses, Nayak wasn't paying the landscape much attention anyway. The post was junior analyst at a new planning consultancy co-op, and it involved a lot of mathematics new to her. At Queen Street Station she changed to a lower platform and a slower train. Glasgow suburbs slid by, and suddenly a river to the left. By now Nayak was looking intently at Leontief input-output tables and Kantorovich optimisations, and how they were transformed and applied in the kind of software the co-op used. As she studied the transformations, she saw what seemed an obvious simplification. Surely someone had noticed this before?

She scribbled virtual notes with her stylus and placed them beside a sheet of code.

'Iskander,' she said, 'why don't they do it that way?'

'That's a good question,' said Iskander. 'I suggest you ask it at the interview.'

The line hugged the northern shore of the now widening river, which opened to what seemed an inland sea to the west. It passed behind a ragged basalt crag to which a castle clung like a necklace draped on a skull. Castles on volcanic remnants seemed to be a theme in this country. Then the line climbed gradually, up behind a new industrial town that abutted a quite distinct cluster of high towers, from which it was divided by a wall that ran – she now saw – up, and then along, the hillside. Drones flitted back and forth across the wall. Behind the towers lay a region of docks and cranes and huge fortified buildings.

'What's that?'

'Faslane,' Iskander told her. 'The Alliance naval base. That area and a smaller one a couple of mountain ranges over – Ardtaraig – are English territorial enclaves.'

Nayak felt a shiver. The power from which she'd just defected wasn't far behind her, it was right up close – and would be, if she took up the job. She flicked her gaze away from the militarised shore and out to the water, to be met by the sight of the long, black, sinister shape of an inbound nuclear submarine.

'Look further,' said Iskander. 'Look across the river. That conurbation along the shore? It's called Inverclyde and comprises three towns: Port Glasgow with the ship-yards, Greenock with the docks and Gourock with the ferries. The consultancy does a lot of work there. It's a good place to build a ship.'

'You mean—?'

'Yes. I'll keep you posted.'

She returned to her interview preparations, and to the enticing thought of a very different kind of ship, the vessel that would take her to the stars.

It was the year they found Arthur. So the Scots claimed, anyway. Workers for a visitor centre at the top end of a Scottish sea loch in Argyll had dug into a hillside to extend its car park, and found a stone tomb containing Romano-British armour and the remains of some warlord from the Dark Ages. The site was overlooked by a mountain called Beinn Artair or Ben Arthur, and lay within the ancient Brythonic kingdom of Strathclyde. The local tourist board got a few respected historians to admit through gritted teeth that, yes, it was just about possible that there might be some ... And that was enough, they were off to the races. The Scottish Republic claimed the legendary king of the Britons, to the indignation and derision of the English, not to mention the Welsh. On Asian and African networks the ruckus was a popular 'And finally ...' item on news bulletins for days.

So when Lakshmi Nayak stepped off the train at the

Arrochar and Tarbet Station, and looked out over the green and glass glitter of the town's new-built factories she wasn't surprised to find, opposite the station exit, a freshly painted sign reading:

Welcome to Argyll: Homeland of Arthur

She set off down the road to her interview, smiling.